I0652873

DEDICATION

War is when the government tells you who the bad guy is.
Revolution is when you decide that for yourself.

—Benjamin Franklin

THE WAR OF US

A NOVEL

CHRISTINE RACHEAL

EST. 2010
AIRRIS
BOOKS

The War of Us
Copyright © 2021 Christine Racheal
Published by Airris Books

All rights reserved.
Printed in the United States of America.

No portion of this book may be reproduced in any form
without permission from the publisher, except as permitted
by U.S. copyright law.

This book is a work of fiction. Names of characters,
businesses, organizations, places, events, and incidents either
are the product of the author's imagination or are used
fictitiously. Any resemblance to actual persons, living or
dead, events, or locales is entirely coincidental.

Cover design by Christine Racheal.

ISBN: 978-0-578-93768-7 (print)

First Edition: June 2021

CHAPTER ONE
THE ILLUSIONS OF HOPE

FACEMASKS clashed with the elegance of the women's gowns. Still, laughter echoed the room. The heels of their shoes clacked against the dull wood as they moved from the elevator and directly to their seats on the 17th floor of the Liberty Centre. Saturdays after hours rendered the building completely void of the thousands who worked within the major banking institutions housed within it.

Amara's fire red dress swept the floor. She blushed, but glimpses of her perfectly aligned teeth could only be imagined. Her cinnamon-shaded hand gracefully caressed a man's shoulder. Towering nearly a foot over her, his response to Amara's flattery could not be concealed; his smooth, white skin turned bright red at her touch. Her husband was Jabari, and he had the essence of a prize-winning stallion, but the man drenched in her affection was not him. It was George. Amara liked to believe he was a friend of the family; he was only a friend of hers.

For Monika, their interaction was difficult to ignore, and pacifism was not her style when it involved her sister, or the upstanding reputation of their father's ministry and business endeavors.

"Hi, you two," Monika said as she shimmied between the pair. Their dialogue instantly ceased.

"I was just leaving." George chuckled as his brows saluted the deep-plunging neckline of Amara's gown. "But it's so good to see you again, Monika."

Monika smirked.

"Goodnight, Amara," he said.

The women watched George turn the corner before Monika looked at her sister with disapproving eyes. The elephant seated in the room daintily crossed its hind legs.

"Don't trip." Amara removed a tube of lipstick from her clutch and was reminded of her face accessory. "I'm going to the ladies' room. Hopefully, it'll give you enough time to forget whatever little speech you've prepared."

That evening, the Mask-Her-Aid Ball would raise at least a hundred thousand dollars to support female business owners weathering the pandemic's storm. People arrived in colorful droves, found an empty seat in properly distanced tables or went up to the rooftop for fresh air and breathed deeply without caution. And as Monika watched her sister step lightly in the same direction George had walked moments earlier, she could use the release. However, a familiar face gave her pause.

Monika was hesitant to approach. The olive-skinned woman's black dress fully covered her chest and arms and slightly touched the floor, yet her entire face was exposed, unlike the others'. Perhaps the glass of champagne she carried was cause enough to remove her face covering, but she never drank from the glass. She held it as though it had accompanied her to the ball and gave her hands purpose. The woman closely examined the painting of a white mare mounted near the elevators and reflected on its textures and shades.

"Mrs. Shamoon," Monika said as she approached. "This is unexpected. You look amazing."

"Call me Fatima." She smiled. "I couldn't miss the chance to help with this cause. Besides, I was running out of DIY projects at home."

"I can imagine. I think we all grew weary staring at the same walls day in and day out. I'm grateful you decided to come."

"You're one of the event's organizers?" Fatima asked.

"You can say that. Bishop Dyer is my father," Monika explained. "I help wherever I can."

"As a good daughter should."

There was silence. "How have you been since...?" Monika began.

"Rebuilding day by day. It's a slow process when there is nowhere to plant your feet—more variables than certainties—more hate than compassion."

"I understand."

"Do you?" She pulled the full champagne flute close to her chest for a heart to heart. "Then you know what it's like to love someone who is completely blind to your love for them. That's what it was like for me."

"I saw Amir almost every day, Fatima. I can't say I agree. Nothing about him said that he didn't love you."

"He didn't love me enough to...be *good*."

"Goodness can't be taught or demanded—just hoped for. You did the best you could. It's what we must accept as mothers."

"If that was my best, I'd hate to see my worst. And I'm sure that 43 families across this city would disagree with you."

Monika's name was called from a table across the room, and several hands waved excitedly for her to come over.

"I'm glad you are here." Monika said gently. "I hope you enjoy the evening."

"Likewise." Fatima moved the glass of champagne towards her face, but still did not drink from it.

A collage of local businesswomen was displayed on several screens throughout the room, and each of the fifteen tables were nearly filled with guests of various ethnicities and cultural backgrounds—a genuine reflection of Atlanta's melting pot of residents if each ingredient was organic, grass-fed, and premium cut.

Dancing was forbidden. The rhythmically challenged Monika quietly celebrated the absence of pressure to take part in a shuffle. A single pianist set the atmosphere for the evening's event, but the chatter nearly muted his efforts— especially at the Dyer table where Amara led the discussion of Monika's future. She was queen of controversial topics, especially when it involved those closest to her. That way, the line between herself and the lesser-thans was more distinct.

"We all want to know the wedding date. Seems your groom doesn't know it himself. Figured you could shed some light."

Monika took a seat between her fiancé, Calvin, a balding man of dark complexion, and her sister. "We don't have one yet," she said sweetly. Her teeth glided along the lining of her cheek.

"Why not? You have the baby. So, what could you be waiting on?" Amara continued to pry.

"Maybe for you to get some business of your own."

"I have plenty business. Six figures worth. I'm just trying to get you settled already. Forty is knocking." She shrugged.

Monika and Jabari's eyes darted pass each other. No one noticed.

"I think what she means to say is that life has been great for the both of us so far, and we're not pressured to marry right now," Calvin said as if he believed it.

"Though you should," an authoritative voice spoke from behind the group.

"Daddy." Monika radiated with pure excitement. She stood and hugged her father tightly.

"I keep telling them, Daddy," Amara added.

Bishop Michael Dyer lowered the mask from his gray whiskers and stooped to kiss Amara before he moved to his seat at the table. Each extended a hand to greet him as he passed.

Nearing 70, Bishop Dyer could physically pass amongst Generation X, but his vibrancy, and the passion with which he lived each day, exceeded that of other men his age.

Calvin whispered to Monika, "Looks like I'm not the only one who needs answers."

"You're the only opinion that matters," she responded. "Barely."

"It's been four years—a baby. Can't you tell I'm in this for the long haul?" She smiled politely as their exchange caught the attention of others at the table, but Calvin was less discreet.

"Don't pretend he was intentional. I won't let you drag me along." He sat back in his seat and folded his arms firmly at his chest.

Monika heard Calvin's pleas for a promised future, but there was nothing more to say that she had not already shared with him—and in a more private setting. She attempted to refocus on the evening's cause and ignore the man whose pouting would be more obvious if his face were not partially covered. Her eyes landed on Fatima, quiet and alone at the rear of the room, and babysitting the full glass of champagne. After a moment, and adding to Calvin's growing frustration, she signaled for her to come over.

"What the hell are you doing?" Amara asked as she grabbed Monika's thigh, but her actions were ignored.

"Everyone, this is Fatima, a law professor at North Georgia. Her son was a student of mine."

The introduction was unnecessary. The entire table was knowledgeable of the little lady in black and would not soon enough forget the evil act her son, Amir, had committed two years prior when he gunned down innocent shoppers in a local mall. He swallowed the final bullet himself. Respectfully, they resisted the urge to cringe, and each of them raised a hand or nodded their heads to greet her.

"There is an empty seat near my father if you would like to sit with us," Monika suggested.

Fatima smiled and accepted the kind offer. As she shifted to the opposite side of the dinner table, Amara leaned towards her sister.

"Are you sure about this? It looks like Daddy's breaking bread with a terrorist."

"He's having dinner with family and contributors. Nothing more," Monika assured her. "Besides, didn't Jesus do the same?"

"It's obvious he had horrible PR."

Monika resisted laughter. "I'm not doing this with you."

"Seriously, reporters are here. Look there." She pointed. "They don't speak Bible." Amara sat up tall and placed a black napkin across her lap. "The backlash of even holding the event during the pandemic is bad enough. Then again, as long as people are talking, business is good."

"I don't think that applies to people in ministry. Either way, Daddy doesn't care much for what people think of him. He can handle it."

"Of course. You're a stich on his sleeve, so I'm sure you know what you're doing." She pressed her red lips together.

"But do you know what *you're* doing?"

Amara leaned in. "Meaning?"

"I saw you with George..."

Amara whisked her head around and noticed Jabari was distracted by his cell phone. "That's nothing—not anymore," she said to her sister to quickly ease her concern.

"Good. Then where did he go?"

"His shift is about to start at the hospital."

"To know that, and to allow it to roll off your lips so easily makes me wonder if you understand the cost of Jabari finding out."

"What I can afford is never a question." She raised a stern eyebrow.

"What was that?" Jabari asked. He sat forward and lowered his phone to the table.

A server who carried a warm basket of bread placed a hot roll on each white, glass saucer, and shoved a bowl of individually wrapped butter into the table's center.

In near unison, they all removed their masks. Removing them to eat made the act of even wearing them to the event laughable, but only few had considered the idea while others saw their compliance as critical.

"I was just commenting on Monika's dress." Amara grabbed the steaming roll from her plate. "Where did you say you got it again? Never mind." She bit down. "I have a stylist you can borrow…if you can afford him." Amara had the air of a Poodle, and the savagery of a Pitbull.

Monika looked down at the blush-colored garment draped loosely from her shoulders, and back to Amara, puzzled.

"Being stylish can't be easy on a teacher's salary," Amara continued.

"Babe," Jabari interjected.

"What?"

"I think you look amazing, Monika," he said.

Eyes wide and warm, she mumbled, "Thanks, Jabari."

"What does he know about fashion?" Amara spoke with a mouthful of crusty bread. "The compliment should be void if it comes from a man whose daily accessory is this cheap jasper bracelet," Amara said and flicked the bracelet on Jabari's wrist.

"That's enough," Jabari said, and she lifted her hands slightly in surrender.

"I'm going outside for some air." Monika left the table without extending an invitation for anyone to join her.

Alone, she leaned against a rigid, concrete post and stared up at the star-speckled sky. She breathed deeply and sorted the thoughts that insisted she separate from the others. Her behavior was not out of the ordinary. Monika was frequently alone, and she preferred it. It had only been six months since she was introduced to the one inescapable person in her life—her infant son, Michael, named after her father.

She never thought she would experience motherhood, but a lapse in contraception forced her to accept what grew within her. Monika would not call herself a good mother. It was beyond definition. However, she loved her son, and was sure of it.

Amara approached and interrupted Monika's moment of solitude. "Mad at me?" she asked.

"No," Monika responded.

"Good. That would make you quite petty."

Monika clenched her teeth. "Do you need something?" She placed her hands within the side pockets of her A-line dress.

"That thing has pockets? How practical are we?" Amara joked.

"Why don't you go back inside?"

When she noticed her sister's heightened aggravation, Amara became serious. "They're about to serve dinner. You don't want to eat?"

"I'm not hungry."

"It's selfish to hang out here by yourself all night. Calvin is in there." She used a hand to fan herself in the post-sunset heat.

"He knows where to find me," Monika said, but hoped he would not.

"Are you going to tell me what's wrong?"

"Nothing."

Amara thought for a moment. "You know, you've said that since Mama passed."

"That's because it's true. I'm fine. Not everyone expresses emotions the way you do."

"So, I'm the cry baby of the family?"

"I'm not saying that. You're quite sensitive."

"That's not true," Amara insisted.

"Being the loudest one in the room doesn't prove otherwise."

"If you think I was too sensitive after she died, fine, but you weren't there."

"No, I wasn't, but with the number of times you've rehashed it, I feel like I was. I'm hoping for the day you would just let it go. Then we can all move on."

"Like you? Emotionless and tough? Or like Daddy, who hasn't taken a single vacation since she was here? She didn't have to die."

"My God!" Monika said, annoyed. "It was a car accident. You got free, but he…" She sighed. "She couldn't get the straps off fast enough to get him out. That's it. They drowned."

"But she was free. She could have swum out behind me."

"As much as I want to sympathize, the other side of the coin is that you believe she should have abandoned our brother to save her own life. You may have been ten, but I thought you knew her better than to assume she would intentionally leave any of us behind."

"But she did—she left us behind."

"Perhaps at the root of your agony isn't even this idea that Ma gave up, or that she chose him." Monika breathed deeply. "Maybe there's the guilt of knowing you didn't help her. You were afraid, and you left them there. That's what burdens you."

Amara backed away from her sister. "No matter how tough you pretend to be, I can see through it." A gentle breeze gifted them with a moment of cool air. "Calvin can't...just like Travis couldn't, or anyone before him. What tragedy— growing old and alone."

"Tragedy? I'm not the one cheating on my husband," Monika fired back.

Amara gasped. "But you don't understand."

"Exactly. It's not for me to understand. It's none of my business what you do—but I can't watch it destroy you."

The sentiment of Monika's words smoothed over their altercation.

The faint sounds of rally chants were heard in the distance, and the women turned towards the source. A few blocks away, city lamp posts lit the pathway for the thousands who flocked downtown from various cities and marched the streets to protest the unjust murder of two, black teenagers, brothers—Desmond and Dante Jones—at the hands of a local police officer. On its third day, the protest continued peacefully as it grew in number; but it was far from quiet. "No justice, no peace" seasoned the night air, and left a bitter taste in the mouths of those who preferred the peace of inaction.

The women could vaguely see police officers strategically positioned to control the crowd and minimize disruption, including the evening's ball, which had been organized weeks before the latest cause for protest had arisen.

Blue and red lights flashed against buildings and lit the night sky like fireworks on Independence Day, but nothing was worthy of celebration.

"I wonder how long they'll keep this up." Amara moved close to the cement wall. "Traffic is even worse with them blocking off the roads."

"Did you know those boys were just leaving a party when they were shot to death?"

"Yeah? But what did they do?"

"They ran."

"Why? They must have been hiding something."

"No. They hadn't done anything. I'm sure they knew better, but in a moment of panic—walking a dark road with an officer yelling to put your hands up—you can't know for sure how you would respond."

"I would stop and put my hands up," Amara said casually. She considered, and was nearly convinced, the boys' suspicious movements provoked the officer to shoot, and her sister was unwilling to meet her halfway.

"Let's go back inside," Monika suggested.

The energy in the dining area had shifted. Partygoers were fully settled and enjoyed an entrée of glazed salmon or roasted chicken with a side of fresh vegetables and rice pilaf. Without masks, very few were comfortable enough to uninhibitedly inhale within the space or hold a conversation. And what was once a good idea had become unsettling as attendees considered the deadly result of having an infected person amongst them. With the pianist on a short break, the quiet permitted the sounds of protest to penetrate the room.

"Are you okay?" Calvin asked when Monika returned.

She nodded her head and pulled her chair closer to the table.

"Where did Jabari go?" Amara inquired.

"Maybe the same place as the rest of your dress," her father said when, even without his glasses, he noticed the thigh-high slit on the front of her gown.

"Or the men's room," Calvin offered.

"Well, Daddy—I would have you know he didn't marry me for my master's degree." She cackled, and most of them ignored.

"With all the protesting—is Jabari on standby?" Bishop Dyer asked his daughter.

"I don't know. Maybe."

"How surprising," Monika whispered towards her sister. "Yet she has George's full schedule converted to memory."

"He's always on call—like other SWAT officers," Amara openly corrected herself as Jabari rejoined them.

"It's an honorable mission to truly protect and serve. I am very proud of you, son." Bishop smiled with glistening eyes.

Amara spoke sentimentally, "There are a lot of crazies out there. There's no greater relief than when I hear his car pull into the garage—even if nightmares won't let him rest. It's scary."

Fatima, the group's semi-welcomed late comer, adjusted in her seat and gently tugged the collar of her dress.

"Let me not start on fear, young lady," Bishop Dyer said. "We'll be here all night." He wiped his mouth with a napkin. "And I have to get out of here."

"Already, Daddy?" Monika asked.

"Yes. I must prepare for the memorial service. Everyone will be at the church at 7 a.m., and I can't let them beat me there."

"I'll meet you at 6:30. I'm sure the kitchen staff could use the help," Monika offered.

"Such a daddy's girl." Amara mumbled and then pressed her lips tightly.

"Are you mad that he loves me more?" Monika smirked.

"I love you both the same," Bishop said, and excused himself to depart.

As Bishop Dyer exited the ballroom, he passed a childcare attendant from the first floor who escorted his grandchildren towards their parents.

"Pop Pop!" Shiloh hugged her grandfather.

"You be good for your parents, you hear." He smiled and continued down the corridor after he gave James a soft pat on the head.

"I love you!" Shiloh called after him.

"Love you, baby."

Their parents were puzzled when they turned and noticed their children stood nearby.

"What's going on? I thought we were good until 9," Amara said to the nursery worker.

Shiloh walked over to Monika and hugged her tightly.

"She said she has a stomachache," the attendant said. "And James refused to stay in the nursery without his big sister."

Arms wrapped around her aunt's neck, Shiloh whispered, "I tried to go to the bathroom."

"It didn't work?" Monika whispered back to her.

She shook her head.

Amara called loudly to her daughter, "Well, come here then." The girl moved close to her. "You alright?"

She looked to Monika with drowsy eyes before she answered, "Yes."

"It's fine. They'll just stay here with us," Jabari said, and placed James on his lap.

"Wait a minute. We've been locked up in the house with all this quarantine business. I'm still on a break," Amara spoke assertively to her husband.

"It's fine." He dismissed the attendant, and a fully blossomed pout appeared on Amara's face.

"Look at you, little girl." One of Bishop Dyer's colleagues acknowledged Shiloh's growth. "She's what now—6? 7?"

"7," the girl said. "And my brother's 3."

"That makes you a first or second grader?"

"First," Amara answered.

"Second," Jabari corrected.

Amara caught herself in a frown and recovered with, "Oh yea, that's right. You see they grow up so fast," and a chuckle.

To continue her contrived interest in her children, she reached for a sheet of paper rolled in Shiloh's hand. "What's this? You draw something for Mommy?" She opened it.

"It's a horse. They ran out of crayons, so I only had red."

The connect-the-dots image was indeed a horse colored in red.

"It's nice baby."

"Hey, I'm going to the restroom," Monika chimed in. "Shiloh, you wanna come?"

"Yes, please."

Monika grabbed the girl's hand and led the way down the hall.

Amara looked over to Calvin, who added more sweetener to his tea. "At least *you two* still have a few hours of freedom."

"It's not like we'll use it," he responded.

* * *

THE neighboring protest was a minor distraction for those who attended ball. Most of them found it amusing and remarked on the dedication of individuals who took action. However, the front line was different. The well-lit city block illuminated the faces of protestors as they passed beneath light posts, masked, and chanted "I can't breathe." Armed officers lined their path to ensure the demonstration was contained to permitted areas, and that violence and looting would not ensue. The crowd's unpredictability was a burden none of them would choose to carry. They were deceived to believe the scope of their duty was limited to what they could see and would be surprised to discover the plot of those they could not.

The Wolves, white men and women who strongly objected the notion of equality and justice for minorities, were not shy to make their presence known as they had done since the late-1800s. A severe distaste for people of color fueled the Wolves' desire to instill fear, and their primary method was the threat of death. For generations, their threats were real, and were affirmed by the brutal murders of innocent, black men, women and children across the American landscape, but primarily in the southern region.

Their guise to safeguard the rights and livelihood of white people was permitted, constitutional, and a valid social cause. Although horrific for American citizens who were targeted and tormented, the Wolves were protected—if not fully embraced—by lawmakers and government officials. They possessed the right to light torches, incite violence, and spew hate just as much as a girl scout is permitted to sell cookies in front of a market.

What did they defend? Economic loss, or danger at the hands of marginalized people, was just cause. The truth was that the Wolves' greatest threat had lain unacknowledged within their own fear. To see past fury and hatred, and to relinquish their anger, they would first have to admit they were afraid. Instead, for over a century, this group's operation was rooted in their fear of diminishing resources and their disgust to share with those they deemed unworthy—those stolen and enslaved by European ancestors. In addition, the possibility of retaliation due to said history unnerved them. Their distress was numbed at the transfer of fear to those they feared most while they feigned their own fearlessness.

For hundreds of years, enslaved Blacks and their "free" offspring assumed most white people upheld the same values as the Wolves. And although beliefs had been deeply engrained, there were many who better valued and humanized black people and were willing to coexist with them. The tolerance of equity-giving Whites was despicable amongst the Wolves. To them, Black oppression meant human domestication, and these were dogs. Therefore, throughout history, progressive-thinking whites clashed with Wolves, and, on occasion, death was a consequence.

While many were isolated and limited their social interaction to those in their pack, there were just as many who existed amongst the least suspecting individuals. The Wolves were able to thrive in close proximity to those they despised if resources, positions, and power were abundant and worked in their favor. On occasion, a hint of revolt, or the disturbance of their traditions and habitat, would ignite a deadly response in defense of their beliefs.

By the second day of protests, the outcry lured the Wolves from the dark crevices of several southern cities, and they secretly scattered themselves along the trail of peace marchers.

* * *

VALERIE Kemp cleared her desk at the precinct and grabbed her car keys and wanted nothing more than to drool into her satin-covered pillow. Her dark, thick hair was pinned into a tight bun and drew the eye to her firm jawline and full lips, which she joked was wider than most; but enabled her roar. Her feet pitter-patted against the steps in front of the station as she approached a fellow officer who stood guard and watched the crowd as it passed.

"You look good in blue. Trinkets and all," Valerie joked.

"Ha! Heading home?" he asked from behind his facemask.

"It's been almost two days. Now would be appropriate." The whites of her eyes were most distinguishable in the dark.

"They'll have another hour before we shut this down and I'm able to call it a night. I missed my anniversary dinner with the wife yesterday. Trying to come up with a way to make it up to her." His soft, green eyes bounced from the march to his compadre.

"Good luck with ending this on time. They say the count has exceeded any other state."

"That's it?"

"What do you mean? That's a lot! It's touching on almost 400,000 people in a single protest. Record-breaking."

"Not that. You won't help me brainstorm a fix to the anniversary situation?"

"Oh. That." She hesitated. "Whatever advice I could offer you—I would first use it to get out of the dumps of my own marriage."

"Damn. You wanna talk about it?"

"No."

While they spoke, Valerie noticed movement in her peripheral vision and turned to see what it was. Two men, dressed in t-shirts and slacks, followed the long walkway carved in the lush grass towards the station's entry. One wore a baseball cap and had his hands tucked tightly into his pants' pockets.

"Is that...?" Valerie began, and the officer turned to look.

"That's Doyle," he finished. "Why would he come here?"

"And come *this* way?" she asked curiously.

"The back entry is protocol."

Officer Robert Doyle, already guilty in the eyes of the downtrodden public for the teenagers' murder, had no affinity for the rules. From a lineage of military veterans and law enforcement officers, his air of superiority was seldom unnoticed.

Confused, the officer in uniform continued to watch the men; however, an individual who hid in the darkness caught Valerie's attention. Tall and stocky, he stood in the shadow of a tree. His skin nearly blended with his dark clothing and facemask; he wore a bookbag in reverse—across the front of his chest—and boots.

He was clearly out of place, so Valerie began to approach as his strides quickened in the direction of the plain-clothed officers who neared the station's entry. The dark man wiped sweat from his forehead, exhaled and, behind the mask, suffered the stink of drunkenness. He reached for his bag with clammy fingers. When he could barely grip its zipper, he wiped his hands on his mask, and removed it before he tried the zipper again.

Valerie's eyes narrowed on the handgun he brandished from his bag, and before she could yell "gun", three shots rang out as the man aimed steadily at Officer Doyle. The crowd shoved past each other to get away but were caged between officers who stood post and oblivious marchers who kept their pace.

Weapon drawn; Valerie pointed it towards the armed man.

"Drop it now!" she yelled. Seeing her, he immediately released the gun, and it fell to the ground before the sound of six shots were heard. Eyes wide, the man went quickly to his knees, and laid back on the grass.

Valerie quickly turned to the source of gunfire as officers rushed over to contain the scene. Elbows locked, guns in grip, they yelled, "Get back! Get back now!" to anyone who did not move with enough haste.

Seeing the stiffness of the officer's arm as he held his weapon, and his slow-blinking gaze, Valerie knew the officer she'd engaged with only moments before had pulled the trigger.

"What the hell was that?" she asked as she approached.

"I had to shoot. He fired his weapon."

"He dropped it!" Valerie said, hands firmly locked around her gun.

Across the courtyard, a female officer radioed, "Officer down!" as she examined Officer Doyle's motionless body.

There was more for the severely ethical Valerie to say, but the moment would not permit it. Instead, she joined the uniforms that hovered over the suspicious man who lie bleeding on the ground.

He stared up at the night sky, past the leaves of the trees that towered overhead and gasped for air, which could not remedy his condition. He gurgled and choked as they watched him suffer through his final moments. At his departure, they lowered their weapons.

"He looks familiar," an officer spoke.

"He's the father of those boys." Valerie holstered her weapon. "Darius Jones."

A hush fell over them, and they noticed the somber expressions of comrades gathered around the fallen officer a few meters away.

Brave protestors who lingered near the scene fired up camera phones to capture the moment the conflicted father surrendered his life. Video was truth, compassionate and concerned, and could bring back to life those who no longer lived.

Amid several city streets, protestors dispersed to escape the chaos, but officers pushed them along in a single direction, and would not permit them to deviate from the planned strategy. The slow and weak were trampled; but even the swift seemed to chase their own tail.

A young, black woman, anxious to overcome the stampede, shoved pass one person after another before her attempt was met by one of the easily triggered Wolves in their midst. His abdomen received a forceful blow from woman's elbow in her attempt to get away.

He painfully grabbed his belly. "You nigger bitch!"

The woman slowed enough to respond. "I got your 'nigger', bitch."

There was a slight break in the crowd, and the isolated altercation caught the attention of others, already outraged, who passed them.

"Show me," he taunted, and then shoved her to the ground with the force of both palms.

Two men went to her defense. One moved close enough to the Wolf to breathe in the man's air as it filtered through his dark facemask.

"You wanna put your hands on a woman?" the guy said as he pushed the man backwards.

The aggressive touch of a black man was the catalyst Wolves needed to move from intimidating observers to a blood-thirsty militia, and they were ready. He quickly removed a firearm from his waist.

"Watch what I can do," he said, and fired two shots into the man's torso.

The less confrontational hero and the woman chewed on the moment's severity, and attempted to flee, but would not get far before they were shot down.

Armed and in protective gear, ninety-three Wolves dispersed amongst the unsuspecting crowd, removed their weapons, and fired at random.

* * *

THE pops of gunfire were heard within the Mask-Her-Aid event a few blocks away, and immediately alerted occupants that something was awry.

"Is that what I think it is?" Amara asked Jabari. She lowered her fork onto the plate.

"Stay here." He removed the napkin from his lap and tossed it aside. His robust, 6'5" frame towered over those who sat in amazement, and his swift action gifted them with a sense of safety.

Before Jabari could reach the window that overlooked York Avenue, the roar of an explosion confirmed their suspicions. They gasped, and immediately gathered their belongings. Someone was under attack, but who was uncertain.

Plumes of smoke clouded the night sky; flames rose above the marchers' heads as they flooded the streets, and the heat hindered their progress. Jabari's eyes darted from one runner to another—one tumbled to the ground, and then another: one pop, and then another, and another. Curious about the turmoil on the streets beneath them, gala attendees parted with their tables. A few started towards the exit when the evening's host grabbed the microphone and moved to the center of the room. The short train of her cream gown trailed behind her.

"Everyone let's stay calm. Don't go outside until we know what's happening." Their blatant disregard nudged them towards the elevators. "Please. Don't leave before you know what's going on out there." They continued to ignore her plea.

Amara's heart raced when she joined Jabari at the window. "What is it? Can you see what's happening?" She looked towards the flames, and instantly hid her mouth behind her hands. "What is that?"

"I don't know. Stay with the kids, and don't leave the building," Jabari said with authority.

"Where are you going? Come with me." She grabbed his forearm and attempted to pull him closer. "Come on," she insisted.

Jabari looked adoringly at his wife when his phone rang and disrupted his gaze.

"Yeah," he answered. Amara watched as his countenance exposed his displeasure. "I'll be there." He started to walk but Amara followed.

"No, wait! Who was that? Work? Where are you going, Jabari? Don't leave us here."

"I have to. I'm not going far. Get the kids, take the elevator to the 20th floor. I'll find you there."

Stretched between annoyance and fear, Amara went back to the dinner table where her husband displayed no regard for his bewildered children, grabbed his keys and tucked them into a pocket.

"Calvin, keep a good eye on my family." He loosened his red tie. "I told Amara what to do."

"Okay, but..." Amara began to protest.

"Monika." Jabari petitioned the icy-eyed woman who sat stoically in her seat, but she did not budge.

"Don't worry." Calvin stepped up, but his machismo paled in comparison to Jabari's natural masculinity and strength. "I'll have eyes on them both, Jabari. Go ahead. They'll be fine." Calvin stood. "Monika, let's get Michael from the nursery."

Monika's face, saturated with sorrow, turned towards him, and she swallowed the saliva that had accumulated in her mouth. "I can't."

"What do you mean?"

"Just go. And give him kisses for me," Monika said with suffocating sadness, and then stood from her chair.

"I don't understand." Calvin's brows nearly met in the middle of his forehead. "Where are you going?" he called out, but Monika hurried away and disappeared in the path of Jabari's shadow.

CHAPTER TWO

ARMED IN THE HOLY CAUSE OF LIBERTY

THE men grew cold and rigid on the fresh cut lawn of the police station and waited for a break in the turmoil before their bodies could be collected. Valerie's throat tightened and she sensed pressure between her pulsating ears. The stench of the shooting officer's ethics was difficult to pacify. As policemen within precinct rushed out to address the protest's worsening condition, Valerie was not among them. Instead, she went inside and retrieved a vest from her locker.

The station's panic mirrored the madness beyond it. No one could passively observe, so immediately engaged. Their territory had been infiltrated by a madman, and their priority was to secure the premises. The momentous entry of a newborn baby would pale in comparison to the urgent need for defense. Valerie knocked shoulders with a few as they hustled to an exit, but stopped short of her superior officer, armed and ready to take to the streets.

"Sergeant," she called.

"What is it Kemp?" the man asked as he moved quickly towards the exit.

Valerie followed as she spoke. "The shooter...I got him to lower his weapon *before* he was shot." She shoved through the doors behind him.

"And...?"

Shots were heard from some indistinct place, and they both ducked, but Valerie was persistent. "It's wrong."

They moved down the walkway onto the road.

"The man fired a weapon and killed an officer. He's dead now. That's the end of it," he said.

"He shouldn't have been gunned down on the lawn," she argued.

The sergeant yielded at her comment. "There is a war going on out here. Do something useful. That's an order." He rushed away.

Her well-organized desk, and the necessary documents to thoroughly and expediently express her disgust, were within the building behind her. In front of her was the scene of a conflict similar to those illustrated in history books. Gunfire interrupted her thoughts, and rendered them jagged, and short of useful. The urge to act rose above the conflicting thoughts, and she strapped on the vest she carried in her hands. The hope of justice would have to wait until she ensured those yet to encounter her quick-acting, fellow officers were appropriately guided to safety.

"Let's go! Move!" Valerie yelled, weapon raised and eyes sharp for gunmen.

Thousands of feet pounded against the asphalt. No one listened, or perhaps no one could hear above consistent explosions, but the radiant fires illuminated their panicked faces.

A woman and her two young sons cowered against an office building. Her eyes were closed tightly as though she would soon awake in the comforts of her bedroom, but she was in the middle of a waking nightmare, and the night still had milk on its warm breath.

"You can't stay here," Valerie said loud enough to be heard over the commotion.

"I hurt my knee," the woman said. "I can't walk on it. And my boys can't help much."

"Come." Valerie holstered her gun and extended her hand to the woman.

They moved slowly as she hobbled with her arm wrapped firmly around Valerie's shoulders. She cut through a barricade intended to control the protestors, and took a sidewalk lined with shops. Most of them were dark inside, but when Valerie noticed movement in a t-shirt printing business, she stopped and pounded on the door.

"Police!" she announced. "Open the door!"

It creaked opened slightly and a middle-age black man with beady eyes appeared. A young woman lingered in the dark nearby, and she pivoted nervously from one foot to the other.

"We're not getting involved in this," he said. "It's hard to get to our car with everyone running around."

"And you won't be able to move it once you get there." Valerie responded. "Can these people wait with you? It may be a while before this is cleared up."

Boisterous snaps of gunfire vibrated against the building.

"Come in," he said, and opened the door just enough for the family of three to step inside. The door was quickly shut and locked without any further exchange.

Valerie breathed deeply, and knew they were merely three of thousands who would attempt to escape the chaos. It was like she collected a single cola can from the waste of a massive landfill. So, she moved with haste to do more.

* * *

BOMBS exploded, and the glow of fires brightened office buildings and reflected from their windows. To avoid the congested elevators, Jabari and Monika took the stairs to the bottom floor and emerged in the foyer as couples frantically collected their children from the nursery.

Monika could hear the whining youngsters and crying babies as parents gathered them with urgency. The security camera that eyed the exit—omniscient and true—captured Monika's hesitation. Her own son was a few strides away.

Jabari noticed her slowed pace and grabbed her hand. "We have to go," he said.

What she lacked was his promise that her son would be fine—or that his own children would be safe. If he had, it would have been a lie, and Jabari never fell short of sincerity.

He tightened his grip of her hand and led her onto the sidewalk. The foul smell of fuel, burning wood and rubber, saturated the air, and made it hard to breathe. They took shallow breaths. Partygoers who made a dash for the flooded streets quickly discovered that random cars had blocked most of the roadway, and the garage was inaccessible. They were trapped.

A car passed on a cross street and hit several vehicles in its path. The passenger positioned himself from the window and erratically fired his semi-automatic rifle as the horrified people scurried to safety. Jabari and Monika hid behind a metal trash can until the threat passed but were mostly without fear. Soon, the pair was on the move again; three others were not as fortunate.

A community center, once the church where Monika's father began his ministry 35 years prior, sat on the corner a few blocks north, and they were determined to get there. Monika's high-heeled shoes hindered her ability to keep pace with Jabari, so she swiftly removed them, tossed them aside, and continued barefoot. Jabari never stopped to look back, and he sped along confident Monika would keep pace.

The building was dark inside and out, but people moved about like a colony of black ants without a queen. The foyer had old wooden floors that creaked with the slightest movement, and it wreaked of mildewed carpet and old linens. In darkness, it was easy to make out a few tables and chairs sprawled throughout the space, but there was little order. Light emanated from a doorway that led to the basement, and they followed it.

On the bottom floor, large boxes—cubby holes—had been installed along each of the walls, at least two hundred of them. Each had a numbered sticker, but no names.

Monika's—18. Men moved swiftly through the space, grabbed the contents of their boxes, removed their clothing, and then redressed. Jabari and Monika followed suit.

Monika placed a gold bracelet, and the diamond earrings Calvin gave her for her birthday, into a plastic box. As she removed her gown, she heard it split, but it did not matter. Nor did it matter that she was surrounded by men as she stripped down to the panties beneath it. Her breasts were full, beautifully bronze, and sat perfectly within her strapless bra, but no one noticed. Perhaps when her gown fell to the floor the man who tightened his boots next to her caught a glimpse of her round backside, but nothing more. She pulled on a pair of loose-fitting, black pants, a black t-shirt, and secured her vest to her chest.

Monika grabbed a pack of chewing gum, nearly empty, from the contents of the plastic box. She popped a stick into her mouth and placed the one that remained into her back pocket. She removed combat boots from the built-in and placed them on her feet. From a second pair, she removed a single shoestring and used it to tie her hair back into a ponytail before she sat down to lace her shoes.

The scuffle was a rhythmic dance of ups, downs, clicks, clacks, grunts, and deep sighs. Few talked, none touched. Within three minutes of entry, each man and woman set out again, and left an empty hole where their gear had been. They moved robotically through the room and readied themselves for battle.

The time for which they prepared, but never desired, had come. These were the men and women of TAAR. The African American Revolutionists was a secret organization birthed in the shadows of the Million Man March two-and-a-half decades before.

A daring alliance of radical intellectuals who attended the momentous gathering were not as civil in their progressive thoughts as the event's leaders and was outraged by what seemed a "pleasant" and "submissive" approach to improvement, justice, and equality. Gone were the days they would quietly accept circumstances that demeaned them. The inferior mindset that plagued generations, free and enslaved, would be reprogrammed. And victory would come at a cost none could afford.

To some degree, they believed the solution to mistreatment was suggested decades earlier with the ambitious idea of a massive exodus. They had grown weary in their peaceful pursuit and settled on the impossibility of a rewired American system. They desired to completely erase the history of black people to enable fresh perspective and acceptance. Gathering what was left of their pride and sailing east towards the land that birthed their ancestors would yield the best outcome. However, many pondered where they would go, if they would be accepted or would ever have ownership. The men and women in their lineage had labored against their will, against their physical and emotional strength and ability, and against their own identity to build the country that held them hostage. Those who met secretly demanded the right to dwell there, have ownership, and be treated as citizens of the land. And they agreed they would never taste freedom without a willingness to die for it. They believed the paralyzing response to intimidation must be completely obliterated, or control would be unlikely. They prepared to be beaten, incarcerated, *and* killed.

"We're not here to rally, or party, or to encourage, enlighten or uplift, or to comply. We're here to die protecting our own to emphasize the need for change," a faceless founder was rumored to have spoken during their initial meeting.

The men took specific measures to ensure they would not be exploited or infiltrated and preferred to remain unknown to the world around them. To make their existence public would mean the assignment of a leader—whom they were certain would be the immediate target of every government agency that sought to silence rebellious speech, or those who posed a threat to national security and their way of life. Secondly, they knew that a leader could not be controlled. Therefore, decisions were made collectively.

There were no allies except those they groomed themselves—black or white. No one joined. They were ordered by their parents or were recruited—most of them initially under the guise of some community development program. And *community* was emphasized over any political or religious affiliation. There was no room to bicker about religious doctrine when a vital organ of mankind suffered death and mistreatment due to a single unifying trait: race. Very little mattered more to those who organized the group, and its followers learned to give no attention to factors that could create division amongst them and weaken their cause. They would only agree that Blacks had consistently suffered injustice, and they were ready to do something drastically different to end it. Lost between the hope of previous strategies and their acceptance of continued oppression, they made peace with the proposed method—fight.

There were several campuses where members were trained and educated. Adherence to strict rules ensured their secrecy. They took busses, walked, or hitched a ride to avoid detection and anyone who could keep record of car tag numbers. No one was called by name, even if it was previously known amongst the group. The organization was not spoken of beyond meeting places, and especially not through phone conversations. Very few were privy to the organization's structure. Most were in the dark, but their reach stretched nine states within a few years, and by year twenty, they had spread throughout sixteen states and could account for nearly thirty-six hundred men and women.

Like eagles, nameless TAAR organizers swooped in and snatched the young from the enjoyment and innocence of childhood. Small institutions were erected specifically for them to learn the origin of their people, their true ancestry coupled with the trauma of the transatlantic slave trade, the history of false promises spoken by their nation's leaders and the system built against them, and the suffering they were certain to experience in the future without their allegiance to the cause. They became familiar with bombs and firearms, and learned to bear deafening pops of gunfire, and the roar of explosions. TAAR-babies were desensitized to violence and grew immune to the fear of it.

Sons were encouraged to join the National Guard, every law enforcement entity, or pursue careers in politics. The girls were also prepped for roles in education, law enforcement, and politics. They were able-bodied equals and trained for combat alongside their male counterpart—an essential strength. As a result, TAAR fully infiltrated even large organizations, except federal agencies that seldom hired minorities.

These men and women slept un-peacefully for nearly 25 years until the spark of conflict that peppery June evening of 2020. In that time, they witnessed the deaths of countless men and women who could never escape their blackness—the crime for which they were punished. Frequently, and with the formation of younger civil justice groups, TAAR considered if they should reveal themselves; but ultimately their stance was for everyone else to march for black lives to matter while TAAR's actions proved they already did.

"We're not activists; we're revolutionists," they would say.

Monika was handed three weapons—two were strapped to her waistband and the other, a larger, heavier rifle, was carried close to her chest.

"Remember," a voice called out from the hustle of preparation, "Wolves aren't the only enemy we'll have out here. Anyone with a gun and badge can take you down. Be alert and watch your back."

As he strapped his boots, a man said, "No one has a face, or a name. If they're not one of us, and armed, I'm firing first."

"Fear give you amnesia, brother?" another man said as he lifted his rifle to his shoulder.

"I won't be killed before I see the end of this."

"Never take aim at the law. You know that."

"We can say what we should do while we're in here. Let's see if the tune changes out there." He tucked a pistol into the holster on his waist. "The revolution will mean bloodshed and not boardroom meetings," he quoted. "Remember?"

Monika overheard the men's exchange and slowed her preparation to digest the severity of the moment, and to contemplate the value of a life, good or bad. They were all her allies, but none were closer to her than Jabari—number 27.

Focused, he ensured ammunition was properly loaded into the weapon he cradled lightly in his arms.

"27." Monika got his attention, and then spoke in a low tone. "How can we be sure this will work?"

"What do you mean?" His eyes narrowed on the gun in his hands.

"People will die."

"Yeah."

"What if our cause is overlooked? This would all be for nothing."

"What we'll show them and what they choose to see may be different, but that wouldn't be anything new." He finally looked to the delicate face painted with apprehension and sadness. Jabari grabbed Monika's arm firmly and whispered, "No, you're doing this." He spoke with authority. "Right now—check your weapon, 18."

Monika stared with empty eyes. She would not budge.

"Check your weapon," he commanded. "Or go out there and hand it over to the Wolves. There would be no hesitation to use it on you."

Monika reluctantly checked her ammunition as she considered as many of the evening's "what ifs" she could conjure. Her hands wrapped around the cold steel and life seemed to drain from her. Numb. Jabari was her voice of reason, but his words conflicted with a subtler voice that spoke from within her.

She settled on the idea that fear had risen to distract her from a cause greater than any other she could possess— one that had possessed her since adolescence. She patted her face with damp fingers as if to wake herself from hesitation.

"You ready?" Jabari asked in his velvety, deep voice.

"Let's go."

Equipped, they rushed back to the ballroom. The lower levels were partially lit as those who hid in the dark peered from windows and avoided discovery, or the risk of luring others inside. As Monika and Jabari passed, observers gawked at the armed pair who made their way towards the elevators in the corridor. They moved in silence and seriousness, and no one stood in their way.

On the 20th floor, a few of the ball's attendees were seated in the dimly lit room—scattered here and there while others gathered near the window for a distant glimpse of the commotion below them. Between bursts of gunfire, they could hear each other's breaths.

Amara and the children squatted near the exit to the stairwell when Jabari spotted them. Shiloh noticed her father immediately and was determined to pounce playfully on him; but with the weapon strapped across his chest, halted her pursuit and stared inquisitively.

"It's alright, baby." He nudged her chin and kissed her forehead. His words were soothing, but the girl was far from comforted.

"Jabari." Amara stood to her feet, initially excited. Like their daughter, when she noticed the weapon in his arms, she paused. "What's all this? What's going on?" Once serious, Amara could not contain her laughter when Monika joined him. Each pair of eyes in the room narrowed on the melanin-soaked GI Joe and Jane.

She chuckled. "For real—what is this?"

"Let's talk," Monika said.

"But not here," Jabari added, and looked around the room. "I thought you would be alone," he said to his wife.

Calvin, amongst the scattered, creeped closer and sized his fiancé from her boots to her rifle-strapped chest as he held their infant son.

"We were, but others trickled in for a quiet place to figure out what the hell is happening. Lucky for them they just caught an eyeful of you two—Beat Down Barbie and Black Man."

They politely ignored her juvenile comedic moment.

"The conference room across the hall," Jabari suggested once Calvin joined them. "Shiloh, can you stay here and keep an eye on your brother?"

The girl nodded, and the group exited with haste.

The conference room had a single, narrow table in its center, and was surrounded by several swivel chairs. It was cold. Jabari and Monika placed their rifles on the table while Calvin and Amara sat partially in their seats.

Amara looked at her hands. "Shoot! Another broken nail. That's what I get. I swear she swapped food benefits for that whack hairdo," she said to herself and rolled her eyes.

The baby gurgled and whimpered as he squirmed for comfort in Calvin's arms. When his father pat him gently on the back, Monika noticed, but withheld any show of concern.

The building rattled after an explosion, and flakes of debris sprinkled from the ceiling onto the conference table.

"Okay. Talk!" Amara rushed them.

Coolly, Calvin added, "It seems there is a real-life battle on York Ave, and here we are with the black Avengers. Tell us *something*."

Amara giggled, but Calvin's words were sincere and devoid any playfulness.

Monika and Jabari looked to each other to encourage one to speak.

"We've trained for many years," Monika started nervously.

No one had prepared them to deliver their truth to loved ones. The explanation seemed silly as she assembled the words in her head before she parted her lips to say them. "Almost twenty-five," she added.

"Twenty-five years, Monika?" Amara chuckled in disbelief. "Well, that's a lie. I've known you all my life. Then tell me when. Where?"

"That doesn't matter right now," Jabari interjected. "Right now, we have to get you out of here safely, and without going into the street."

"It's crazy right now, I know, but it'll calm down soon. The police are out there," Amara spoke confidently. "I'm not leaving my car parked down here in all this mess."

At her comment, deep creases surfaced across her husband's forehead.

Calvin sat quietly and stared at a Monika he had never known.

"It won't pass in the way you think. This is beyond random violence—and deadly."

Amara's eyes widened. "So, you're going out there to kill people, Jabari?" She sat up high in anticipation of his response. "You're an officer of the law. Where is your SWAT attire?"

"It's not what you think. I have to protect us—our children."

"We're fine. We're all here together."

"Not just us, Amara. Our people…Black people."

"If this is some extreme activism bullshit, I won't stick around for it. This is not the way to do it." She stood partly from her seat.

"Sit down."

She plopped back into her chair.

"We're beyond suggestions, Amara. Just listen to me."

Monika, more assertive, spoke again. "Out there are Wolves who planned this attack on innocent people."

"But none of them expected a fight—at least not from us. We're ready to respond—to do what we've been trained to do," Jabari added.

"Die?" Calvin asked.

"Yes," Monika responded without a gulp of hesitation.

Amara spoke slowly, "Oh, my god."

"Why you?" Calvin asked with tense brows.

"I can't explain that now." Monika said, and then redirected. "There is a way out of downtown, but you have to follow very specific instructions."

"And leave you here?"

"Yes. Take the baby as far as possible. Amara and the kids too," Monika said.

"Wait. You knew for 25 years that you would do this, and never said a word?" Amara asked as she pounded a fist against the table.

Jabari ignored his wife's inquisitive rant and reached for the weapon strapped to his ankle.

"Here, Calvin. Take this." The steel clanked against the table, and he pushed it closer to the stunned man with the baby.

Calvin looked at it with hollow eyes. "I guess I can fire with my right hand, and carry my son with the other," he said mockingly. "Are you serious? Monika, you're not leaving us."

"I can't stay here."

"If you know how we can get out of here, then we are—and together," Calvin insisted.

"And along the way I'll pass countless others who are committed to seeing this thing through. I won't do it."

"Who gives a damn what they think?"

"I do. They can't lose courage knowing they've been left behind."

"And it's okay for you to leave *us* behind?" Amara yelled. Her lips trembled, and nearly caused Jabari to bend under the weight of her expression.

"I'm getting into position, Monika," Jabari said. He grabbed his rifle and was gone in an instant.

"That's it?" Amara wiped her eyes.

"I'm sorry," Monika said in a whisper.

"Are you really?" Amara stood from her seat. "Anything you say right now may very well be a lie. And I've never known my sister to lie to me."

"I know."

Amara paused next to her sister. "I wish you the best with all of this, but I have to check on my children. While you're both out here playing vigilante, you forgot you have your own to look after." She glanced at Calvin before she walked away in disgust.

The room bore a moment quiet enough to hear hearts breaking. Calvin's breath synched with the rise and fall of his son's chest, and he briefly imagined the life the boy would have without his mother. His despair called for a calculated approach to pull Monika from her outlandish commitment, but the words would not come to him—at least there were none profound enough to give him confidence, so he went with what he felt.

35

"What do you want from me, Monika? Whatever it is, just tell me."

"It's not about us."

"Then can we make it about him?" He patted the drowsy child on the back, but Monika refused to look.

"This *is* about him."

"Is that what they told you?" He asked, appalled. "Tell me how."

"Our people die at the hands of law enforcement and racists in this country every day. Who's to say that one day he won't be one of them?"

"Our people. This boy is *your* people. And you're okay with him growing up without you?" He paused a moment and endured the silence. "Monika, you're sure to go to prison for this—if you're not killed first. Please tell me that's not okay. I want you to say it, and we can leave right now."

"It has to be."

"You have a choice."

"I don't."

"Wow." He clenched his jaw. "I always admired your loyalty, but I never took you for brainwashed. This is crazy, Monika. Can't you see that?"

His pleas were met with silence. The climate caused Monika to shiver. Her teeth chattered.

"I have to go," she said.

He reciprocated her cutting silence.

"Take the gun. Use it. Protect him."

Insulted by her false concern for their son's safety, he scowled at her, but managed to calm himself before he opened his mouth to speak. "It's no secret that I've never fired a gun before. I'm a math teacher, not a militant. Before now, I thought you'd never touched one either, but as I sit here, I'm trying to count all the lies you've probably told me over the years. And as much as I want to be angry, I don't want them to be the last thoughts I have of you." He stood. "I may not be foolishly trained and brainwashed, but I have my own plan for getting out of here. Goodbye."

As Calvin slithered by with their son, whose eyes were closed gently—completely unaware of the tension in the room or the chaos in the streets—Monika grabbed the back of a chair as her legs buckled beneath her. Although the moment pained her, she never wanted her son to know what it was like to march in a protest for equality, to bury a friend, or to be cut down himself, and those thoughts rekindled her purpose for the fight.

She grunted to clear her throat and stood erect after a few moments. As she turned to leave the room, her sister approached—eyes red and heavy.

"Tell me where he is, Monika." She removed the designer shoes from her feet and placed them on top of the table.

"I can't."

"I won't stop him. I promise. I just want to tell him 'Goodbye'. With all I'm losing, at least give me that."

Monika sensed her sister's desperation, and the need for closure to prepare for worst-case scenarios that circled her psyche.

"Come with me." She grabbed her rifle from the table and led her barefoot sister down the corridor towards the stairwell.

As they ascended, Amara's ball gown swept across the concrete steps and snagged on the railing's chipped paint. Suddenly, she squealed in pain as they neared the exit door to the rooftop. A small piece of metal pierced her foot.

Concerned, Monika halted. "You okay?"

Amara examined her bleeding foot, and then took another step towards the top. "Nothing's okay."

Outside, fumes and smoke caused them to choke on the suffocating air.

Between breaths, Monika mustered, "Stay here. He's on the other side."

It was the same space where, hours earlier, Amara and Monika conversed with a pleasant celebration as their backdrop. Since, everything had turned on its side, and Amara struggled to piece it all together. Neither of her college degrees could help her to discover reasonable answers; nor could her experience in advertising, or her knack for analysis, result in anything that could give her comfort, or some level of understanding. The fact that two people she loved most led secret lives made her a stranger to herself. She struggled to discern what, if anything, was real.

Jabari bent the corner and, upon seeing her, lifted his hands slightly in silent surrender. "We can't do this right now. Not here."

"Then when? Where? Your gravesite?" she snapped back.

"You have to leave. It's not safe."

"You're still here. I'm not going anywhere."

"Then what?"

"I deserve a better goodbye than you've given."

"I don't have time for the dramatics."

"Then just tell me why—why are you doing this?"

He huffed. "Come here." He grabbed her arm and walked her to the edge of the roof. "Look."

She could count at least a dozen people in the road who lie limp or lifeless, and countless others who swarmed frantically before they hid briefly behind a pillar or parked car. The wails of women were heard from various places. And out of ambiguous, dark places, shots were fired; but Amara could not bear to see if the bullets reached their targets, so turned away and clung tightly to Jabari.

"This is real, Amara."

She could see into the sincerity of his soul, and there was nothing more left to say.

"It won't just blow over."

"This is not who we are," she said softly.

"Very few of us know who we are. We're who this world forced us to become. They will see."

She had never known the man in front of her. "Please, Jabari."

"If you want to get out of here, go down to the first floor. There is a man waiting at the first entry point. We call him 39. Tell him you're the wife of 27."

The words rolled from his lips as gibberish to Amara. Since adolescence, she had known him as Jabari Rushing, but somehow, he had been reduced to a number.

"You don't love me, do you?"

"Don't let a moment rob you of the joy we've experienced for nearly 18 years." He pulled her chin nearer to him and kissed her. "The kids need you. Go."

Amara tried to memorize the places on her face where his hand pressed against her skin, the firm yet gentleness of his touch, the warmth of his breath, the softness of his lips, and she was determined to never part with it.

CHAPTER THREE
KNOW THE WHOLE TRUTH

October 16, 1995

THE long day of events, the sweeping crowd of black faces, and the call to improve their communities—beginning with their own homes—was enough for anyone to crash into bed before the privilege of a hot shower; but five men resisted the urge for rest. Instead, they assembled near midnight in the grandest suite of a popular D.C. hotel.

The room's furnishings were crimson and mahogany, dark, and dimly lit by a small lamp on a short, end table. Each chair was perfectly positioned to engage with those seated comfortably on the sofa.

The evening's host poured whisky from a stout bottle into short, frosted glasses and handed them out one by one. He grabbed one for himself and took a seat near the others. His name was Jacob Spencer, a New York-based lawyer whose kindness in social settings balanced the monstrous perception most people held of him. To them, his defense of thugs, dope pushers, and murderers was as atrocious as the crime itself. After 18 years in practice, he had made peace with others' opinions if it kept men out of prison.

Jacob had no interest in technological advancements, so blew the dust from a Nina Simone cassette he carried in his car for years and inserted it into the dual player. Her melodic voice, piano chords, and a trumpet, filled the silent space as they settled in their seats.

One of the men grunted from the sting of the whisky as he lowered his glass.

Robert Hudson's glass was nearly empty before the host could take his seat. He was a writer, and the son of a famous Harlem Renaissance literary figure. No one truly knew his father's identity because he would never say, and no one pressed the issue. It is possible that he was the product of an affair and had not known the man; or perhaps there was no truth to it at all. Most people were swallowed up by his tales, and that one may have been amongst them. Despite curiosities that surrounded his origin, he easily drew people to him. Women found his light complexion and tall stature appealing or could not bear to ignore the dysfunctional drunk. Intellectuals found elements of Black pride engrained in his works and were easily intrigued. He was a natural teacher, and many flocked to him—or at least his words, which flowed freely and consistently from his lips just as alcohol to his glass.

Robert spoke slowly to minimize the slur of alphabets that bubbled from his lips. "I've had enough time to reflect. I am a man—have always walked upright and taken care of my family. I didn't have to come here for this."

"Wait now. I can understand the man's point. Get the house in order is first. Real change can't come from disunity. Not all men are where you are," Jacob offered.

"But what more? After meditation and prayer, what then?"

"Back to the drawing board, I suppose." Jacob lifted his glasses to his face and squinted for better focus.

"We should have made some demands—asked for something. We came all this way to talk about us black folks and how we can be better amongst ourselves. I say, we'd be quite alright if we worked our jobs, took care of our women, fed our kids, and wasn't afraid to get locked up or shot at. It's not one or the other. All sides need addressing."

E.J.'s glass clanked against the coffee table, and then he slouched quietly on the crimson sofa. E.J. Rushing was not a "man of few words", though he gave many the impression. He had conditioned himself to speak only if what he had to offer would make a difference. Otherwise, he was an observer. From a lineage of proud Igbo people, he made no apology for his ancestry. Although some had embraced American ideologies and customs, they never lost sight of their identity as warriors, priests, and kings.

E.J. spoke from behind loose fingers covering his lips. "Seems to me he wants to create a better perception of the black man. And that's good, but who rights the perception Blacks have of Whites? I don't see them making speeches about how they could be less perceived as racists, bigots, or oppressors. Why are we so concerned about what they *think* when most of them couldn't care less about what they continue to *do*?"

The man closest to E.J., spatially that evening and in friendship, was Michael Dyer—a pastor from Georgia whose ministry had grown to nearly eight thousand members since taking over an abandoned building in downtown Atlanta ten years prior. The climb was continuous, steady, and plentiful, but was overshadowed by the loss of his wife and young son eight months earlier. He channeled the ache of their loss into his ministry, or his desire to implement change by pushing the Black agenda. Still, there was always sadness in his eyes— one that existed long before the loss of his wife. Something had bubbled to the surface, but instead of spilling over, he pulled it back and contained it. His love for his daughters— Amara, who was 12, and Monika, 14—was seldom spoken but often felt. They adapted to the void of their mother's absence but could never fill the emptiness within their father.

"I'll tell you: we're a trapped people. Stolen from our homeland, forced into slavery, and then taxed with the duty of proving our worthiness to be here," Michael offered. "Anything—character, personality, hair, lips, nose, work ethic—that's unlike their own kind, they find a way to change it, even make us hate it ourselves."

"Seems like we need their approval—a pat on the head to show we've been good boys and won't cause no trouble. And still—no peace."

"You need no approval," E.J. spoke, but his dark features were barely seen in the shadowy room. "Be confident in the man you are. Black people make themselves small to comply with what's acceptable to Whites. It won't be until we express who we are openly and proudly that they can learn to just accept it. They try to change us because they know they can. They have no respect for us, or our culture. We may never see the end of it."

The room grew quiet as the men fully grasped the comments or waited for the burn of their liquor to pass. The question that plagued those victimized by the American system, and those who desired to remedy its brokenness, was: how to end racism? It was quite optimistic to believe that America could be cured of the deep-seated illness that oppressed its Black citizens and, at one point, deemed them disposable. A truth more readily accepted was that it was impossible to eliminate racism without dismantling the entire system. Therefore, it was more likely to witness an echo of times past than the establishment of new, peaceable conditions for Blacks.

Adam Chaskel wasn't Black. He was a Jew who sympathized with the anguish of black people and earned the trust of otherwise untrusting men. His father's role as a political science professor at an HBCU in the 1940s and his unspoken connection with his students' affliction, was the springboard for his affinity. He sat forward in his chair but had not contributed to the discussion up to that point, so saw the silence as his chance to engage. He took a swig of his liquor and hissed as he clenched his teeth.

"Let me pose this age-old question," he started. "As black men in this country, would you rather be respected or feared?"

Initially, none of the men spoke. It even seemed they dismissed his question altogether. Perhaps his lack of melanin had given some of them pause.

"So, which is it?" Adam petitioned. "Respected or feared?"

Throughout history, there were Whites who rallied against the marginalization of Black people, but the divide ran so deep that neither changes in legislature nor constitutional rights could guarantee a shift in mindset. Many were oblivious to their own racist beliefs. Not Adam. He was confident in his love for all people, and never stretched himself to prove it.

After a moment, E.J. responded as casually as someone ordering takeout. "Because I am feared, I can never be free. And the idea of having respect is merely a dream. I'd rather be free."

"Why would you say that you're feared?"

"No one would dedicate so much time, energy, and resources to keep something in line they were not already afraid of."

"Innocent as doves..." Michael mumbled.

"What was that?"

"It's a scripture. Matthew 10:16. Jesus says he's sending the disciples out like sheep among wolves. He told them to be as wise as snakes and as innocent as doves."

"But black people aren't the twelve disciples."

"No, but they expect you to take heed to Jesus's words. The majority of Blacks are Christians."

"Wolves are cunning, swift, strong, deadly—run in packs. It's even been said they don't just kill to eat." E.J. took a swig of liquor from his glass. "They kill for sport. Not threat, or danger."

"Very true."

"Yet the response should be gentleness—like doves?" Robert asked.

"It's scripture," Michael affirmed.

"Wait a minute. You've missed the other half of it. 'Wise as serpents,'" Adam added.

"Snakes are very calculated. Can't hear. Vibrations let them know when something's coming."

"In human terms, you would avoid being distracted by what people say, and mindful of what they do."

The men nodded as they understood the collective breakdown of the verse.

Jacob lowered the glasses from his face. "Their eyes are always open too—even asleep," he said. "Always on guard to respond to subtle movements." He lifted the frames back to his nose.

"Think about it: the way they avoid danger in the first place is to hide themselves. If they strike, they wait for whatever it is to get close and enter their space."

"I'm all in for the serpent, but a dove... I don't know," E.J. said.

"We've all had enough to drink. Wolves, serpents, doves—maybe it's time to call it," Robert chuckled. "But I'll have another for the road." He went over to fill his glass as the others laughed at the odd trajectory of their conversation.

It was after 1 a.m. and exhaustion had nearly pinned the men to their seats. They knew the shades of the evening were fully drawn.

"Maybe that's what was missing," Michael said. His eyes had grown weary, so he removed the wide, metal frames he wore. "Each black organization throughout history has been infiltrated and destroyed. They made their public demands, exposed themselves as organized Blacks across media platforms, and soon after came tumbling down."

"I see where you're going," E.J. said. "They didn't have the wisdom to keep quiet; prepare to strike instead of announcing it—and only when danger was close, attack."

"The notoriety that comes with being the front man of a Black organization makes him a target. Could mean his ruin for sure, and the organization's. Leaders should remain nameless."

"While you're at it, *everyone* should remain nameless," Robert gestured as though he'd said something spooky, and then chuckled at himself, but no one joined in. "We're kidding, right?" He looked to each of the men who seriously contemplated what was unspoken between

Michael's words. "Y'all starting a super-secret sauce society?" He laughed and lifted his glass playfully into the air.

"It could work," Michael said.

"An organization based on these principles. Why? What would be the purpose?" Jacob asked.

"Come on. The slavery mindset has been passed down from one generation to the next. We are not slaves. When will we move pass slavery Stockholm syndrome and see this treatment as unnatural? We're teaching our children to quietly accept and adapt to what we know is wrong." Michael gulped the saliva in his mouth. "Sometimes pain precedes victory."

E.J. agreed with his friend. "For a long time, we didn't have the sense or the skill to organize, or access to weapons, or even a militaristic mindset. We can now."

"Again—why?"

"Complete freedom."

"That's all? No demands? New legislative bill? Forty acres? Mule?"

"Where would they find forty acres? Probably couldn't dust off four. Asking for a separate state for black folk would be pointless. Besides, desegregation destroyed the structure of the black economy. However, it is possible to rebuild it."

"No, we don't want any of that—just to be recognized as a people willing to die for their freedom."

In an instant, the thought of death halted the development of their audacious plan. Yet, in their hearts they knew that something which had never been done must be attempted. Freedom Riders and protestors of previous decades understood the risks involved in their stance, and they accepted whatever fate would befall them. The near promise that death would result from participation in such a radical movement was far from appeasing.

"What's the alternative?" Jacob asked.

"More of the same injustice, the same fear, the same bondage," Michael said.

"If we don't die fighting, we're sure to get locked up for our involvement."

"So, what?"

"My job is to keep men *out* of prison. How could I then encourage them to commit crimes that would give them a one-way ticket to rot there?"

"Conflict of interest. I understand. If the details of this conversation aren't something you should have any knowledge of, we can take it elsewhere."

Jacob took a sip from his glass as he considered a response that would not force him to bear the weight of their rejection, or the label of a black man resistant to change. "No. Stay. I think we equally share in conflicts of interest — Pastor."

"Is there anyone who feels they should not be here?" Michael surveyed the men, and each of them locked eyes with him to affirm their willingness to at least be a part of the conversation.

"I just want to say this," Jacob added, "a violent fight against oppression has always backfired. Consider Nat Turner's rebellion."

"No one is talking about killing white people in their sleep. First, I don't believe I would be wrong to say that no one in this room hates white people; we hate oppression. Second, we would only organize to create a strong defense against an attack, which may or may not come. Think more along the lines of the Chicago riots, or Black Wall Street."

"It's been decades since those attacks." Jacob pondered. "Unless this is retaliation for historical wrongs."

"That's not it. Think about it. The Red Summer in Chicago sprang up because of injustice. The black folks who witnessed that boy get killed pointed out who'd done it, and police did nothing. Neither side started dropping bombs outright, but once it started, no one could put out the flames for days."

"Who won?"

Michael thought about it but wanted to maintain his air of confidence without an overly delayed response. "Neither side," he said. "People died, lost homes, lost peace and hope. But if history is bound to repeat itself, which it will, I want to be ready."

Michael seemed to take the lead, but no one would call him the leader—if anyone dared to acknowledge his involvement at all. He was very take-charge—borderline controlling in most instances—but people respected his ability to push the envelope. Such charisma drew a following and was demonstrated by the swift success of his growing church.

"You're the preacher man. How do you justify telling people to be ready to die in a fight?"

"What if it's not a fight, but a surrender? We've exhausted every peaceful option. If it takes the death of well-meaning people in a battle for equality to get the world's attention, it will be well worth it."

"Are you serious?" Jacob asked. "What could people out there do to help? I'm sure Adam can attest to how slow help came to assist Jews who were being extinguished in flocks. I mean millions! That's not the case in America."

"I hope to see the day when we value the life of one slain as much as we do one million if their death was unjust. Wrong is wrong no matter the scale. I just hate that the world sees this place as the land of freedom and opportunity. America is home of the brave, but nothing about it is free for people of color."

Jacob removed his glasses again and scratched an eyebrow with his pinky. "It still doesn't make sense to me."

"Your concern is jail or death. Regardless, any move we make will be misjudged and labeled a threat. Protests are a threat to daily functions; armed and organized men of color are a threat to safety. I find it funny that white supremacists have been armed and organized for decades yet pose no threat. Perhaps it's because they pose no threat to the system that enables them to function, parade around antagonizing us, while our people are kept in line and docile. We have to stop being afraid and face the truth."

E.J. added, "There comes a time when a man chooses to do something—or nothing. The choice is his own, but he cannot then lie to himself, pretend all is well—that social injustice hasn't plagued our people since we were brought over as cargo. A man has to own up to his decision to ignore it."

A few nodded slowly, but to differentiate between a nod of agreement, inebriation, or fatigue had become more difficult as time passed.

"You ever lose anyone in the system?" Michael asked.

Jacob sat back in his seat and pushed his glasses towards the ridge of his narrow nose.

"In '67, I was getting ready to graduate high school. My older brother, Anthony, had gone off to college the year before and was waiting for me to get there. We didn't grow up with much, so we were used to being close, always shared space, and damn near ripped the shirts off each other's backs for a chance to wear it.

"He was walking back to campus one night after a basketball game close by. Police grabbed him. Said he looked like a suspect in a burglary at a couple's house a few blocks away. They whooped my brother's ass. And they would've tossed him in jail, but his injuries were so bad they dropped him at the emergency room instead. It breaks my heart to say I'm grateful. They dropped him off after they nearly beat him to death and he's still alive, so I must be grateful—right? Lost his vision in both eyes; gets around in a wheelchair.

"Nothing happened with the officers. Claimed he resisted arrest when he denied his involvement. I know my brother. As youngsters, I couldn't accuse him of anything without him fighting to clear his name when I was wrong. But knowing his character doesn't make what happened to him right."

To avoid the onset of a therapeutic atmosphere, each of the men lifted their glasses and took a sip.

"I became a man sooner than I should have when both of my parents were taken from me. That won't be my children's stories," was Michael's declaration.

E.J. leaned forward and squared his shoulders. "My grandfather started a small drug store in Virginia. Left it to my daddy when he died. He did well for himself, and we always had plenty. They planned to redevelop the land near the drug store and, at first, offered him a little money to uproot. Stubborn as he'd always been, he refused it, but they understood all their niceties were unnecessary, and burned it to the ground." He sipped his liquor. "Quick resolve. He had nothing left. Not even memories. My mama's comforting wasn't enough. He poured a glass of bourbon with a cooking-spoon full of cyanide and left for the other side."

On cue, the men lifted their glasses and took a swallow.

"I want true freedom. Just once," Michael said.

"What would we model the program after? Or who?" Jacob posed a new question, and by his shamelessly inquisitive nature, the men sensed that he would probably make a better investigator.

"Nothing like it has ever existed. There isn't a mold for it to fit into. It will break them all," E.J. spoke confidently.

"It doesn't matter if you'd side with Booker T. over Dubois, or King over Malcolm, or the ideas of Frederick Douglas, Martin Delany, or Marcus Garvey," Michael added.

Adam shifted his weight in the chair. "I can't deny that Garvey may have been on to something. There may be no liberation on this side of the Atlantic for Blacks."

"Where you going with this?"

"Garvey's message was to prepare for exodus—return to Africa. It makes sense. Some were able to do it. Listen, the laws of the land are based on the Constitution. It wasn't written in favor of black people. They were property when it was drafted and the details that keeps them oppressed have not been edited out. It's the fine print of the Black demise. Leaving may be the only way to rise above it."

"Africa isn't home for most of us, but Whites would like to believe it is. I have just as much of a right to be in this country as the next man."

"I know what it's like to be forced into a land you've never known, but you find your way eventually." Through the sliding balcony door, the moon's light reflected against Adam's pale skin and casted shadows of the furniture against the walls.

"That was different. You had to flee for your life."

"So, the issues Blacks face aren't life or death? Someone need to light a city-wide fire under your ass for you to feel the heat? Or has the normalization of death at the hands of police and bigots given you cause to relax. I believe many Blacks are hindered by their own sense of entitlement. Don't get me wrong. Your ancestors can lay claim to this country a hundred times over what my family can, but the truth of the matter is this: despite *that* fact and because of my skin color, I'm also regarded in a way that your people may never know. Is it then worth it to stay? If the acres and mules haven't come in all this time, it's just not. Those who promised it are dead! What's disheartening is for someone like me to watch as you wait for it with your ignored demands and consistent outcry. I'm not saying to return to Africa, but I can recognize a sensible solution when I hear one, and Garvey was possibly in the right vein."

"What you've missed is the other side of Garvey's argument. Blacks could build a steady economy that allows others to see us as equals. That perspective is reminiscent of Booker T's approach."

"It makes no sense! Why must I labor to prove I'm human. I must become industrious! The white man can walk the streets with a guitar case in his hands, play a tune for a few coins, and no one cares. Oh, how industrious! If one of our sons does it, by God! He must be searched! He must be up to no good! There must be drugs in there! Or weapons! They criminalize our every move—our existence. Why can't we just *be*? I don't know who the notion of working to earn their favor hurts more: Blacks, for believing it's even possible to earn their acceptance, or Whites for—actually, it either gives Blacks false hope, or it conditions Whites to believe they can only accept us based on deeds, and not our humanity. Lose-lose."

"Okay, guys. The point has been made! To model ourselves after any intellectual would mean rejecting a practice or perspective that could be equally as good. Historically, taking sides didn't generate results that kept bullseyes off the backs of black people," Robert slurred, eyes a burning red hue.

"You're right." Michael waved his finger as thoughts flooded in. "It was after Booker T. and Douglas that the bombing in Tulsa, the Red Summer of Chicago, and the killings in Rosewood happened." He smirked. "Talk and taking sides has done its job of dividing us."

"There are no systematic *steps* to equality. If we want freedom, we have to send a message," E.J. said and slouched against the sofa again.

The silent wheels reeled within them.

"Adam made a good point," Michael spoke slowly as he processed his thoughts. "Leaving here may be the best thing to do; but *where* we go would be our choosing."

CHAPTER FOUR

TRANSFORMED INTO BEASTS

VALERIE was robbed of any moment to pause, collect herself, or respond to the phone that vibrated in her back pocket. Besides, she could accurately predict the body of each message from her husband, Charles. "Where are you?" "Are you okay? "Please call me." Each line was the broken record of an entire decade and was translated in the most damaging ways. She had not seen or spoken to her parents since her adolescent years, but it seemed her husband stood in the gap. However, his inability to control his wife's movements, or protect her, was a significant blow to an already fragile ego. Once an officer himself, a bullet to his knee forced him down a different trail but had not deterred his wife from the crime-riddled streets.

Officers struggled to pinpoint the origin of gunfire; there were many. When they drew nearer in one area, and assumed they had cornered the culprits, shots would ring out in another, and forced them to take cover and regroup. Although the Wolves were organized, it was not their strategy that plagued officers, but their undeterminable reach—how widespread they were. It seemed their method was to lurk in darkness and fire at unsuspecting passersby, or corner as many as they could and detonate explosives—which stretched nearly ten city blocks. Even the ability to see through walls would only slightly aid in their quest to end the massacre.

"Parker," Valerie called out as they hid behind a parked squad car. "Get inside."

"I think the shooters are on the sixth floor. I can almost see the weapon jutting from the window," the rookie officer responded.

"There is nothing you can do alone. We're spread too thin."

"I can shoot him down."

"You don't have a clear shot, and he may return fire."

There was another blast, and a body dropped a few yards away.

"I can do it," Parker insisted. "I can see the muzzle flash from his weapon."

"You still can't get a clear visual. We don't have ears out here. Let's use wisdom."

Parker looked at the man who collapsed, bloody, nearby; and it made the idea of retreat unbearable. "I can't."

"Okay. I'll head back to the station. I know where to find you."

"Where's Samson?" he asked.

"I don't know," she said as she looked around.

"Garrison?"

"Not here."

"Okay."

"I don't want to leave you out here alone."

"Think about it, Kemp," he started. "It's been over two hours. Who plans an attack this long? I think we've somehow cornered them. They can't just hightail it out of here, or they would have by now. There are enough bodies in the street."

"We don't know their motives."

"It's not obvious?"

"We don't know the facts."

Nearly insulted, he slightly lowered his weapon. "A peaceful protest—black bodies in the streets."

Valerie could have easily made the connection, but even as a black woman, she spared most opportunities to make assumptions.

"Listen," he continued, "if we back down, it will be easier for them to escape—blend with the rest of the crowd."

"What if they never planned to get out of here?"

"I don't think they want to die, or they wouldn't hide. Columbine—totally open, plain sight. They knew how it would end. The church in Charleston—clear targets, in and out. These guys here just can't get out. They would even be a better shot if they walked the street."

"You could be right," Valerie agreed. "We can stay here—try to push people back to safety. The runners are easy targets."

"Stay back!" Parker yelled at a man locked hand-in-hand with a woman. "Stay there! Don't move!"

The couple could not digest the scenario—one where they faced an officer's loaded weapon as they ran from snipers hidden behind dark windows—but they dared to be defiant if it meant a safe return home.

"Don't move!" Parker yelled again to help them avoid unseen danger.

They ignored, gripped each other's hands a bit tighter, and dashed for an adjacent building that would move them further from the core of conflict.

Pop! Pop!

The man fell to the ground and took the woman down with him; but her instincts would not permit her to remain there a moment longer than it took to jump back up to her feet and run.

"Get out of there!" Valerie yelled as she watched the ordeal.

Takka-Takka! The sound was not one the officers had heard all evening and came from a direction other than where they had focused their attention. The woman scurried across the street and out of danger. She was clearly visible, but no one fired at her. The officers who stood by looked to the sixth-floor window—nothing. They checked other buildings, the streets, scattered cars—nothing.

Parker's squinted eyes locked in on the rooftop of a different building. He could see movement, but the figures were dark and small from his ground-level perspective.

"What they hell is that?" he asked Valerie as he pointed in the direction of the gunshots.

"I don't know."

Pop! Pop! Pop! rang out in the distance, followed by *Takka-Takka-Takka-Takka!* and the officers knew that someone had returned fire.

"Is that us on the roof?" the rookie asked.

"Can't be. We've all taken cover—haven't gone in. At least I don't think we have. We have to know for sure."

"But we can't leave."

"We're sitting ducks," Valerie explained.

"I don't think it's us they're after."

"If your theory is right, badges won't speak for our skin color."

"Let's just say there are two opposing forces—not police—in such close proximity. It's possible they may even occupy the same building."

"If true, that is where the real fight will be."

The gunman on the roof was none other than Jabari, son of E.J. Rushing, and he was a professional in the best sense of the term. After nearly 18 years in the force, and an expert shooter, TAAR was equipped with the precision of a highly-trained assassin; but his credentials were not exceptional when juxtaposed with other TAAR members who were ex-military, war veterans, or had trained as sharp shooters since they were old enough to complete a set of pull-ups on a playground's jungle gym.

TAAR worked in pairs. Monika was Jabari's yin—and had been since adolescence. To divide and conquer was to *be* conquered, so the adage did not apply. As one identified the target, the other kept watch to ensure they would not be caught unaware and snubbed out. There were two pairs of eyes, four hands, but a single heart that trusted the other's skill and alertness—one that had sworn to protect at any cost.

"I think I got him, 18," Jabari said to Monika whose eyes searched the darkness. "Quiet over there."

"Reset, 27," she said. "Check the road. The others will come out at some point."

Jabari lifted the rig from the floor and changed positions on the rooftop with Monika in high-five range.

The call went out for additional armed units from nearby jurisdictions to assist police who were already on the scene, or to replace those who had fearfully abandoned ship. They arrived with sirens ablaze or in silent, armored trucks. Charged, equipped, and decked out in protective gear, their presence was evident. They joined the other officers around the perimeter.

When it was clear the sixth-floor gunman was no longer a threat, Officer Parker and Valerie ushered as many people across the road to safety as possible. They waddled past like ducklings until the sound of distant shots caused them to halt, and then continue once convinced they were beyond the scope of danger.

Upon proper orders, the National Guard created a more secure barricade around the conflict zone. Blockades were erected in a three-mile radius to contain the violence. Exit points were created to control movement in the core. There would be no escape without confrontation, which was just as deadly with doubtful officers who found it impossible to differentiate between an innocent bystander and a deadly invader.

Valerie assisted a group to safety, and briefly returned to her position near the squad car to catch her breath.

"Officer…," the new guy searched for a name.

"Kemp." Valerie placed a hand at her waist and bent forward as she panted.

"Don't bring them out," the man said. "We're taking a different approach."

"By leaving them in there?" Her mouth gaped open for air as she spoke.

"The goal is to contain the situation. It's spread far enough. Without knowing who's who, you could enable them to increase their range."

"These people just want to go home. They don't want to die here."

"I understand that. There are thousands hidden in these streets. I get it. But there are nearly 6 million in the city. We have to plug the hole. Eventually, these terrorists will run out of ammo."

"How many will die until they do?"

"Following orders." He shrugged.

He noticed Valerie's glare across the street and sensed that she would attempt another rescue when he saw the two heads that poked from behind the corner of a building. Their eyes scanned the scene to see if it was clear.

"Orders, Officer," he reinforced.

"Damn those orders."

Valerie ran closer to the bobbing heads, and they revealed themselves with the nervousness of a toddler taking her first step towards her mother.

"Hurry! Come on!" she yelled.

Pop! Pop! whirled the air, but the sound did not come from the sixth floor. There was a new shooter, and he was close enough to have them in his crosshairs.

"Take cover!" the officer yelled to Valerie, who immediately returned to her position behind the car as the runners landed face-down on the asphalt.

"Dammit!" Agony and frustration sent fire through her veins.

"That's it, Officer. No more."

Her nose wiggled and pulsated as she fought to contain her fury. With fierce eyes, she watched the final twitches of those who had been shot as they lie dying in the street.

By 3 a.m., those within the perimeter were without escape; the prey hid among hunters. Beyond it, people locked themselves in their homes and were alerted to possible infiltration of terrorism within their communities. Their defense made a noise of its own as shops across the city were looted for weapons to safeguard against imminent danger, which perpetuated the madness. And there to provide a front seat to viewers in each time zone were news crews who salivated to capture the chaos as it radiated outward and created hysteria. Helicopters swarmed over bodies that stiffened in the streets, and the steady eyes of their lenses experienced the tumultuous event in real time. By day and by night, they hovered unapologetically from one direction or another—always present.

✳ ✳ ✳

GOVERNMENT officials were awakened to the news of the massive assault by perplexed officers who failed to quickly regain control.

As Mayor Sharon Oakley met with an assistant and a few staff members in the basement office of her Atlanta home—where her children slept—she received a call from Georgia governor, Lewis Spalding, who rose from the comfortable bed of his Florida beach property when he heard the news. Tensions between the two officials were impossible to conceal; the Black public chewed on it and spit out the bones with pride. Right or wrong, Mayor Oakley consistently upheld the interests of black people, and never wavered despite the pressure—and this was no different.

"Governor," she spoke, and adjusted the phone to hear clearly.

"Good morning, Sharon," he replied.

"I can't say it's been 'good'."

"We are prepared to end this—within reason."

"We?"

"President Couper has given us the greenlight to take necessary measures and restore peace in Atlanta."

Mayor Sharon Oakley had proudly piloted her city's recovery in the aftermath of six police shootings and three major protests while she served dual terms in office; but her response to that evening's events resembled the onset of frostbite—cold, numb, immovable, and others noticed.

"Since I didn't get the dial-in code to the meeting regarding *my* city, tell me what was discussed." As she spoke, she quietly excused herself from the room and stood in the stairwell.

"We wanted to ensure you were equipped to..."

"I think I'm only missing one vital piece of equipment that would get me on an actual call than for you to relay plans sketched without my input."

"It's not us versus you, Sharon."

"I know how deep this runs. Tell me, what's the plan?"

"Couper wants a quick resolve." There was silence. "We'll use gas."

"Absolutely not. Aren't you watching the news? There are fires and explosions down there. It will be an inferno for miles. You will kill them all."

"They'll do that anyway. I just want to stop the spread."

Mayor Oakley removed the phone from her ear and looked at it. "What? Your rich comrades put in a call? There are innocent people down there. Answers are slow to come, but I know protestors are not responsible for this."

"You can't be sure of that."

"Would they be less disposable if they were of a lighter pigment? Perhaps covering them all in white paint would get them out unscathed." She did not attempt to sugarcoat her thoughts, and her audaciousness left nothing less than a bitter taste in the governor's mouth. It was the unapologetic roar of Oakley's voice which caused people to flock to her.

"I'll pretend you didn't say that."

"Don't. I meant it."

He released a sinister chuckle. "Let me explain something to you, girl. Even the cutest puppy can outgrow its owners and become wild beasts without proper training. Some owners would just stash them in the backyard, let them destroy it—dig holes, trample over plants, kill the grass, intimidate neighbors. The moment an owner fears going into their own backyard, they will realize something must change—even if it means completely destroying the cause of the disruption and fear."

She gulped nearly loud enough to be heard on the other end, but after years in the White, male-dominated political arena, the middle-aged woman had grown skin as tough as an armadillo and was immune to the deadliest venom.

"Now that you've shed the wool, we can speak candidly. I don't give a damn about your agenda. I will do everything in my power to stop it and ruin you in the process if you go forth with this."

He paused a moment, and then released a deep sigh. "Listen, I don't know how many Blacks are wounded, or dead, but so far I have two officers hospitalized with severe burns, and the risk of many others who will choose to flee to save their own lives. Lower *their* risks, restore order—that is how we will do this. If not…"

"We'll watch as people burn alive. That's your plan, right?" she asked rigidly. "Turn on the news. They can see everything, and we can damn near plot our point of attack by tuning in to Channel 5 News."

"The people will want to know that it's over, and that they're safe."

"But would you get the votes of people who watched their loved ones burn to death in the street? I don't think so."

He chewed on her words. "Listen, I'll talk to Couper, and give you until sun-up to bring it to an end—and without injury to even one officer. Otherwise, I'll pull the trigger."

"You've held your weapon against me for so long you don't remember what steel feels like cold."

She ended the call no clearer of her next action and sensed the time she was afforded might come at the expense of additional lives.

* * *

AMARA'S children fell asleep on the floor beneath the large windows as she watched the violence on the streets below. It was a wonder they could sleep through consistent pops and booms, a building that rattled, people who cried, fear that would not relent; but they surrendered to their exhaustion and found a moment of rest. On the contrary, their mother paced the floor and stared from the 20th-floor window for over six hours. She grew more anxious as each victim in view collapsed from their wounds and, for a while, melted weightlessly into the chair.

The quiet of her children's slumber enabled her to plot an escape without distraction. Amara seldom experienced the robust nature of children at play, or their ceaseless inquisitiveness, or what they were like when they felt afraid. She had absented herself to pursue a career that would make the average woman blush and, any man who was tempted, bow to her. She did not know that James' frequent trips to the restroom meant that he was afraid and needed to be in small spaces surrounded by light—and not due to the juice pouch provided in childcare. On occasion, Jabari would find him sound asleep in their bathtub, and wrapped in a blanket. He would simply pick him up and return him to his room.

If Amara was attentive, she would have known that when Shiloh would occasionally burst into song, it was not as misplaced or awkward as she assumed. The girl would do so to soothe her discomfort—usually at the onset of nervousness. So, Amara sifted through the lies for some solid sense of identity beyond her marriage—to know a part of herself untainted by her newly discovered truth. She realized she barely knew them.

Pieces of perspective fell into place, and hers was completely renewed. She had not mustered a strategy to know her children better but was determined to get them out of there so that she could try.

No one came or went. The elevator doors had not opened for hours. She draped a white tablecloth over her children, and then went away to find Mr. 39.

She went down to the bottom floor, but no one was there. The windows stretched from floor to ceiling and could not conceal anything within the space. The lights were bright and exposed the sensitivity of Amara's haggard eyes. She walked from one end to the other. Nothing. After an explosion that was close enough to shake the ground beneath her feet, she wondered if it woke her children, and if they would be afraid to not find her nearby. Her mission was short-lived.

Suddenly, she heard a faint sound amid the night's clatter. Someone whimpered, and then groaned in pain. With caution, she followed the muffled sounds like a hound on the stench of a fruitful trail, and found a woman nestled behind the reception desk. The woman's pale, white skin was smeared with blood. She held her hand firmly over a neck wound—the result of a ricocheted bullet, which drove her into the building. Her eyes were closed tightly as sweat beaded on her brow. She waited, and hoped she was invisible.

Initially repulsed by the sight of blood, just as she had been since childhood, Amara hesitated to go near. After a deep breath and the terrible thought of a role reversal, she went for it.

"Do you need some help?" The earthy color drained from her voice, and she spoke above her natural octave.

"Were you shot there?" she asked as she tip-toed towards the woman to minimize the pain of the cut on her foot.

The woman's eyes were hard and frightful. Her laser stare could not burn holes through Amara, but it was her silent command for Amara to stay away. Yet, she failed to pick up on the woman's cues, and aggressively ripped the tail end of her soiled, red gown to use a tourniquet. The woman's feet shuffled quickly as she backed into a corner beneath the desk. As Amara prepped the homemade bandage, the bleeding woman reached into the bottom drawer. Her hand glided along a metal, three-hole puncher, and she concealed it while she kept her eyes glued on Amara's movements.

"This should work," Amara said, relieved, and prepared to stomach the bandage's application.

When the women locked eyes, Amara's paranoid patient raised up her weapon and flung it towards Amara with all the strength she could muster. It collided with her cheek and knocked her to the floor. To prevent a second attack, Amara jumped up just as quickly as she had been laid out.

"What the hell is wrong with you?" She massaged her throbbing face and eagerly backed farther and farther away.

The woman's slight cough evolved quickly into an unbearable gag, and then gurgle.

"I'm not one of them. I wasn't going to hurt you."

Amara realized that an act of kindness, or the tenderness of her voice, was not enough to set her apart from a people marked "dangerous". She made herself vulnerable to death at her refusal of a black woman's aid. Ironically, just the day before, she joined the march against Black injustices. Had she meant it? Or had her actions been a ploy to remedy deep-seated prejudice? She would die before Amara could know — a casualty of her own pride and despair.

* * *

ROUNDING 5 a.m., many officers had gone at least 24 hours without sleep; their vision began to blur, and their bodies were overwhelmed by a natural intoxication. As reinforcement arrived, their veiny red eyes begged to be swapped out. Yet, even the most energized would not dare to enter the deadly zone.

The night transitioned slowly, and Valerie hungered for answers — insight on the shadow men, and those postured on the rooftops. Gunfire had not completely ceased, but fewer people were scattered targets. Shots were more sporadic.

"The next one in, I'm taking off," Parker said to Valerie.

"You should. Your eyes are barely open."

"You're leaving soon, right?" he asked.

"I don't think so." She second-guessed the thought to let him in on her private plan. "I want to go in."

"Why? You don't have eyes in there."

"And we never will if we stay out here."

"How will you pull that off without being shot at? They'll see you coming."

"The 6th-floor shooter is down, or no longer in position. Shots fired from this building," she pointed, "are not as consistent, and had more misses than hits. My guess is *that's* a novice shooter who struggles with the weapon. Odds are, I'll get past them both."

"And then what?"

"I want to know who they are."

"So, you'll just walk over and ask to see some ID." He hissed.

The truth: many of the officers were well-aware of one group's identity—Wolves. Eyewitness statements at the spark of the conflict placed the white gunmen amid the protest before they were scattered; but their testimony was weakened, if not fully discredited, by a helicopter's footage of armed black men on the roof. The contradiction left them clueless, but Valerie wanted to discover the truth for herself.

"I'm going now—before sun-up—when they'll have a better visual, and I'll have less strength." She secured her gun within its holster. "I'll follow the line of cars until I'm close to the building. Stay in the dark as much as I can, enter the building, and see what happened with the shooter on the 6th floor."

"You won't need backup?"

"Too noticeable. It's best I go alone."

"I can't leave knowing you're in there."

"Then don't. Take a nap on the pavement. I'll see you before sun-up," she said, and then walked away.

Valerie followed the trail of cars and was within 200 feet of her target when she quietly stepped into the darkness. Others noticed, but no one called attention to her, and minimized her risk of discovery. Each step, she stared sharply in the direction of the adjacent building with the active shooter. In the building's dim light, she could see a figure pace back and forth before he stopped suddenly and came towards the window.

Instantly, Valerie dropped to the ground. The high beams of a squad car made touchless, yet blinding, impact with her eyes. She laid there motionless until colors and shapes were more than white specks, and she noticed she was not alone. The fallen were beside her. She dragged her weight upon her elbows, and her small movements went undetected, but was captured by a dash camera still active within the car. She was in perfect scope its eyes, and safe.

When she entered the unsecured building, she drew her weapon. It was an abandoned office space that had been overlooked for nearly a decade. The carpet was shabby, worn; and the light fixtures were yellow and outdated, which barely mattered since there was no power in the building.

Valerie located the stairs and proceeded to the 6th floor. Occasionally, she shook her head and blinked her eyes quickly to suppress the swift onset of exhaustion. She walked the corridor and checked each room with her weapon drawn until she stumbled upon exactly what she had hoped to find.

Her heart pounded erratically. "Police! Get up from there now," she said to the motionless figure on the floor. The sound of gunfire in the distance unnerved her.

She took a breath and waited a moment before she moved closer, and kept her weapon properly aimed.

By Valerie's observation, the man could have been in his late 40s to early 50s, was White, and had long goatee. Upon closer examination, he had been shot through the chest with a rifle powerful enough to burn through his vest like a match to paper and had long expired.

His rifle remained mounted near the window. She stepped over his body and placed an eye against the scope. She could clearly see the officers along the makeshift barricade, who were easy targets if they were the focus. However, the fact that none of them were shot on post made it clear that these delinquents had a specific target, and it was not police.

She swung the weapon towards her left shoulder for a look at the rooftop of a nearby building. Initially, there was nothing. She slowly moved the scope along the roof's edge to spot Mr. Goatee's killer. Indeed, she saw them. And they were Black. A man and woman stood nearly shoulder to shoulder, alert and armed.

Valerie moved her face from the scope. "What are they doing?" she said to herself, and then went for another look.

She increased the scope's magnification and focused on the man and woman's features. Consumed by her quest, she did not notice she had gained the attention of an onlooker whose scope had also narrowed on her from across the street. She was hunted—like a deer beneath a city lamp post.

She continued to stare at the man behind the rifle on the rooftop. In an instant, one of the lanterns illuminated his face as he turned to speak to his female counterpart. Valerie was astounded.

"Rushing?" she said, and a bullet shattered the glass above her head.

A finger-sized shard cut a small dash into her forehead, and she immediately dropped to the floor and crawled down the corridor. Across the road, the shooter continued to fire towards the building, which distracted him as she ran down the stairs and quickly to safety.

Valerie's butt collided with the concrete when she sat to catch her breath. Three officers surrounded her—desperate to learn of her findings—including Parker, who had caught a fresh wind and no longer functioned on fumes.

"We need a medic!" he called.

"I'm fine."

"Your head is bleeding."

"It's just a scrape," she insisted between breaths.

The crowd's patience grew thinner by the second.

"What…who was it, Kemp?" he asked frantically.

"White," she panted, "guy. Goatee, middle age."

"And the roof?" he asked excitedly.

"Black male." She took a breath. "And female."

"What?" The officers were puzzled.

With manageable breaths, she said. "That's not it. I know the man on the roof."

"How?"

"He's one of us."

CHAPTER FIVE

FORCED INTO SUBMISSION

FRESH flowers lined the sanctuary at Wanderer's Refuge Temple. Preparations were made for the teenagers who lost their lives days earlier, but none of the intended guests would come. Only a few miles beyond the conflict's core, Dunbar Street was within earshot of the chaos. Slowly, the city and its functions were shut down.

Bishop Dyer awoke on his office chaise to a news stream displaying random explosions and the crack of gunfire in real-time. His proximity to the core caused the television screen to merely echo the sounds he heard with his natural ear.

There was a faint tap on the door before it opened. "Want any coffee?" Patrick, Bishop Dyer's assistant, asked.

The elderly man sat erect and placed his feet on the floor with a grunt. "I'm fine."

With the cancelled memorial service, only three other men were in the church, all TAAR. Their purpose was to prepare for the next stage of the plan. They would also serve the bishop's needs which, due to his level of focus, were few.

He increased the volume on the television—eager to hear how the story of what transpired downtown had evolved. Helicopter footage had Black men and women, bold and lethal, strategically positioned on rooftops; and he silently celebrated to see them in action. To him, these were boys and girls who, for decades, trained as young soldiers for a cause that was finally realized.

A news anchor spoke from the comforts of her desk with a live view of the violence sprawled across the screen. "Due to recent attacks, flights in and out of Atlanta are temporarily suspended. If you plan to travel, be mindful of long lines at the pumps. A few of our reporters said they waited for over an hour and a half for fuel."

The male anchor chimed in. "At this rate, gasoline within the city will soon be in short supply."

"It may be best for drivers to wait until they've driven beyond city limits to gas up if they can manage it," the female anchor suggested.

"Sheri is on location and can give us an update on what's happening. Sheri…"

A nervous reporter stood center in front of a police car with lights that flashed dimly against the sun's rays. "Police are still baffled, and no closer to identifying the armed men and women planted on the rooftops behind me," she said.

"Would they say this is a terrorist attack?" the man asked from the newsroom.

"It seems that way to me, but again, they are not sure at this time," Sheri responded. "With the aerial footage captured this morning, the shooters appear African American."

"So, these violent agitators surfaced from yesterday's protest and started firing at innocent people?"

"It appears that way."

Bishop Dyer frowned at the screen. "That wouldn't make sense. Why would they do that?" he said to himself.

"What provoked them?"

"A few accounts taken from those who managed to run free emphasized the Wolves' involvement as well."

"…who have the freedom to exercise their first amendment right and demonstrate as much as anyone else," the man clarified.

"Eyewitnesses also noticed men sporting the Wolves' insignia near the protest prior to the eruption of violence. And one recalls a white male who threw what appeared to be a homemade explosive into one of the buildings."

"But the people on the roofs—that's quite odd," the anchor's puzzled countenance flashed across the screen.

"Again, officers here are just as stumped, but one thing is for certain—terrorism is approached with extreme caution and utter seriousness. We hope to soon witness an overdue turn of events."

"We hope so too."

"God be with everyone affected by what's happening down there."

The cast signed off for a commercial break as Bishop Dyer, disappointed, processed the news report. To him, the people of TAAR were far from terrorists. They were responders. He was certain the act itself would usher in a new voice that rallied for Black equality; but at that point, their mission was overshadowed by mere speculation.

"Bishop," Patrick called as he entered again.

"Yes?"

"There are at least a dozen people outside—even more crossing the parking lot—wanting to come inside."

Bishop Dyer stood and went over to the window. A pilgrimage of injured and exhausted individuals encroached upon the massive campus. The nearly 8,000-seat sanctuary had the capacity to safely house the refugees, and it was obviously well-considered.

"We can't," Bishop said, hidden in the shadow of window drapes.

"Do we keep the doors locked, and cause them to go elsewhere?"

The people pounded against the doors and yelled, "Help us!"

"Sir?" Patrick continued.

And then it came to him—quick and sinister. "Let them in," he said.

"Yes, sir."

"Give them water, and whatever there is to eat in the kitchen—medical supplies for their wounds if you can find the nurse's closet."

"Yes, sir."

"And when you're done—storage room B3. Grab as many of those chains as you can," he said casually.

The man looked to Bishop Dyer with inquisitive eyes, nodded his head, and left the room. Bishop continued to monitor those who crossed the parking lot into a land more dangerous than the one they had escaped.

* * *

THE sun had already risen before Amara nestled next to her children and dozed off. The hour-long recharge was enough to improve awareness of her children's voices as they discussed the bodies in the streets below.

"They're still sleeping, Shiloh," James said to his sister.

"They're so small from up here," she said. "Maybe they're dead."

"No, they're not!" James insisted. "They're not, right?" he wondered.

Amara wrapped her arms around her children and moved them away from the window. "Have you gone to the restroom?" she asked.

"Yes," Shiloh said, "James had to go, and I took him."

"Is it time to go yet?" James asked.

"A little while longer," Amara responded.

When he noticed she was awake, Calvin, who had camped out on the other end of the room, walked over to talk with her. A solo conversation with Amara was unusual for Calvin. Because he seldom agreed with any perspective she offered, he typically shied away from any interaction that involved her. He sought to avoid one of her volcanic confrontations to save himself the drama and disagreement with Monika, who consistently defended her sister's actions.

Michael, the infant, was fully awake in his arms, and gnawed on his tiny, wrinkled fingers.

"I'm down to a half bottle," Calvin said as he approached. "There's nothing left in the can."

Amara sighed helplessly. "Maybe someone here with a baby has some extra."

"I've asked around—this floor, and a few others." He noticed a bruise across her cheek. "What happened to you?"

She pressed against her skin for a tender reminder. "Tried to help someone. I'm okay. Wish I could find my diamond earring though."

From the window, Amara could clearly see the garage where her car had been parked the previous night—possibly the 9th or 10th car on the second aisle. Cars were spread randomly in the street, but she figured it was possible to maneuver around them if she could just make it to her vehicle.

"Let's run for it," she suggested.

He looked from the window. "It's hard to say what's down there."

"You have a hungry baby, and I have kids anxious to get out of here." She grabbed her small handbag from the chair.

"What about Monika? Jabari?"

"What about them? They left *us*."

Calvin drew the baby closer and patted him on the back as drool cascaded down his fingers.

"Let's go down to the first floor," Amara continued. "We'll get a better feel for what's going on."

The elevator arrived quickly and, children in tow, they landed on the bottom floor. It appeared that no one was there. The sun made it bright enough inside to run for shade, but they shielded their eyes and moved forward.

Near the entryway, Amara looked from the glass towards the garage. She gave no attention to the horror sprinkled in between.

"I have a pretty good idea where my car is. It shouldn't be hard to drive right out of here."

"There are at least three cars in the way that could stop you—unless you plow into them," Calvin said.

An imagined glimpse of Amara's pristine luxury vehicle rammed into a parked car made her shudder.

She concocted a new plan. "What about the other cars? Maybe the keys are still inside. It would be a faster getaway."

"If that were true, I'm sure someone would have driven away in them by now."

"Okay. Then come up with something yourself."

"See, I told you they were dead," Shiloh said to her brother.

By the time Amara noticed the lightless shells of random bodies, activity along the roadway caught her attention. One of the parked cars that blocked the garage was not vacant. A man and woman hid in the backseat, and when their heads suddenly popped up behind non-tinted windows, they were immediately spotted by a group of approaching Wolves.

"Get down," Calvin commanded.

"Down where?" Amara pulled her children close, but the bare, contemporary lobby offered little more than a reception desk, and she was fully aware of what was on the other side.

"There." Calvin pointed to an alcove with recess lights and tall, artificial plants, and they scurried over quickly.

"Let's just take the elevator back up," she said.

"No. They'll see us through the glass. Wait."

Amara and Calvin watched, wide-eyed, as the pack taunted the frightened individuals within the vehicle and circled them like sharks closing in on a school of feeble fish. First, they shot out each of the tires, and then started on the windows. The couple held each other and refused to look in their tormentors' direction.

Amara grew more anxious with each bang but could not spare the blink of an eye. From the 20th floor, the appearance of bodies as they dropped like flies was literal. These were human beings. And when it became real to her, she screeched.

"Quiet," Calvin warned.

She panicked. "I have to go. I'll go alone, press the button, and when the door opens, we'll all get back on."

"No, don't move."

As they watched, the mob forced the man from the car and onto the street. He was punched and kicked before several bullets pierced his chest. The woman begged for her life and screamed as she was pulled from the car by her ankles. Snow in the summer sun would be more real than the scene enacted in front of her, and Amara could no longer conceal the tremor that rose in her bones.

"I can't." Amara's children cried after her as she made a dash for the elevator button. In an instant, the elevator chimed, and then opened. "Come on!" she yelled, and her children ran to her immediately.

A shot rang out in the distance and, instantly, one of the Wolves near the couple hit the ground. After a second shot, another was thrusted against the car, and he released a dreadful *yelp*. The woman from the backseat managed to run away while the remaining Wolves raised their weapons to the sky in search of the shooter and began to unload each of their bullets.

"Calvin, let's go!" Amara called from the elevator.

One of the building's many surveillance cameras looked upon them and judged without words as she urgently waited.

"I need milk," he responded with renewed confidence. "Go back upstairs with the kids."

"Give me the baby!" She opened her arms as if she would receive him.

"If I'm getting out of here, so is he."

The elevator door closed on his words, and Amara was on her way to take cover on the 20th floor once again.

* * *

THE precinct overflowed with people who sought safety amid armed officers. However, there were too many to house and maintain conditions to meet, strategize, and operate. Many of them were ordered to go elsewhere—and occasionally at gunpoint.

Valerie wrestled her way through the crowd gathered on the lawn and found only a subtle difference once inside. The air was thick and humid, and the chatter was inescapable. The office was flooded with men and women who were permitted to take up every chair and inch of carpet in the room. Officers who remained in the building were pushed into smaller quarters—conference rooms where they normally met for daily meetings.

"Sergeant!" Valerie called when she noticed her superior officer.

"Make it quick, Kemp." He scurried.

"How many officers do we have out there—you know, in the core?"

"What?" he stopped. "There are no officers in the core—just along the perimeter. It's not easy keeping you all abreast of these details. Stay out of the core."

Jabari was not commanded to take the position on the roof, and it deepened Valerie's bewilderment.

"Are you sure?" she asked.

"Sure of the order to stay in the perimeter, or that there are none of us in the core? It's both, Detective." He hurried away.

Valerie entered the zoo of an office, and stepped over exhausted, lethargic people who sought rest and solace. "Excuse me. Sorry. Excuse me," she said as she passed.

She ordered a man from the chair at her desk and browsed her computer—a quest to discover information on her comrade. Her most recent *exceptional service* plaque had shifted on her desk, and she returned it to its proper place beside the computer.

"High school class of 2000," she spoke to herself. "AA in Criminal Justice. Academy."

There was nothing peculiar about Jabari in the database, so she took to social media for clues. There, she observed pictures of Jabari with Amara, and their children—

all of them dated months apart, which indicated his minimal use of the account. And then, she remembered.

She reached for her nearly-drained cell phone and pressed the callback button on her most recent 12 calls—Charles, her husband.

"Val?" he answered.

"Yes. I'm okay."

"God. Can you get here?"

"I'm not leaving, Charles."

"I'm watching the news. There is nothing you can do to stop this."

"I can't run away like the others. Soon enough, there'll be no one left."

"They're the smart ones. This is why the military exists. It's above local law enforcement."

Valerie refocused on the purpose of her call. "Jabari. Do you remember him? Officer Rushing?"

"What does this have to do..."

She asked more intensely, "Do you remember Officer Rushing, Charles?"

"Yes. He made SWAT the year before I retired. What about him?"

"What else do you remember? Anything stand out about him?"

"Not really—but he wasn't like the rest of us."

"What do you mean?"

"Didn't fraternize. Kept to himself mostly. Why? Tell me what's going on."

"I can't."

"I've been blowing up your phone for over 24 hours, and you call to ask me about a man I haven't seen in years—and in the midst of everything that's going on down there. You at least owe me an explanation."

"I saw him," she said.

"Okay. You should if he's still on the force."

"No. He was a shooter."

"One of the people on the roofs?"

"How did you know?"

"We can see them from the helicopter footage on the news. Do you think he's responsible for all of this?"

"I can't say. There is nothing in his background that indicates his involvement with any terrorist organizations."

"It shouldn't. His nose is clean."

"How would you know?"

"His wife is Bishop Dyer's daughter."

"Bishop Dyer of Wanderer's Refuge?"

"Yes. That's her. He's an upstanding guy."

"You said he was quiet."

"Quiet doesn't make you a criminal."

"If you're a vigilante or a terrorist, it can be the perfect bullseye."

"You think a group of Black vigilantes has been brewing under our noses? That's ridiculous!"

"But not impossible."

"Listen, we can discuss the existence or nonexistence of a Black terrorist organization when you get home."

"It may be a while. Thank you," Valerie said as she ended the call.

She plugged her phone into the charger connected to her computer and contemplated the idea of a contemporary group of black men and women, trained and equipped for battle on American soil.

"Where did they come from?" she thought.

Valerie was well-aware of the power and influence of the Black Panther Party through the early '80s. Her thoughts drew back to their structure and mission, and the faces of those ready to die for their cause. Yet, they had been known, respected, and impactful before any blood was shed in their defense.

While Valerie learned to esteem the bravery and progressiveness of the Panthers, she never fully agreed with their tactics. A peace-lover, she silently sided with nonviolent movements and the law when it came to retaliation, so the idea of this group was bittersweet. She understood their cause but was certain it could never end well for them. Whatever transpired in the core of violence was a new beast—one that raised its head at the cough of criminal acts incited against Blacks.

"Kemp," a voice called above the babble and interrupted her thoughts. Two uniformed officers approached and stood next to her.

She turned. "Yeah?"

"Sergeant wants to see you in Room B."

She unplugged the minimally charged phone and followed the men as they stepped over dreary survivors sprawled across the floor. They went down the corridor to a room that swarmed with officers.

"Kemp," Sergeant began, "They tell me you got a good look at a few of the shooters in the core."

Valerie considered the truth of Jabari's position on the roof but struggled to tell it.

"So, what did you see?" he urged her to speak.

"Nothing more than what news channels are showing its viewers. Just people on the rooftops."

"Armed?"

"Yes."

"Did they fire at you?"

"No."

"Have you seen them fire at any officers?"

"No."

"Protestors?"

"No."

He frowned. "Then why are they there?" he asked.

Although Valerie had an answer, she withheld it. "I'll head out to learn as much as I can."

"No. You should go home. Take 8 hours."

"I'm fine, Sergeant. I can get back out there."

"No. You're not sharp. We have help from all over. I can afford to give you a break."

"But I'm..."

"That's an order, Kemp."

She left the room with full knowledge that she would not adhere to her sergeant's commands and went down to the locker room where there were cots and pillows on standby for the weary. She plopped down in a dark corner and laid her head back when there was an alert on her cell phone. When she opened it, a text message from Charles with a picture of Bishop Dyer, Jabari, Amara, and another woman was displayed. They stood in the pulpit of Dyer's mega church. The message read: "These people are saints."

Her fingers spread over the image and zoomed in. She responded immediately, "Who is the second woman?"

After a moment, he replied, "Bishop's other daughter."

And then, Valerie knew the identity of the woman on the roof.

* * *

ABOUT a half hour passed before Calvin crawled behind the reception desk on the bottom floor of the Liberty Centre and realized he had not been alone. The corpse of the woman who died there the night before remained in its somber position as Calvin hid a few feet away. The baby had grown weary of the wait and fell asleep in his father's arms. Calvin started to plot his semi-solo escape.

The silence was brief. Pops of gunfire were heard from adjacent buildings. A mob of Wolves, on foot, forced many from hidden places and into open range. They were easily gunned down. The pack moved close together and entered one door after another to lure inhabitants into the street to face their doom.

Calvin's eyes swept over the room and towards the window for a look at the threat. He ducked quickly when two heavily armed Wolves looked inside. When nothing within their sight gave them cause to enter, they continued past the entryway. Suddenly, shots were fired from rooftop rifles, and prompted the Wolves to take refuge inside the building.

Calvin heard the door swing open and caught a whiff of smoke and decay from outside. He did not breathe.

"Dammit!" one said as he looked from the glass.

"You okay?" the other asked.

"Fine." They breathed heavily.

"We gotta get back soon."

"Stay close to the wall. It's harder to see us in the shadows."

"Got it."

"Ready?"

The infant started to stir in Calvin's arms, and gurgled faintly as his eyes focused on his father. Sweat beaded and dripped down Calvin's forehead as he held his son tightly. With a subtle shift of his shoulders—left to right, right to left—he rocked the infant into a quiet state. When the baby could not deny his hunger, and needed to communicate his desire for sustenance, there was but one method. Calvin could see his son's chest rise and fall as he began the silent panting, which he had done countless times in the past. It was the calm before the screaming-baby storm.

With his features scrunched close together, the boy stared up at his father, who attempted to "shush" him with his gaze. When his lips parted, he released a sound that was silenced by his father's hand.

"You hear that?" The men stopped.

"Yeah."

One of the Wolves walked further into the space and looked around as the other continued to search the skies for snipers along the path back to the others.

"Who's in here?" He aligned the rifle with his eyesight and caressed the trigger.

Calvin tucked his legs close to his body as the sound of the man's footsteps came near. He closed his eyes and released a silent prayer.

"Let's get out of here," the other called.

"Okay." He pivoted in his partner's direction and they both took off.

When he heard the door shut behind the departed hunters, Calvin opened his eyes and breathed heavily. His prayer had been heard, and he was spared. Relieved, he looked to his son. Fear and panic caused him to forget the position of his hand over the boy's face. He quickly removed it, but the damage was irreversible. His chubby face bore a red imprint of his father's hand. His delicate, pouty mouth did not move, and he looked as if he was asleep. He would never make a sound again.

∗ ∗ ∗

THE sun vanished completely. After nearly 24 hours on their post, Monika and Jabari prepared to swap positions with a pair who stood guard on a less-active region of the rooftop. First, they would take a 2-hour rest—just as they were trained to do.

Drained, they gripped the rail of the stairs to help carry their weight as they descended to the 20th floor. They haggardly entered the room where Amara, her children, and two other families attempted to wait out the violence.

Once she entered, Monika nearly collapsed to the floor but was held up by a wall.

Alert, Amara heard the door creak open and noticed her husband.

"Jabari!" She ran to console him, but he could barely muster a smirk of pleasure.

He embraced his wife with what strength he had left. "I'm okay."

"Tell me it's over."

"I want to."

"But you can't."

Jabari shook his head and, when he noticed the injury to his wife's face, cupped her chin with his hand and pulled her closer.

"It's fine." She gently pulled away.

Jabari made his way to the nearest seat in the room and plopped down. His children's attention was focused on the turmoil in the streets, and they had not noticed his return.

"They shouldn't see this," Jabari said.

"Not much of a choice."

"Kids," he summonsed, and they approached with grim, hope-drained faces.

"Can we go home now?" Shiloh asked her father.

"Not yet."

"I want to get out of here, Jabari," Amara insisted.

"What did I tell you?"

"I went to the first floor. No one was there."

"Where is Calvin and Michael?" Monika spoke wearily with bloodshot eyes.

"The last I saw them, they were down there," Amara said.

"You should have stayed with them," Jabari said.

"People were being killed right in front of us. I couldn't."

"What?" Monika stood.

"I asked for the baby, but he insisted on taking him to get milk. We came back here."

Monika started for the elevator.

"Want me to come with you?" Jabari asked.

"No. Stay with your family. I'll be fine."

The elevator lowered an anxious Monika down to the bottom floor, and she stepped off with her weapon raised and ready. She moved with ease through the quiet room, which appeared empty. After ten steps into the space, she heard whispers. She raised her weapon a little higher and looked for where the sound had come.

As Monika turned the corner, Calvin's dress shoes stuck out as he rhythmically tapped his toe against the floor. His eyes were closed, and their son was nestled in his arms as he whispered the boy's favorite nursery rhyme.

"The doors on the bus go open and shut, open and shut, open and shut; the doors on the bus go open and shut all through the town," he whispered.

Monika lowered the gun and tucked it at her waist. "Calvin," she said as she approached.

He raised his sunken eyes to see her, and instantly choked on his words, "I don't know what happened." He shrugged. Mucus dripped from his nose and alarmed her.

Monika walked nearer and noticed the purplish complexion of her baby's face. A spear had pierced straight through her lungs, and she was suffocating. She silenced her dismay with a single hand over her nose and mouth and fell to her knees.

"What's wrong with him? What did you do?"

"He was going to cry. I didn't—," Calvin wailed. "I wanted to stop him from crying." His sobs intensified. "If those guys heard him, they would find us. I was afraid. So, I—I stopped him from crying."

Monika's hands trembled and resisted her intent to keep them still. She parted her lips to speak, but nothing came out. She opened her hands to receive her baby and Calvin placed him in her arms. Her sobs were pulled inward as she stared at the once vibrant infant.

"I'm sorry."

"That will never be enough."

"What can I do?"

"Get the hell out of here. Go!"

"Where? I'll be killed."

"Fair enough," she said bitterly.

Calvin gathered his thoughts. "If you had been here with us, this wouldn't have happened."

As she traced her baby's features with the tips of her fingers, Monika's mournful moment turned to silent disgust. She tried to summon the memory of his giggles and toothless smiles but landed back at the moment she longed to escape.

"I asked you not to leave us."

Calvin wiped snot from his face with the sleeve of his dress shirt.

She cradled Michael closer and kissed his forehead before she lifted him to her shoulder as though he would speak into her ear. She caressed his cheek with the tip of her nose and inhaled the remnants of his scent.

"Talk to me," Calvin pleaded.

Monika stood with her baby in one hand and reached for the gun at her waist with the other. Calvin leaned away, and feared an irrational act was awry.

Monika placed the gun against the cold floor. "It is better to die than to live in fear. Use it however you're led."

She walked towards the elevators, stepped inside, and it lifted a solemn Monika back up to the 20th floor.

CHAPTER SIX
NO TIME FOR CEREMONY

1995

THE first time Monika stood on a roof she was afraid. The pressure as she faced the enormity of a 30-story building paled in comparison to her father's awkward behavior as he led her there. It was December, cold, and the 14-year-old Monika spent most days in deep contemplation. She questioned her ability to push through her first Christmas without her mother.

When her father arrived at school mid-day and explained he would sign her out early for some mysterious doctor's appointment, it was out of character. Normally, a trusted friend or employee would accompany the girls to appointments, so Monika sensed that something was amiss, but had no clue what awaited her.

It was difficult for the bishop to find his way back to himself after the accident that claimed the lives of his wife and son, and his girls were well-aware. They seldom saw him. He was often buried in his studies and surrounded by ministry leaders who supported his vision. There was barely a pinhole of space for his girls but, to soften tragedy's blow, they made sure to behave themselves, make good grades, become upstanding ladies—anything that would appease him and make life easier in the wake of heartbreak.

Monika left her jacket behind as she hopped from the passenger side of the car, but the walls of the garage shielded her from the crisp wind that would unkindly greet her on the rooftop.

Bishop Dyer grasped her hand as they rode up in the elevator, entered an "employees only" area, and walked onto the roof.

"Daddy, what are we doing?" Monika asked, and folded her arms for warmth. A cold draft brushed against the scalp-exposed parts between the braids she wore.

"Come on." He walked closer to the ledge and stepped up fearlessly.

Monika looked over. Cars moved slowly through intersections; people strolled the sidewalks, moved briskly if poorly dressed for the weather, sipped coffee, stopped to tie a shoe, smoked a cigarette.

"Step up here," he said, and reached for her hand.

"I don't wanna fall, Daddy."

"You won't."

She shivered, and hesitantly grabbed his hand. Monika hoped the moment would pass more quickly with her compliance.

"See. It's not so bad." He held her hand firmly and inhaled deeply.

"Why are we here?"

He looked at her with intense eyes. "I want you to jump."

"No!" She snatched her hand away.

"What are you afraid of?"

"I don't wanna die."

"Why not?"

"I don't want to." Her terror provoked tears that pushed through searching eyes.

"There is nothing to fear. I can't see down there. I don't have my glasses." He turned to look. "One thing that's for sure—the end of this life." His eyes squinted towards the sky. "There is another side that's beyond what we can even imagine."

"I can see it, Daddy." Monika referenced the roadway below and ignored her father's imagined afterlife experience. "I wanna get down."

"Stay there!" he demanded with authority.

"Please."

"Your mother and brother transitioned. They're in a better place." He laughed faintly as though he was fully convinced. "There is no pain."

"Even if I land in Heaven, I'm not ready, Daddy. Please. Let's get off."

"You'd rather stay on this earth with me?"

She nodded her head. "And Amara too." She chewed the inside of her jaw. Tears zig-zagged from cheek to ear as they were guided by the cold wind.

"If I jump first, would you come down after me?"

Her father's condition was worse than she assumed, and Monika was afraid to respond. For months, he hid behind locked doors or "the work of the Lord", and his girls respected his need for privacy—but the man who stood next to her was someone she had never known. It seemed her father morphed into a maniac inside those walls; but as much as she wanted to scream for help, run for her life, she understood his pain.

She locked eyes with the man she had loved since she knew time, and sensed the sincerity of his heart, but said nothing. He extended his hand to her again, and it lingered there a while as Monika replayed the memory of her mother— the tragedy that shattered her family, the holiday she would spend without homemade sugar cookies in the shape of stars and a round-belly Santa, how nothing that year felt like times past, how no one could promise it ever would again, or offer a remedy for the guilt she carried—and she extended her hand. Deep within, she felt she owed him as much. Monika closed her eyes; her throat became a restricting mechanism, and she found it hard to breathe.

She would not see the smile on her father's face before he gently kissed her cheek.

"Thank you for trusting me," he said.

Monika opened her eyes, and her father stepped back onto the floor. He helped her down and wrapped his arm around her shoulders as he led her back to safety and warmth.

"You want pizza?" he asked.

She never told anyone—not even Amara, whose immature method to make sense of ridiculous scenarios was to argue that it never happened. Simple. Bishop Dyer and Amara were all Monika had in life and, since the moment was spent, she decided that peace among them was most important.

A week later, Monika found herself in an unfamiliar facility after school, and surrounded by dozens of youths who ranged in age from 9 to 18. Stranger, her father arranged the drop-off across town with a man Monika did not know. The commute was quiet, but as they crossed the final intersection, he warned her to never speak unless spoken to, and to never use her name.

"Where am I going?" she asked from the backseat.

"I can't speak on it. You won't either."

Monika was baffled, and her thoughts stretched beyond the realm of reality.

"If I can't say my name, what do I tell them?" she asked the man as he pulled into an empty parking lot.

"Nothing. You're here to listen—not talk."

"Is it a class or something?"

"Sure."

"Are you coming too?"

"No. Someone else will pick you up from here at 10 tonight. They'll find you. Just wait inside until you're called to come out." He put the car in park. "Head in now. Wait! Take this."

He handed her a black, light-weight full-face mask that only revealed the wearer's eyes—like those worn by motorcyclists to shield their faces from the elements. "Put it on," he ordered her, and she did.

When she entered the muggy room, the others were seated in folding chairs situated in two circles, one enclosing the other. They were all masked. A man stood at the center and stared at his audience, puzzled and silent. Each of their hands folded together on their laps. So, as Monika took her seat, she mimicked their behavior, and placed her hands atop her baggy jeans. Of the 36 who sat nearby, she counted only 9 girls—all near her age, give or take a year or two. The boys were better poised than most pre-adolescents. Monika was curious and contemplated the cause of their docile demeanor.

"You were chosen," the man spoke.

The nameless, near faceless man wore a thick winter coat, but it could not conceal his muscular physique. His gruff tone commanded attention and submission to each demand. Besides, there was not a parent in the room, nor the promise they would come if needed.

"You will better understand what we are here to accomplish in time. What I need is your commitment to give your very best."

Monika observed the blank stares, and knew she was not alone. If there was ever a moment to raise a hand and pose a question, that was it; but she had been warned not to speak and had no desire to know the consequences.

"Your folks placed you here, but nothing that happens or is discussed in this room will be shared with anyone—not even them."

As The Man spoke, a brave, bubble-eyed boy raised a hand slightly into the air. Either he completely ignored, or warning had not been properly delivered to the oblivious soul.

When The Man noticed, he broke his sentence to address him. "Yes?"

"I have a question—sir."

"Who are you, son?"

"Gre—."

"Quiet!" The Man yelled and halted the boy's response mid-vowel. "You are not a name. We will not use them, and neither will you learn them—mine or your own."

The youngsters looked to each other with more questions than they dared to ask.

"You are kings, queens, gods, warriors," he continued. Their eyebrows raised. "Never speak or write the names you were given by your parents when in this room. Soon, I will more likely recognize your unique squeal of exhaustion, or the shallow sounds of your breath, than know your names."

At the thought, bodies squirmed in their seats, feet tapped against the floor, legs shivered; and then a woman, whose presence was overlooked, stood from within the first circle. Her hair was cut as short as most men, and she wore a baseball cap and loose-fitting jeans.

"You will be referred to by number," she added. "These numbers will not be written or placed on your person. Remember them."

As the woman circled the room and named them all aloud, Monika wrestled with the reason she was there and silently questioned the need to shrivel to a number. Nothing made sense. However, her father knew of her whereabouts, so she felt secure. Monika never failed to trust his judgement and was certain he would not bring her harm.

"18," the woman said as she pointed to Monika, and then continued around the circle.

A dark-skinned boy who sat in the outer circle caught Monika's attention. He wore a collared shirt, and the tails of his cornrow braids peeked from beneath his mask. His eyes followed the woman who steadily approached. A unique scar—left from six stitches he received when a rock was thrown at his face in elementary school—stretched across the boy's dense eyebrow. The girl beamed from within as his presence saturated her heart with peace. Finally—a familiar, though covered, face. And she knew his name.

"27," the woman announced, but his name was Jabari.

He was not a friend of Monika's per se; their parents were. In the past, they had dinner in each other's homes, but were both too timid to branch off into their own discussions and listened intently to their parents' conversations instead. Since her mother's death, friendly meals came to a halt, and it had been almost a year since she had seen the boy.

Monika shifted in her seat and sat up high to alert him of her presence, but he kept his head down, and had only raised it to receive his name.

When the count reached "36", The Man spoke again. "Do not forget your number. In a moment, you will also receive a partner. Do not forget them. Now stand."

The chairs screeched against the floor as the young people rose to their feet. He pointed randomly and made a horizontal scissor motion with his fingers for them to stand together. They moved two-by-two like submissive animals onto the ark.

Out of the silence, someone snickered as they connected with their new ally.

"Who was that?" The Man turned abruptly.

Silence. The guilty party—14—kept his eyes steady to avoid detection, but his partner's gaze in his direction was an immediate tell-tale. The man found the partner's reaction more repulsive than the disruption itself and approached *him* instead.

"Why did you look at him?" he asked.

The boy was no older than twelve, and his natural expression teetered between tears solemn bravery.

"I don't know." He shrugged.

"You do. You wanted to tell on him. Am I right?"

The boy's eyes shifted.

"That's what we do." The Man loudly addressed the room. "We panic, we fear, and then we point fingers. Not in this room. You are guilty by association. Your partner screws up—you screw up. There is no way around it."

He turned back to the boys. "Suicides," he ordered them. "Over there."

The boys hustled over to an area of the room where the floor had been pre-marked with duct tape and got on their first mark.

"Don't stop until I say." He continued to point and pair the rest of the group.

When he reached Monika, it was as if her heart was swallowed up by her belly. She followed his eyes across the room towards those who remained uncoupled; and in that moment, Jabari noticed her. As the man's fingers directed, the teens were relieved to grasp something recognizable within the strange, new world. They joined together and immediately aligned themselves with the others.

Although they were the same age, Jabari stood nearly 5 inches over Monika. And when the man turned his back, Jabari offered her a quick smirk of friendliness, and she responded with a slow blink of the eyes.

The pair entered an experience for which they were not prepared, but was without the option to quit, resist, or protest. Even the evening's first assembly delivered a hands-on lesson in Krav Maga. No time was spared. The knowledge of what took place in that room—take downs, choke holds, history lessons, weapon-handling, suffering—was first shared between partners, and then with the others in the room, and no one else.

After years of secrecy, training, and bonding, it would be easier to loosen the knot of a single thread than to break the alliance between Jabari and Monika. There were moments when Amara, naïve and protected, assumed her father played favorites when he would permit Monika to come in after 10 p.m. several days each week. Monika's extracurriculars exceeded the two ballet lessons their father permitted Amara to take; however, Amara's jealously was rooted in her lack of awareness. She could not know that her sister was moved by obedience, and not will.

Although the youngsters were certain both of their fathers knew of their training, and were indeed close friends, they would never again see the two men in the same room.

Jabari was an only child. His father, E.J. Rushing was a direct descendent of the Igbos of Nigeria. A proud man, he relished his ancestry and the strength of his people. And Jabari's mother, Nnenna, had immigrated to America in 1968 to escape the Nigerian-Biafran War. She was 17 years old. During the conflict, African students were sent by Christian missions and churches to Historically Black Colleges and Universities in America, which is where she first encountered Jabari's father—Ejofa, as she called him. Jabari's mother had known hardship and fear, but not slavery. However, she bore witness to the persistent clash of America's Black citizens, white-sided laws and bigotry, and understood her husband's irrepressible urge to vindicate victims of the prejudice government system.

E.J. had a knack for enterprise and opened a tax service, a car wash, and had a successful hand in stocks and bonds. Yet, he was a champion for the voiceless. Every chance he could, he openly expressed disdain for those who controlled the system that perpetuated his ancestors' travail and continued to oppress Blacks. His means knew no bounds, and he went blow for blow with political figures whose reach was just as limitless.

Brown, and intimidating in stature and deeds, there was no wonder he became a suspect in the shooting death of a known enemy. The most recent target of E.J.'s venom was a school board official who casually refused to fund academic programs and provide better resources for predominantly Black schools. The two men engaged in heated debates and vicious attacks on public platforms—two of which were televised town hall meetings. By June of 1996, there was no more suspicion. Police had packaged a few details to indicate some level of E.J.'s involvement and arrested him; but he would not stay long. Three months later, while he awaited trial in a cold jail cell, they found him dead on the floor. He suffered a fatal heart attack at 46 years old.

For Jabari, the excitement of high school was overshadowed by his father's death. The one who groomed him for manhood, one of integrity and dignity, would never witness the outcome of his influence. The foundation of Jabari's straight and narrow path had been laid, but his mother knew the power of a village, and the impact men have on the lives of adolescent boys.

Closest to them was the Dyer family, and they were reunited soon after E.J. was buried. The two empty seats at the dining room table made it a challenge to partake in any merriment, but the occasional dinner and casual conversation was enough to make the adults feel that they were no longer alone.

* * *

IT was carnival season, and every young person who enjoyed the exhilaration of rollercoasters, greasy cuisine, cheap stuffed animals, or a chance to socialize, made plans to go. Monika was no exception. Although recently submerged in the hormonal dramatics of the high school experience, none of her grades had touched below a 'B', and she used the fact to bargain for what she wanted.

Bishop Dyer entered the front door of their home and helped a limping Amara to the couch.

"What happened to her?" Monika asked when she surfaced from her bedroom.

"Sprang my ankle, I think."

"The child is only 12 and has had more injuries than I've had over my entire life," their father said. "She'll be alright. You might want to give dance a break."

"Not if I have a choice, Daddy." She smiled.

"The aspirin should kick in soon. Just stay off your feet. Monika, let's get ready for bible study," he said as he passed.

"But Daddy..."

He turned to her.

"I was wondering if I could go to the carnival," Monika said sweetly.

"What? Not on a church night. No." His answer was final, so he started to walk away.

"Then when?" she asked in a more serious tone.

"Not tonight. Maybe not this year. There's too much to do."

"I know."

Monika looked to see how invested her sister was in their conversation; and Amara had the focus of a patron who purchased a front row seat months in advance.

"There's never any time, you know." Monika hoped her father would catch on.

"There's time for what matters."

"And I do my best. Six 'A's'; two 'B's'. My grades are better than last year's, and almost twice as good as before Mama—." She stopped short of the thought's completion.

96

"I'm doing better now. School, track practice, church, home—that's it."

It was undeniable. She had managed to juggle each of her obligations and almost nightly sessions with the youth of TAAR. It was impossible for a sensible man to be uncompelled by her argument; but within their home, sensible was not a word used to describe their father. Monika anticipated the reinforcement of his "no".

"Just one night," she pleaded.

Her desperation to experience girlhood softened him. "With who?" he asked.

"I wanna go too," Amara whined from the sofa.

"You're not going anywhere."

She folded her arms and sulked.

"I don't know, Daddy. I wanted to ask you first," Monika continued.

"You're not going out there alone. Call Nnenna. See if she'll let Jabari go with you."

Monika gleamed, and sprang for the kitchen's cordless phone.

There was a chill in the air, and as Monika and Jabari climbed from the backseat of Nnenna's car, she offered the girl a sweater to keep warm. It was brown and beige with patches of green, an irregular pattern of triangles, and was three sizes too big for Monika.

"Here. Take it," Nnenna said.

Monika flashed to the future of the ugly-sweater-carnival-night—the kids in the park, the boy at her side—and would rather suffer frost bite than be seen in the garment.

"I'm really not cold," Monika insisted, "but thank you." Before Nnenna could say anything more, Monika shut the car door and proceeded to walk away.

"Yum...You smell that?" she asked Jabari with a wide smile and a springy step, but her energy was unmatched.

"Yeah," was all he said.

"I can't decide if I'll get a corn dog, or one of those polish sausages—no onions. Can't stand those things."

Jabari did not respond but moved sluggishly through the gate of admission and slowed to await Monika's guidance.

"So, what you wanna do first?" she asked.

He shrugged.

"Let's see. There's the spinning top thing over there, or the mini coaster that goes backwards, or that huge swing."

Still, no response.

"Okay. I guess I'll choose." She huffed. "Come on."

Jabari followed her to a fast-moving ride that caused whiplash or temporary hearing loss from the loud, trending hip hop songs that blared from its speakers. They sat, locked in, and took off but, afterwards, Jabari was no different. From one attraction to another, his demeanor remained. Monika noticed, but the excitement of a night of freedom overshadowed the emotional state of her friend.

When she was ready for a break to massage the ache from her neck and shoulders, she traipsed over to a caramel apple stand.

"Want one?" she offered as she reached into her pocket for cash.

"No."

"You don't know what you're missing."

The decadent treat was wrapped delicately with plastic, and the white stick that poked from the apple's core was tied with a bow. She wanted to ravage the package and get to the succulent goodness within it.

"You wanna sit down?" was the most Jabari had spoken all evening.

The pair sat at an empty picnic table surrounded by other carnival cuisine diners. The cellophane crinkled and crumbled as Monika ripped open the caramel apple. Her mouth watered when she lifted it to her face and took a bite.

"So good." She crunched on the tart, crisp fruit beneath the thick layer of velvety, brown confection.

"Looks like it."

"Want some? I can share."

"No. I don't like it."

"Caramel apples? What?"

"I like candy apples."

98

"Same thing."

"Yeah, maybe. They're both candy, but I like the crunchy outside better."

"Have you ever eaten a caramel apple?" she asked.

"No. It gets stuck to your teeth."

"So does the other kind."

He agreed but did not respond.

"Here. Bite it." She moved it close to his face.

"No. I'm cool."

"Here." She made engine noises with her mouth and waved the apple in the air as though it were an airplane. "I won't stop until you bite it. I can keep going." She chuckled.

Jabari noticed they had the attention of a few onlookers and conceded to Monika's playful insistence. "Okay!"

He gently pressed his lips together and then parted them for a bite of the fruit. Juice dripped from his chin as he chomped. Monika used her hand to wipe it away.

"Good, right?" she asked, and examined the apple's massive indentation.

"Yeah." He licked his lips for any remnant of sweetness.

Monika took another bite. "You know, you can say more than one or two words."

"I am."

"We spend so much time being quiet. Here, we can talk—like normal people."

He nodded.

"So... What's the deal with the sweater your mama tried to give me?"

Jabari chuckled. He had concealed his reaction to the moment between Monika and his mother since they entered the park.

"Don't front. You look like you could use a little covering up."

"Not with that! No diss."

"That's exactly what it is." He cleared his throat. "She got the sweater from my grandma—on my dad's side—when

99

I was a baby. She made it for her husband before he died, and just wanted to hand it down, I guess. I'm surprised she would let you wear it. Maybe she didn't want me around a hoochie."

Monika playfully punched him in the arm. "Whatever."

She examined her loose-fitting jeans and top, which hung from her thin torso and revealed an inch of skin below her navel. "I'm good."

"I was just playing."

"Mm hm." She took another bite. "Seriously, people don't knit."

"My people different."

"How so?"

"They like to work with their hands. Do things the old-fashioned way. They're from Africa."

"Tis! We *all* are. I know they're not gathered around knitting sweaters in Africa."

"We're not from there in the same way. My mom is still connected to it."

"She go back there sometime?"

"After she left, she lost contact with everyone she knew."

"Her mom and dad too?"

"Yep. I never met them."

"And she won't go back to find them?"

"I don't think she wants to know—you know—if they didn't make it."

"That's sad."

"She says it stopped worrying her a long time ago. A lot of people got killed, or they starved to death. So, either way, she feels she's better off not knowing." He shrugged.

"I didn't know that happened to her."

"She told me stories growing up that most kids around here won't hear. And so did my dad." His expression shifted at the sound of his own words.

"Like what?" Monika was curious.

"There are a lot things they don't mention in our books. Slavery happened for hundreds of years, but there's only a brief mention."

"History—it's my favorite subject." She gnawed down on the apple.

"Do you know about Igbo Landing?"

"Who?"

"It's not a person. In the 1800s, they brought a fresh shipment of Nigerians over here as slaves. Instead, they took over the ship, killed the white men, and then they all drowned themselves—75, maybe 100 of them."

"That's depressing."

"And true. Not in the books though. They would rather die than to be a white man's property." He shifted in his seat. "The story goes, my ancestor—a great, great, great grandfather –changed his mind, was captured and, until the day he died, said he regretted not going through with it. I don't know how true it is, but it would make sense to me."

"And your dad told you this?"

He offered a subtle nod, and Monika could no longer pretend her friend was not in agony.

"You miss him, huh?"

"All day," he said in a whisper.

"It'll get better." She touched the back of his hands that were clasped together on the picnic table, but he moved them in a manner to not offend her.

"I don't see how."

She thought for a moment, and then jolted in her seat when the thought came to her. "Conditioning is starting for baseball pretty soon. It can help take your mind off of it."

"I don't wanna play."

"Okay. Then is there anything else you like to do?"

"No."

He was a lost cause, but Monika was eager to speak life into her friend and make things better for him.

"I had track."

"What?"

"I started track in the 7th grade—the year my mama died. It helped."

"That's why you do it now?"

"No. I love it—just like you love baseball."

"I *did*."

"You still do. You just don't wanna show it right now."

She took a final bite that cut into the apple's core, and then rewrapped the remains as Jabari digested her words. It was the first time he discussed the devastation of his father's absence with anyone. And through their exchange, he discovered that normalcy after pain was possible. Monika's words—though playful—had given him hope.

"Wanna ride some more?"

"If I say 'no', I think you'll make me do it anyway."

"And you're right!" She jumped up and grabbed his hand to diminish any thought of protest. "Come on! Three more!"

* * *

THE one-year anniversary of their training arrived quickly. The youth, still oblivious to their cause, had become skilled in physical combat techniques and the assembly of several weapons. They were made tough through hours of gruesome activities from which they were never permitted to relent.

Rain, hail, ice, fever, or stomachaches were never an excuse to miss sessions, and they did not. They were forced to push through their conditions—vomit if they must—but could never miss a night's training. Monika assumed her partner had finally gone against this principle when he was not present at roll call one evening. And since 11 was feverish and forced to watch from the sidelines, she was paired with 21. The boy was a little older than Monika, had a beauty mark near his right eye and preferred to wear shorts—with a jacket if it was cold outside. His bulging calves were always properly moisturized with shea butter and glistened, which caught a few glimpses from the girls in the group.

Monika was indifferent. It was not an "anti-boys" phase; she did not fully know how to engage with them beyond friendship. Her mother and father had kept her and her sister busy with school, activities, ministry, and their favorite pastimes so they would barely have room for boy-crazy chit chat. Monika never thought to move beyond investing in a well-deserved stamp of "cute" but, with what little she had to go on, 21 was an immediate "denied" in her book.

Nearly a half hour late, and while the group was already gathered around the mat to witness a wrestling scrimmage between partners, Jabari walked into the room and tossed his bookbag in the corner. A masked woman greeted him before he made his way to the circle.

"What happened to you?" she asked.

"Missed the bus home," he said.

"Discipline. Responsibility. Promptness. What have you learned, boy?"

"I know. I was talking to my teacher, and —."

She put up a single hand. "That's enough."

She looked around the room to determine where Jabari should go but knew the others were already paired. Jabari noticed Monika near the mat as she waited her turn.

"Take a seat over there." The woman pointed.

"But Moni — my partner, 18 — is about to go in."

"She's not your partner tonight. Go."

As Jabari drew near the group, he noticed 21 at Monika's side. They both squatted at the edge of the mat; their shoulders touched. At the conclusion of the previous match, they turned their heads, and their faces were close enough to kiss if masks were not a barrier. Jabari's focus was not on the wrestlers, but on his partner and the boy next to her.

When the match ended, 21 stood and offered Monika a hand. Her black sweatpants fit snug around her tiny waist. Her t-shirt, tied in a knot at the back, revealed a small section of skin. The pair took their positions in the middle of the mat, locked eyes, and then dapped each other's hands before they posed in an attack stance.

Monika planted her feet and shoved at the boy with all her might; he could not gain an inch and had underestimated her strength.

"Let's move," The Man yelled. He checked the timer in his hands. "Enough playing around."

The boy leaped to action and pushed Monika backwards. Jabari's fists clenched tightly on his lap. In one fluid movement, 21 dropped down, stepped forward, and placed his knee on the ground between Monika's legs. She resisted and locked onto his shoulders to shift his weight back, but it was too late. She hit the floor when her leg was pulled from beneath her. Jabari cringed.

"Get up! And again!" The Man called.

The youngsters breathed heavily but had no room to pause. They got into position. At the whistle, 21 moved towards Monika. She immediately grabbed his glistening calf and raised it to her shoulder. She pressed her palm into the inside of his thigh and knocked him to the ground. Jabari blew a puff of warm air through his mask.

"One more," The Man said.

Her opponent's hands began to sweat, and he wiped them on his shorts before he stood in position. His desire to win intensified. It was one thing to lose to his actual partner— a boy—but he refused to lose to Monika. He gazed at her with rattle snake focus, and at the sound of the whistle, he sprang for her. The boy's ego radiated from the mat, and Jabari knew his refusal to be crushed would charge him enough to win at any cost.

Monika locked her arm around his neck and attempted to pull him in. She failed. The boy wrapped his arm around her waist, swung her around, and with every speck of aggression he could muster, took her down from the rear. She hit the floor harder than ever, and all her upper body weight was absorbed by her left arm as it collided with the floor. Immediately, a sharp pain shot through her shoulder, and it ached.

"Alright. Good job. Next."

Her opponent extended his hand to help her up. She initially reached out with her left hand but drew it back quickly to reverse the tears already internalized from the pain. Any demonstration of weakness would mean more exercise, so they learned to conceal it; but Jabari saw. He knew.

Monika was helped to her feet with her right hand, and she dapped the boy again before they moved back to their seats. Once there, she massaged her arm and shoulder with compresses as strong as her fingers would allow. Jabari watched her. It seemed his gaze was strong enough to lure her attention because, after a moment, she turned around.

Jabari's eyes were sad, concerned. He slightly held up a hand—his thumb and index finger pressed together—to ask if she was okay. She nodded her head and turned back at the sound of The Man's voice.

"No fooling around on the mat. We're moving quickly," he said.

Jabari noticed nothing more than Monika's consistent, self-massage to minimize her discomfort. Regret and guilt welled up within him; but how he felt about himself paled in comparison to what he discovered he felt for her.

CHAPTER SEVEN
NO ROOM FOR HOPE

WHEN the elevator landed on the 20th floor, Monika swiftly turned from where Jabari and Amara sat side-by-side with the children near their feet. Jabari's head rested on his wife's shoulder as he slept; but Monika did not move past her sister unnoticed.

The 20th level housed one of three major banking institutions, and each department and cubicle were for its loan officers and processors. At the end of the walkway was a quiet corner office, and the light from the hallway was all Monika needed to move about with her baby in arm. There was a large desk that faced the door, and two tall file cabinets against the wall—otherwise, the room was bare. She sat on the floor, listened to the pops of gunfire in the distance, and attempted to gulp down the growing knot in her throat.

There were no words to speak, and tears were no option. She unwrapped the blanket from around the baby and held him tightly. As she hummed a mournful melody, she opened the bottom drawer of the file cabinet and placed the blanket inside. Monika was unaware that Amara had quietly joined the ceremony from the doorway.

Stunned, Amara watched her sister memorialize the lifeless boy.

Monika kissed her baby's face from cheek to chin and laid him inside the drawer. She wanted to close it, but her final look lasted longer than she expected it would.

"How?" Amara asked gently as she walked into the room.

"Does it matter?"

"I'm sorry."

Monika continued to stare at her resting son. "I'm not."

Amara gasped. "How does that make sense?"

"How does any of this?" She caressed the baby's face. "I didn't know I could fall in love with something I never wanted."

Amara sat next to her sister. "You regret having him."

"I regret bringing him into a world that would force him to prove if he was a coward or a soldier."

"That's not the world we live in."

"That's not the world *you* live in."

"I don't understand. We're from the same place—the same family."

"You saw what you wanted—what you *could* see. You had that freedom."

"This is not who we are. Daddy didn't raise us to be— this. He would never stand for it. What happened to you?"

Monika looked at her sister with narrow eyes that concealed a decades-long truth.

"Nothing happened to me."

"Was it Ma? Did Mama dying make you become this person?" Amara dramatically covered her mouth with her hands as though she had stumbled upon the right answer. "That's it, isn't it? Ma died, Daddy was in his own world, and you became...this."

Amara's waspish comments salted Monika's injury with insult. She wished her eyes could expose the years of anguish, and preparation for present turmoil, to alleviate her sister's naïveté.

"And you were always his favorite," Amara added sarcastically.

Monika considered each sacrifice she had made, and each command she could not refuse when she desired to walk away.

"No. You were. Rest assured," she said.

Monika finally mustered the strength to roll the cabinet closed when Jabari's head poked into the room. Before he captured the women's attention, he noticed the tiny feet inside the drawer as they moved completely out of sight, and the cabinet clicked into place.

"Amara," he called.

She stood and moved closer to him. "Something wrong?"

"Nothing to panic about. The kids asked for you." He observed Monika's condition—eyes low, body limp—but tried to balance his attention between both partners.

"I'm coming." Amara moved past him in the doorway and left her grief-stricken sister behind.

Monika lifted her head, but words were not exchanged between them. With steady eyes, and lips firmly pressed together, Jabari stood boldly, raised his chin in salute, and then walked away.

Alone, she pressed her face against the cold cabinet and stared absentmindedly at the wall in front of her. The gum in her mouth had become tasteless, so she spit it onto the floor.

That which provided normalcy was no more. She was a trained killer who doubled as a high school history teacher—and not the other way around. Michael's existence allowed Monika to share her authentic self, which could not be ruined by TAAR. Her son could experience a pure perspective of who she was—a mother—without any coercion or deceitful cause, but simply because she loved him. Calvin was merely a temporary-situation-turned-permanent after the birth of their son, who became the glue that bound them all together and opened a new dimension of Monika's purpose.

She grew increasingly numb by the second; her toes tingled until they became mush in her shoes, and she could no longer fight against the mighty blow of exhaustion. Fatigued and overwhelmed, Monika soon fell asleep at her son's makeshift grave.

* * *

THE battle shifted. The Wolves were angered by those who injured and killed members of their pack. Therefore, the quest to slaughter innocent protestors was quenched by their need to locate and take down those who caused their comrades to lie cold in the warm street. However, their original targets were not given a pass. As Wolves fought to gain access to skyscrapers and rise to the level of those who haunted them, they pushed through buildings where people hid away and gunned down as many as they could on their way to the top. By the second night, nearly 400 people were dead or wounded, and the number continued to rise.

Recharged from her rest, Valerie thought to change into her navy-blue officer's uniform since they were least targeted—if at all. She removed her clothes and exposed the gray-shaded tattoo on her left shoulder—the phoenix, a celebration of resilience. She slipped into attire she had not worn for six years and topped it with a "POLICE" vest. She grabbed as much ammunition as she could carry on her person and returned to the battleground.

Casualties had nearly doubled since she was last there. She had not expected to sleep for such an extensive time, but trusted her body knew best. Valerie was ready to face the chaos with renewed energy that rest, and the remnants of a half-eaten granola bar, provided her.

Her thoughts made high-speed doughnuts around Jabari's involvement. And her discovery of Monika Dyer's position on the roof beside the gunman, who doubled as a fellow cop, left her mystified. It was too much to sort through and remain alert enough to guard herself against potential attack, but she was eager to find a solution and end the violence.

As she slipped past fellow officers, her eyes darted the high-rises along the way, and she disappeared into the shadows. Valerie's hand firmly gripped her weapon, and she walked along a backstreet for a few blocks. She hooked a left and found herself in a zone bloodier than where she stood post the previous night. The all-knowing camera lens anchored atop a coffee shop's brick exterior had gotten its share of tragedy.

For a moment, it was quiet. No one moved about on the street; the rooftops were a different story. She counted the gunmen on guard, "two there, two there," as she went. Her eyes were focused so long on the people in the sky that she almost collided with a man—armed and dressed in all black. His back had been turned to her, and she startled him. He turned quickly and aimed his handgun at her.

"Police! Drop the gun," she commanded him.

"No."

"Drop your weapon. Now!" She aimed at the man's head.

"I can't do that."

"You will drop it, or you give me no choice but to shoot you."

"Go ahead."

He looked towards the ground a few meters from where they stood. There was the body of another man dressed in all black. The two were partners and had known each other over half their lives. His gaze offered a final salute.

"There is nothing you can do about him. He's gone. But you can put the gun down now and spare yourself."

He raised the gun higher and aimed it directly at Valerie.

"You don't want to shoot me. You *won't* shoot me. Just put it down."

"No. You'll have to shoot me first."

He bore the cold indifference of Tin Man. Valerie considered the time wasted on the distraught man and was ready to end it.

As she moved her weapon to aim at his leg, he lunged forward, roundhouse kicked the gun from her hand, and it landed near his partner's body. His leg went up again, and Valerie ducked swiftly to avoid the collision. His other leg was thrust out and landed in the center of her chest. She was forced back as her arms flailed in the air. She gasped after she hit the concrete. The man drew near but, in one swift motion, Valerie drew the gun from her ankle and fired a single shot into the man's thigh. He dropped to the ground immediately yet held tightly to his weapon.

Valerie hovered over him. "Drop it."

"Shoot me."

Neither of them wanted to see the other dead; and neither was confident the other would not shoot. Valerie understood that as an officer of the law—a recently assaulted officer—the ball was in her court, and she could unquestionably shoot the armed man who refused to drop his weapon. It was no longer pointed in her direction, but he held it like a toddler's security blanket as he clenched his jaw in pain.

"What's your name?" Valerie asked.

"I don't have one."

"Tell me your name!"

"73," he responded.

Wide-eyed, Valerie's forehead grew increasingly tighter. "And what's his?" she nodded towards his partner.

"95." His words were muffled by pain.

"What did you say?"

"95." He moaned.

"Numbers, huh? How many of you are there?"

"Who am I?" he asked and released a pained chuckle. "Who are we?"

Valerie's gun pointed towards the ground and relieved the injured man. His willingness to die surprised the detective. She strapped the weapon back into its holster and walked over to retrieve the weapon that had been kicked away. As she bent down to pick it up, she saw that the man's partner had been shot through the neck, and his cold fingers were still locked around his gun.

She returned to the living soldier. "I would put it down if I were you, or the next time you might not be so lucky. Pretty soon they'll storm in here and take down anyone with a weapon."

As she walked away, the man said, "Who can kill a dead man?" He grunted, gripped the torn pant leg around the bleeding flesh, and pulled it tight enough to tie it together.

Valerie looked at him a final time and realized that the individuals were like nothing she had seen in action before. She sensed it was only a matter of time before shooters on either side would no longer extend the courtesy to resist the need to fire at officers. Before everything could take a turn for the worst, she hoped to uncover some truths.

* * *

AN explosion nudged Monika from her sleep. She wiped the drool from her mouth. Her vision focused on the room as she recalled how she came to be there. No one moved about; even the hallway was still. She checked her watch, and realized she was overdue for her shift on the roof. Monika nearly panicked, but remembered Jabari knew of her whereabouts, and would have come for her if she was needed.

Her body required more rest. The nap proved counterproductive and made her more lethargic than before, but Monika could not waste another minute and put her partner at risk by waiting for his call. She had a duty to uphold.

Before she stood from the floor, she pressed the palm of her hand against the drawer where her son had been delicately placed and said a silent prayer. Monika left the room without a look back.

She stopped where Amara and Jabari rested earlier with their children, but they were no longer there. No one was. She checked behind the closed doors of smaller conference rooms in case they had hidden there. Empty.

Suddenly, she heard a continuous stream of gunfire. It was the first time so many shots had been fired at once, and it caused the tiny hairs on Monika's forearm to stand erect.

Frantic, she took the stairs up to the rooftop, but when she arrived, no one was there either—not even the pair she and Jabari left on guard hours before. She looked over the side of the building to the street and watched a mass of nearly thirty men and women suffer the pain of fresh wounds, or totally surrender to them. It was as if they had all decided to make a collective run for safety but marched out to their death instead. Monika was horrified. For a moment, she imagined her sister's family had joined the crowd of escapees who were piled in the street.

After twenty-five years of training, she had learned to deliver powerful blows with kicks and jabs, disarm the enemy without the flutter of an eye, shoot with immaculate precision, and endure the most unbearable pain, but nothing prepared her for the anguish she witnessed in those moments. Although considered, a surrender would never replenish the lives already lost. She could only hope her loved ones were not amongst them.

In an instant, the access door flew open, and Monika excitedly assumed Jabari had returned. Instead, a haggard and winded Fatima sprang from the stairwell and trudged onto the roof. Monika had not seen the frail, Arabic woman since she was seated near her father at the ball, but the figure who stood before her was not as poised or polished.

"I can't do this anymore," Fatima cried and shoved past Monika.

Her black gown was ripped in several places, and her once elegantly laid bun had become a disheveled mess on her head. She made a beeline for the roof's edge and climbed up to the ledge before Monika could make sense of her intentions.

"Fatima, wait!" she called.

"I've waited and waited. I can't stay here like this. Afraid."

"Come down. I'll stay with you. I'll protect you."

"You're no better off here than I am."

"I can help. Let me help you."

"Did you see? You see all of these bodies?"

"Yes, Fatima. I see. And I see you too."

"You cannot see the pain within me. There is no fight left."

Fatima looked at the road that seemed a million miles below. "I should have known," she started. "The typical overprotective mother—that was me. Amir's father was gone. I held onto my son tighter than I should have."

"It wasn't your fault—what Amir did. You couldn't have known. I couldn't have known. I saw him every day. Come on. Get down from there."

Fatima turned to her. "I might as well have pulled the trigger myself," she said sorrowfully. "I pushed him. He rejected me, and I pushed him harder. I was blind to what he was becoming—a monster."

That was exactly how witnesses, victims, and their families remembered her son, Amir—the evil terrorist who opened fire on innocent people in a shopping mall. No one mourned his death—not even his mother, who found it more difficult to cope with her part in his actions than the loss she suffered. Society forced her to choose. And to select the part of a mournful mother would have appeared insensitive to those impacted by his ghastly deeds. Either way, Fatima was forever marked, and her peace had to come from some place within herself, or not at all.

"The mall shooting—that wasn't the Amir I knew. He was a good kid," Monika assured her.

As Monika spoke, a glimpse of Amir's smile and random sketches he scrawled across his notebook, came to mind. Although her words were true, she hoped they were effective.

"Who would believe that? I was his mother. I loved him. And I don't believe that. You can't begin to imagine what others think of him. He's died ten thousand deaths in their wicked imaginations. They don't know how he made honor roll each quarter since grade school, or how the only blemish on his record was a fight where he defended a boy who was bullied every day. They can only judge him by the moment they'll play over and over and over again to warn others that people like us should never be trusted."

"That's not who he was. Maybe his head wasn't on straight. Things happen that we can't always explain, but his choices were not your responsibility." Monika extended her hand. "Come. Please."

"I wanted to protect him," Fatima spoke wearily. "They filled his head with death, destruction—told him to stand for something. Now, he can't stand for anything at all. I killed my son."

Monika remembered her off-the-record rants about American greed, inequality, racism, hatred, and knew she was a contributor to the voices in Amir's head, but refused to expose it. She would have to peel back many layers for Fatima to understand, and it was not the time or place for such explanations.

"What does this prove, Fatima? Think about it."

"It proves nothing. That's the thing—I have nothing left. But I won't live another minute afraid I'll be gunned down like the others I saw. They're all dead or will be soon."

Monika understood Fatima's fear, but could not allow her to execute her plan. "You're afraid, Fatima. I know. You don't have to do this. Just take my hand."

Fatima continued her confession. "I should have backed down. Given him his space."

"That was then. You've made it this far. We can get through this too. I promise."

Fatima's wails ceased, and Monika believed her pleas had impressed upon the guilt-stricken woman's heart to finally step down from the ledge. She grew quiet as she took in her surroundings. It was a starless, dark sky saturated with plumes of smoke, but she stared as though a beautiful flock of birds had flown overhead.

Fatima spoke with a stoic expression. "Knowing history incites hate and living in the present incites fear."

"You're right. It's sad. Now, come to me."

The tears in her eyes transported her into darkness. "And I can no longer live between the two worlds. I hope you find peace," she said, and then stepped off into the open air.

"No!" Monika yelled, but it was too late.

She dared not look over the ledge to witness the aftermath of the Fatima's actions, so she squatted near the concrete wall and screamed into her hands. Monika struggled to regain control of her breath, and it tarried.

The sound of gunshots rattled her, and she heard the bullets collide with the building's structure in very close range. The next moment, she could see dust from the concrete as it floated in the air and knew she had become a target.

Wolves, postured on an adjoining rooftop, had a clear shot of Monika's movements. They fired again, and Monika ran for cover behind a pillar. She checked her weapon for ammo. There was none. She was trapped. All that stood between her and the deadly sting of a bullet was a short pillar, so she dared not move.

* * *

VALERIE'S mission to uncover the truth behind the vigilante organization overshadowed plans to help anyone she encountered along the way. She entered one building after another—most with smashed windows and shattered glass—and found many cowered in corners, dark rooms, and broom closets; children cried and were weak without food, water and rest. She was merely equipped with a weapon that could feed none of them.

"We'll get you all out of here as soon as we can," she promised the helpless many who initially saw her blue uniformed presence as a sign of hope—before they realized she was just passing through. However, they were in a better position than the decayed bodies being feasted upon by ravens.

When she exited a law office that housed nearly sixty innocent bystanders, a man ran by her in dress socks, a collared shirt, and slacks. Valerie was not as intrigued by his attire as she was the gun he toted in his hand as he went.

"Freeze!" she ordered and raised her weapon.

The man halted and lifted his arms into the air. He turned in her direction.

"Don't move! Stay right there," she said as she approached him.

"I haven't done anything, officer," the man said.

"Put the weapon on the ground."

He instantly complied with her demands.

"Kick it," she said.

"I don't have time for this. I need to get out of here."

"Do as I say."

He kicked the gun, and it moved a mere two feet in front of him.

"Now, put your hands behind your head."

He did as he was told. Valerie moved near and picked the gun up from the ground. She examined him, unkempt and panicked. It was Calvin, Monika's fiancé.

"Why would you arrest *me*? I'm not the one out here shooting people."

"You didn't bring this gun to the protest?" Valerie patted him down.

"I wasn't at the protest. I was at an event, and then all hell broke loose. I just wanna get out of here."

"There are shooters all over. You won't get far. They'll shoot you before you even know they're there."

"The white boys are down here. And the people up there—," he pointed, "won't shoot us."

Valerie opened her mouth to speak but paused at the prick of Calvin's statement.

"How do you know? Why don't you think they would shoot you?"

"I know them. Can I put my arms down now?"

"Yeah. Go towards the pole."

They moved further out of view.

"Who are they?"

"I don't know fully. Monika—," he started.

"Monika Dyer?"

"Yes. She was my..."

Like a parrot, Calvin was ready to regurgitate every word he had heard when a male voice called from the distance. "Kemp!" Six uniformed officers in a hodgepodge of colors that represented various districts, approached her with their guns raised.

"What's happened?" she asked.

"We have orders to move in. There are vans and busses lined up within three blocks. They're taking everyone to base camp—a parking lot about three miles from here—to sort through the riff raff. Then they'll find somewhere to house them for a while."

"These people will be walking targets if they pile out like cattle."

"We'll surround them—fire at anyone who tries."

"And lose the grace of not being their target? Desperation presses buttons."

"Something has to be done. We can't wait around. Are you coming with us?"

She looked at Calvin, her ticket to truth. "I will. Give me a minute."

The officers rushed into a building to initiate the rescue mission.

"What about her—Monika Dyer?" she asked Calvin.

"That's where I got the gun. She's—*was*—my fiancé, and she's up there," he said.

"Why?"

"I don't know. Something about training since she was a little girl. That's as much as I know—as much as her sister knows. That, and the fact that she was willing to lose everything to be on that roof—even our boy."

"What?"

"Our 6-month-old, Michael—he's dead." He gulped. "She ran off with him last I saw her."

"Where would she take him?"

"She wouldn't come out here for sure. It's like she's chained to that building."

"Who else is there?"

"Jabari...Rushing—his wife, Amara, their kids, some others. Bishop Dyer hosted a banquet, and we've been trapped in there since."

"Is Bishop Dyer in there?"

"No, he left last night before everything broke out."

Valerie was curious about the bishop's ability to escape prior to the clash but knew she had milked as much information from Calvin as she possibly could.

"Stay in the shadows and follow the sidewalk around the corner. There should be officers to help you out of here. I'll keep the gun; they'll shoot if they see you with it."

"With or without it, someone is gunning for me."

Calvin ran as fast as he could, but Valerie was far from satisfied. She took the walkway back to the law office and went inside.

"Officers are nearby. You'll get you out of here soon," she promised as she moved past the people who waited in the dark.

She walked a long corridor lined with offices and entered one. She approached the desk and wiggled the computer's mouse. The screen was locked. She left to find another. Again, no desktop access. She moved up a hall that soon opened to a small library where staff would conduct research for their cases. There was a small desk with a computer at the rear and, when she realized it was unlocked, Valerie took a seat.

Valerie accessed a minimally secure database that only provided an individual's history of addresses, infractions, arrests, and a few other details. She conducted a search for Jabari Rushing again, and discovered his 2002 marriage to Amara Dyer, whose name was changed that year. She was only seventeen at the time. Then, Valerie entered "Michael Dyer" into the search field and made a mental note of the sixteen buildings throughout the southern region he had purchased or leased over the last two decades. Although seemingly excessive, her discovery did not alarm her. Bishop Dyer was a man of power, influence, and business savvy, so his access to multiple properties was self-explanatory.

However, personal addresses on file exposed a new facet of Bishop's story. In forty years, he had only lived in two Atlanta homes, but there was no indication of his movements prior to 1974. There was nothing at all. "Where did he come from?" she thought.

A small icon caught her attention at the top of the screen. She clicked it and fell into the depths of bewilderment when she learned that Michael Dyer was not Michael Dyer at all. Although the man was 65 years old, Michael Dyer did not exist until the mid-70s. Valerie could not stop there. She was determined to know what caused the prominent preacher to assume a new identity. And despite the crack of gunfire that lit the atmosphere, she could not leave until she was fully aware.

CHAPTER EIGHT
THE KISS OF BETRAYAL

JABARI and Amara ransacked offices on various levels on their hunt for food. The banquet room where the ball was held over a day before was already raided, and every scrap left on the plates was devoured by the ravenous stowaways. After all the effort, they gathered a small bag of tortilla chips, a handful of bite-sized chocolates leftover from Valentine's Day months before, and a packet of trail mix—from which, Shiloh picked out the chocolate and dried fruit, but left the nuts she abhorred for her brother.

"What are you doing?" her mother asked as Shiloh chewed the succulent chocolate.

"What?" Jabari turned to them.

Amara examined the bag. "There are only nuts in here. She took the pieces of pineapple and chocolate."

"I've told her about that," Jabari said. "She keeps the things she likes for herself and gives the rest to James."

The raid would have continued if their children had not moved sluggishly from room to room. They batted their eyes slowly, and often held up the wall as their parents scrounged around. Amara dumped the contents of a desk drawer onto the floor and sifted through the pile.

"We should call it," Jabari said. He cupped his daughter's chin with his hand and examined her. "They're tired."

"They're also hungry," Amara said as she continued her search.

"The sun will be up in a few hours. In all this time, we haven't found much. Eat what we have and let me get back to my post. I can learn more there."

Amara halted her search and looked to her husband. "That's what this is about? Getting back to your post? Your children are starving, Jabari. Look at them!"

"I see they need rest."

"Why? To take their minds from the fact that it's been two days since their last meal?"

"I'm doing the best I can, Amara."

"It's not enough."

"For me to know more, I have to go back."

"Fine!" Amara marched by Jabari and the kids.

They all stepped off the elevator at the 20th floor. Amara quickly escorted the children to the area near the window where they slept the night before. Meanwhile, Jabari moved down the hall to check the corner office for Monika. She was no longer there.

"She's gone," Jabari said when Amara approached him.

She glanced inside the vacant room for herself. "Maybe she went back to the roof."

"Without me? She wouldn't," Jabari said.

Annoyed by the unraveled strands of secrecy, Amara snappishly remarked, "Whatever the rules, she definitely could have."

"I have to go." He started to walk away.

"I'll come with you...make sure she's okay."

"What about the kids? No. Stay with them."

"They're exhausted—probably already asleep. Don't make me sit here. I'm all Monika has right now."

"You should get some rest too."

"I can't! I want nothing more than to get out of here, and I'll lose my mind if I sit in that room another second."

With his energy on the verge of full depletion, Jabari could not muster the words to further the disagreement with his wife, so ended it with, "Come on." And they took the stairs up to the roof.

He stopped short of the exit, and spoke in an authoritative voice, "Stay here. I'll come back."

Amara's shoulders released all tension and relaxed as her desire to follow him heel to toe was cut off.

"I mean it," he reinforced.

Monika, crouched behind a pillar, saw the access door swing open.

"Get down!" she yelled and warned her partner of dangers unseen.

In an instant, bullets pummeled against the steel door, which retracted and started to close; Jabari shielded his head and stepped back into the stairwell.

"What's going on?" Amara asked.

"She's cornered. They can see us."

"What?" In a panic, she attempted to shove past her husband. "Where is she?"

He locked his arms around her shoulders and pulled her back. "No! Don't go out there."

"It's my sister," she cried.

"Calm down." Jabari released his wife from his grip. "I have to think this through. She's safe for now."

"Get her back in here!" she yelled hysterically.

"I'm trying. Can you calm down please?"

Jabari went back to the door and opened it wide enough for a single eye to look around a small section of the roof and up to the next building. There was only one shooter, and his attention was divided by the movement on the roof and the commotion on the street.

"Listen," Jabari addressed his wife. "I'm going out here."

Worry immediately washed over Amara's expression.

"I'm coming back—with Monika. I need you to listen for my call." He removed his weapon from its holster and readied it with a click. "When you hear me, push the door open as wide as you can, and get out of the way."

She nodded her head to agree.

He looked through the open slit in the door again, watched as the shooter turned away, and then bolted onto the rooftop. The shooter caught a glimpse of his movements and swung his weapon around to fire but lacked aim. Bullets flew past Jabari, who was quickly out of view, and right next to Monika.

"I'm out of ammo," she said.

"How long you been here?" Jabari asked.

"Hours. Can't say how many."

"He knows we're both here now. It won't be easy to get back inside. I'm sure he's aimed right at us."

"And it's possible the drone floating past here is theirs," she said. When it appeared for the 30th time, she pointed. "There. It just won't go away." There were no labels or recognizable features to attribute the device to one entity or another, but its power seemed everlasting.

Amara made an attempt to see where Jabari and Monika were holed up on the roof. She inched the door open, but her view was obstructed by the door itself, and they were in a blind spot.

"Just shoot," Monika said, "It would distract him long enough to get us inside."

"We've always thought alike." Jabari pulled the gun close to his chest. "And we can also agree that you're a much better shot in the dark than I am. Take it." He handed her the weapon.

Monika considered Jabari's plan of escape—playing chicken with the bullets of an assault rifle.

"Perhaps there is another way," she suggested. "I run faster."

He stubbornly ignored her foolish suggestion, and said, "That's it. No other way." He closed his eyes tight and wiped the sweat away from his forehead. "He'll aim for me. Shoot him before he can…" He looked at wide-eyed Monika. "Just shoot him."

He pressed the back of his head against the concrete and released a *huff* before he jolted up from the ground and took off towards the door.

He yelled, "Amara! Open it!" Instantly, the door swung open.

Monika stood, steadied her hands, and squinted her eyes to aim for the shooter who fired incessantly at Jabari. She fired twice and missed. Her third shot caught him in the shoulder, and the gunfire ceased as the shooter went to the ground. Jabari safely awaited Monika's arrival inside the stairwell, but she knew the shooter was still there, so kept her gun aimed in his direction.

Overwhelmed by exhaustion, Amara's legs buckled. She sat down on the cold, concrete steps—relieved that her sister and husband were both alive.

Monika held the access door open with the heel of her foot and watched for any motion on the roof where she knew the man was likely to resume his position. Jabari stood tall once he caught his breath and saw a shadowy shift on top of a different building across the street. In a flash, gunfire exploded, and bullets cracked the concrete walls near Monika's face. Without hesitation, a tiger-like Jabari lunged out, grabbed Monika at the waist, and flung her to safety before the door shut behind them. As they landed, his brawny stature pinned Monika to the ground, and almost covered her completely.

"You okay?" he panted.

"I think so," Monika said sweetly. "You?"

They looked at each other with penetrating eyes.

"I'm fine."

Monika heard a shuffle and, without knowledge of her sister's presence, lifted her pistol over her head and aimed upside-down in Amara's direction.

"Don't shoot." Jabari said, and lifted himself from the warmth of Monika's feminine frame. "It's Amara."

Amara stood, arms folded bitterly across her chest, and watched as her sister sat up on the floor and placed the gun aside.

"Thank God," Monika said, relieved to see that her sister had escaped the slaughter in the road.

"What should we thank Him for, Monika? Tell me." The spice of Amara's tone demanded Monika and Jabari's attention.

"What?" Monika responded.

Feeling rejected and confused, Amara asked, "How long has this been going on?"

"What are you talking about, Amara?" Jabari asked, frustrated by her consistent inquiries and protests.

"How long have you been fucking my sister, Jabari. You have an answer for that? Or will it continue to be another one of your secrets?"

"Don't do this," he said helplessly.

"Do what? This isn't on me. Seems you two have done enough behind my back. Monika? What is this?"

"It's not what you think, Amara." Monika tightened the laces of her boots to distract her sister from the question at hand and gnawed on the inside of her cheek.

"Well?"

"We've been partners most of our lives," Monika said to her sister. "That's all. Nothing more." She glanced in Jabari's direction and nodded, "Tell her."

He was ready to speak openly to his wife, but he knew the facts would overtake them both like a tsunami.

"Tell her the truth," he said.

"What?" Monika was puzzled.

"Which is?" Amara interjected.

He massaged his beard, and the bracelet of knotted jasper stones shifted on his wrist. "There's a lot that you don't know, Amara," he said as he approached her with caution.

"That's obvious. What, Monika? Your man up and leave you in all this mess—and you haven't even mourned your baby—but here you are with *my* husband," Amara spoke harshly to her sister, who could only shake her head in disbelief.

"Be quiet, and listen to me," Jabari urged her.

"Then tell me—how long?"

"Since they arranged my marriage to you," was dragon's breath from Jabari's lips.

Monika perked up and gave her full attention to the storyteller.

Amara chuckled. "Arranged marriage? Whatever. What are we? Easterners? Miss me with that."

Jabari's expression was constant, serious. "It's not a lie, Amara."

Thoughts, memories, emotions all welled up within Monika, but she resisted the prompt to express any of them.

"No. Monika and I have never had sex. In all these years, we never even kissed—before or after our vows, Amara. Never. That's the truth. There was never an affair but," he paused and looked to Monika, "there was something between us."

"I knew we were all friends since we were kids, but the two of you dated?" Amara asked.

"No," Monika spoke.

"We couldn't. It wasn't allowed." Jabari thought to withhold what was left of the truth. "But I can't promise that if things were different, you and I would be together, and I'm burdened by that."

"You would be with my sister?"

"Saying I never wanted to would be a lie," he said, and Monika beamed from within, but her inner glow was quickly dimmed.

"And you feel the same for him?" was directed at Monika, who was hesitant and could not muster the courage to break her sister's heart. She remained silent.

Jabari continued, "Regardless, I don't want to lie to you anymore."

"How convenient! A whole lie of a marriage and two kids later, you want to be honest. What am I supposed to do with this? My entire life has been controlled by some invisible force. Why? How could they do it? Who would force you to marry me?"

"I wasn't forced. I was told it would be best—for all of us."

"That's unreal. Who would possibly convince you of that?"

Jabari peeled back the final layer of his confession. "Your father."

Both women whipped their heads in Jabari's direction. However, it was only Monika who fought back fiery tears fueled by anger that was certain to scorch her cheek if released.

"*My* daddy?" Amara asked, appalled. "*He* told you to do this?"

"This way, I could protect you. He knew you would be *connected* to the cause without ever joining it. Monika was already a soldier."

"Protect me? Or control me? I didn't ask for this."

"I know," Jabari said remorsefully.

"I gave up what I really wanted—world travel, getting the hell out of his mundane church life. You made me believe I did it for you. It sucks that I thought you were worthy. What 17-year-old would know better, huh?"

Like her sister, anger steadily rose within Amara, boiled over and bubbled from her lips like acid. "Jabari, fuck you—and fuck him too!"

She turned towards the stairs but did not descend before her secretive sister was served a taste of her wrath. "How stupid could you be? Daddy put you up to all of this. You're nothing more than a spineless puppet."

Jabari saw every ounce of vitality drain from Monika's eyes, but there was no remedy for her torment; and he could not linger there too long.

"Amara! Wait a minute!" he called out and followed the sound of her swift exit down the tunnel of stairs.

There was nothing he could offer Amara either, but felt it was his duty to provide whatever she needed to cope.

"Would you wait a minute," he begged as they stepped onto the 20th floor.

"For what? So that you can keep lying to me?"

"I didn't want this for you. Believe me. I know it's hard to understand."

"You can't begin to make sense of this for me, Jabari."

"I can try."

"You'll waste your time." She waddled past him.

"Don't walk away—please."

Amara turned swiftly. "Isn't there somewhere else you should be?"

"I won't go back to the roof until I get you someplace safe."

"So, now it's about me and *my* safety? Funny. But that's not what I was referring to." She paused. "Wouldn't you rather be with her?"

"What I felt for Monika was a long time ago. We were young."

"And those feelings have gone away? You feel nothing for her now?"

"I love her, Amara. She's been like a sister since before I can remember. After all these years, it should be understandable that I could love her."

"Maybe if you didn't just reveal that this whole marriage was a lie."

"What I feel for you isn't."

"You're saying you love me?"

"Yes. You know that."

"But did you love me then—when my daddy handed me over like a dirty rag?"

"I learned to."

"I can't believe I trusted you." She chuckled nervously. "You're such a good liar."

Jabari refocused on the issue at hand. "Call me whatever you want. Only two people can say I've loved them since the day they were born—and they're over there." He nodded towards his children. "And I want to get them, and you, out of here. I'm begging you—just help me."

Cynical, she fired back, "Or are you trying to get rid of us and return to who you love best?"

"Are you serious? Dammit!" He grabbed her by the arm and led her to the window. "Can you see where we are? Look! Those aren't chocolate sprinkles. Those people are dead, Amara, and you're here hoping to resolve your insecurities with insults and rudeness. I know it hurts, but the world does not spin on the axis of Amara. Believe it or not, I love you. Sometimes it's hard to understand how with your consistent spoiled schoolgirl antics and conniving ways."

"Conniving? You are the epitome of deception," she snapped. "You *and* her."

"She didn't know, Amara," he spoke through his shrunken effort to contain frustration.

"Of course, she did! I saw the way she looked at you. What—did you two vow to keep it a secret?"

"She didn't know," Jabari insisted. "I promise I never mentioned how I felt about her. Not to anyone—not even her."

"I'm sure after all these years, she's told *you*—even if you never shared how you felt."

"That didn't happen either." He reached out to grab both of her shoulders. "Monika loves you. I can write volumes on the ways she's shown it without you ever knowing. You don't have to believe that, but if you let this drive a wedge between you, it would be a tragic mistake."

She pushed his hands away. "I'm the one who's been in the dark all this time while you two frolicked around and kept your little secret, so don't tell me how much she loves me. She should have told me about this—all of it."

"She can't tell you what she doesn't know, Amara." He thought for a moment. "Monika is probably just as hurt as you are."

"Really? You want to defend her? Don't you dare try to get me to feel sorry for her."

"She may not have been as in the dark as you were, but she wasn't far from it."

Amara gathered her thoughts and watched as her daughter changed positions on the floor when her sleep was disturbed by her parents' elevated voices.

"That means you blame Daddy for all of this," she said.

"No. Whatever the consequence, he meant well."

"Or you're just as dumb as my sister. He used you." She exhaled between parted lips. "I give him this much, he knew he would have to plot, scheme, use whatever subterfuge he could think of to get me to bend to him longer than I had to." She smiled in disbelief. "He's a smart man—but I always thought you were smarter. You're just a pawn. Thank you for destroying my family."

The sting of her words lasted beyond the moment they were spoken. Like a sponge, Jabari absorbed each syllable and was saturated with offense. There was little left to say.

"I should go," Jabari spoke painfully. "If I'm not back in six hours, do what you can to get to your dad's church."

He walked away without another word.

CHAPTER NINE

HUGGING THE DELUSIVE PHANTOM OF HOPE

1997

JABARI and Monika were well into their sophomore year, yet they failed to form bonds with other high schoolers. It was already difficult to conceal bruises, sore muscles, sprains, and the truth of their ancestry and ongoing oppression as it was told by TAAR leaders, so they were not open to new bonds. Instead, they kept to themselves to better mask their secrets.

Yet very few could say that Jabari and Monika were friends—or knew each other at all. They kept significant distance at school. The warning was clear. Fraternizing was forbidden. And to prove their seriousness, the youngsters were forced to witness vicious, nonstop calisthenics of those who broke the rules, or heard rumors of others who were removed from their parents and dumped in a distant group home. For the most part, they were incredibly obedient youth, but the sudden disappearance of 10, 22, 31, and 36 was enough to make the threat real. Jabari and Monika possessed no desire to know where the absent children had gone or to take part in some mysterious vanishing act themselves.

The holidays—a time for family and ease—were upon them, but their preparation did not match the calm of the season. There were no summer breaks either. It had been a steady two years of TAAR training, and the group of youthful participants still had not discovered its full purpose.

One evening, the adults used duct tape to disable one of their limbs. One partner would have the use of their legs and a single arm—right or left, whichever was weakest. The other would lose the use of a leg, which was bent at the knee and taped ankle-to-thigh. Their limbs fell asleep, invisible needle pricks shot painfully through their flesh, joints ached, or the entire body part went completely numb. Naturally, the idea would unnerve adolescents, but this was not their first time.

"Today, not only will you lose something you've entrusted to defend yourselves, some of you will also fight in the dark," The Man said.

The youth considered how the use of dark blindfolds would block their vision and completely black out their faces, but that evening's training was more sinister and painful. One of the women carried a spray bottle small enough to conceal in her hand and passed it to The Man.

"You'll get in the ring and take down your opponent. Some of you, in the dark and without the full use of an arm or leg."

The young people stared, oblivious to what awaited them.

"13 and 20, you're first."

20 moved into the ring on a single leg and held tightly to the rope for balance. When he released it, he balanced himself with stiff arms extended like the wings of an airplane and hopped to the center. He wobbled as he went. His partner, 13, could already see the victory, and silently celebrated the win.

The Man approached 13 and spoke in a low tone. "Keep your eyes open. Don't flinch."

The boy, no older than twelve, looked to him with a curious gaze. The Man raised the spray bottle to the boy's face and pulled the trigger. A large mist formed liquid specks from his forehead to his nose, and the boy screamed as he used his free arm to swipe away the furious sting of lemon juice in his eyes.

"Fight!" The Man ordered and backed away.

With his partner's pained demeanor, 20 hesitated to approach the leaky-eyed boy.

"Let's go!" The Man roared.

13 constantly blinked his bloodshot eyes to remove the remnants of liquid torture and raised his fist to block his attacker, who moved with speed despite the loss of a leg. With the long-established rule to avoid damage to a soldier's face, 20 delivered as many jabs to the boy's arm, shoulder, and torso as he could before he lost balance and fell to the floor. He thought to lift himself up again, but he noticed 13's failed attempt to kick him—unable to adequately see through his blurred vision—and went for his legs instead. With one swift move, he locked his arms around a single leg and lifted it into the air. His partner crashed down with an enormous thud.

"That's enough. Out!"

The boys picked themselves up and went back to their seats.

Jabari looked to Monika's tightly wrapped arm and knew what was in store for her. So, when they were called to the challenge, second to last, he thought to position her for the win.

They faced each other in the ring and, after she was warned to not cringe or cry, the man released a stream of lemony venom into Monika's eyes. Immediately, she shut them tight and postured herself for combat. She breathed through the discomfort, and grit her teeth, which were exposed behind the mask.

"Fight!"

Jabari, on a single leg, bounced forward and quickly jabbed her taped armed; it radiated with pain. He jabbed the other twice and hopped towards her again. Her eyes were completely closed, but a consistent stream of tears dripped from them and salted her sheer facemask.

With cat-like craftiness, Monika listened for Jabari's movements, and she could sense his position by the direction of the blows. She stepped forward and delivered a kick that struck him in the center of his chest and knocked him to the ground.

"That's enough. Out!" The Man called.

Finally, Monika opened her eyes wide like a tormented child who escaped the dark of a haunted house and noticed The Man's smirk.

"Finally," he said. "Everyone before 18 fought against the *pain* and not the opponent. This young lady accepted the discomfort, walked into the pain. She knew that complete darkness would be better than dividing your focus in an attempt to see. The sting doesn't fade for a while, but behind closed eyelids, you could have found more comfort. Learn to work with the pain and not against it. You would be surprised what you could see in the dark when you no longer care to find a light."

After The Man's praise, Jabari pat his partner on the back, and then helped to remove the tape from her arm just as the others had done.

Sweat and funk saturated their clothing at the close of their Friday night session. Not only had those with irritated eyes learned to defend themselves against knife attacks, multiple opponents, gun threats, and to use improvised weapons, they learned to fight in the dark and through pain.

When the final match ended, the group sat in the circle for an announcement before they were dismissed for the weekend.

"It's been a pleasure to help on this leg of your journey. You worked hard. You've grown. You're stronger than before," The Man said. "But I'm moving on to another group. You will have a new trainer."

The group never learned The Man's real name—or a pretend one for that matter—and they despised each time they were punished with countless laps, push-ups, or suicides, but news of his departure was disheartening.

"Don't hold back. Show him what you know and prove how fearless you are." He stopped to check his clipboard. "Oh. One more thing. Training hours have moved to 4 p.m. to accommodate his schedule. The good news: You'll go home at 9 instead of 10."

They all stared, unbothered; but Monika was immediately distraught by the news. She folded her arms, and her eyes focused upon the nothings on the floor. When they were released, she snatched her bag from the wall hook, and moved swiftly to the car that waited for her outside. With that same energy, she stormed into her father's study when she arrived home.

Bishop Dyer was seated comfortably in an upholstered, high-armed chair and marked text within the Good Book while Amara used his desk to outline an essay for her 7th grade English class. The deadline had already passed but, like everything else, Amara moved at sloth-speed to do what was required of her—even *after* the threat of dire consequences.

"Daddy, can we talk?" Monika shifted her eyes towards her sister, and then back to her father.

"Amara, have you finished?" he asked.

"Not yet. You said you would help me with the Trojan War part," she whined.

"It's after 10 o'clock."

"But it's due tomorrow."

"Tomorrow's Saturday," Monika corrected.

"I meant, Monday. I have rehearsal tomorrow, and you know how Sunday is, Daddy. We won't get home until almost 5. I'll have math homework to do then. I need to finish."

"And you're just now asking for help?"

"I asked last week. You told me to wait."

"Not an excuse to wait until now."

Monika grew impatient with the pointless tennis match of dialogue between them.

"Daddy, please," she whined and stomped her foot against the floor.

"What is it, Monika?"

She was troubled by her sister's presence but knew she could not clear the room.

"I have track practice after school, right?" she started.

"Yes. I know."

"Well..." She looked to Amara, who stared down at her notebook. "That after school program I started a while back changed its hours. It would mean I can't go to track practice."

In anticipation of an immediate answer, she laid it out like oracle cards—and without Amara's detection. Since her father had been supportive of her athletic endeavors in the past, Monika was confident he would side with her and bring whatever consumed her time in the community center to a close.

Bishop Dyer sat tall in his chair. "I've explained to you and your sister before—you can't be in two places at once."

"I know. And I wanna run track, Daddy," she said excitedly.

He lowered his head and removed the glasses from his face. "That can't be your choice."

"But if I can't be in two places at one time—I choose track. I don't wanna do anything else. I promise."

"Believe me, I understand how passionate you are about track. But..."

"Then say I can go to practice." There was still hope.

"No. We agreed you wouldn't *jump* into anything without first thinking it through."

"I'm not. I've done track since middle school."

"And you've been in the after-school program for almost as long."

"But that's not what I choose."

"You will. I'm sorry."

Nothing would be abrasive enough to scrub the disappointment from his daughter's face. Her frustration shifted the energy of the entire room.

"Please," she petitioned a final time with a shaky lip.

"I won't say it again."

Monika harnessed the anger and disgust; it was heavy and slowed her strides towards the door.

In the bedroom, she slid across her heavily pillowed bed, and buried her head beneath them. The conversation had not gone as she intended, but there was a speck of hope for a favorable outcome — even if it required a little finesse, or bold deception. She was open to either method — desperate to hold tight to the one thing that gained some attention, and that she was not threatened to keep secret.

The following week, Monika intentionally mis-read between her father's lines. Nothing was written, but rebellion rose within her. She was dressed and ready for track practice only ten minutes after the final school bell.

The group of young athletes met near the bleachers to bend and stretch in preparation for the gruesome workout ahead of them. As Monika jogged in place and repetitively jumped into the air to activate her muscles, the coach approached.

"Young lady, someone's here to get you," she said.

Monika glanced over to the parking lot; her driver was there.

"I don't know him," Monika said, and stretched her arms behind her head.

"Then why would he tell me he's here to pick you up?"

"He's not my dad, Coach. I don't know him."

Her eyes narrowed. "Should I call security?"

"No! No! He probably just got the wrong person." Monika shrugged.

"Maybe."

The coach blew the whistle, and everyone rushed onto the track. The driver watched for a few minutes after his summons was ignored. Then he returned to his vehicle and drove away.

Over an hour passed, and the discussion between Monika and her father was far from mind, so she was surprised when he casually approached the track during practice. She was already on her mark and prepared to go 100 meters. Despite his presence, she positioned herself and focused on the race.

"Ready!" the coached yelled. Her thumb pressed the stopwatch. "Go!"

Monika took off strong. She was only rivaled by the wind. The swiftness of her movements made her steps impossible to count and appear like a cartoony ball of yarn. Soon the race was over, and Monika, the victor.

"Monika, 11.2. Good job," the coach announced.

"Good afternoon," Bishop Dyer spoke from behind her.

"Hi. Can I help you?"

When she noticed their exchange, Monika shortened her recovery period and went over to where her father stood with her coach.

"I'm Monika's father, Michael." He extended his hand to shake hers. "Today is her last day at practice." He delivered the blow with a smile, and the woman immediately released his hand.

"Daddy!" Monika shrieked.

"What did I tell you? Get your things." He wrapped an arm around her shoulder to hurry her along.

"Can I ask why?" The coach followed.

"No, you can't."

"She's the fastest on our team. With all due respect, I don't want to lose her," she petitioned, but her words went ignored.

Monika grabbed her bag and looked back at her baffled coach and teammates. Her father's grip was firm; she dragged her feet against the asphalt as he led her away.

"Get in," her father ordered as they neared the car.

Monika slung her backpack onto the backseat before she strapped on her seatbelt.

"You disobeyed me. I won't stand for it, Monika." He cranked the car and started the drive. "And why wouldn't you leave with the driver when he came for you? What do you think you're doing? Think you're grown now? Just outright disrespectful."

Monika sat quietly. Her hands gripped the seatbelt, and she accepted the reprimand, which stung like needles through the skin.

"You know what I told you," her father continued. "Why would you go behind my back and do it anyway?"

She wanted to speak, cry, scream—anything to get her father's genuine attention or to have her way. She wanted to say that she had nothing, felt like "nobody", and it was all unfair; but when she opened her mouth, the words were not released with enough haste.

"You're doing it again," her father said.

She looked at him curiously.

"I guess you won't be satisfied until you've put *both* of your parents in the grave."

A lump bobbed to the surface of Monika's throat, and the guilt she thought had gone away for good returned for a visit—as well as the memories that created it. She could vividly recall the week before her 14th birthday—the day of her mother's accident.

Monika cut school, but it was not a habit. A project was due in her science class, and she was unprepared. She detoured from the school building as classes began and, instead, coolly walked off campus. She made her way around a nearby plaza that contained a coffee shop filled with sweet pastries, a bookstore stacked high with classic teen lit, and a burger joint that would give patrons a nearly full, brown bag of greasy fries for under two dollars and a free cup of water upon request.

The adventure caused Monika to lose track of time. She returned to campus as her bus bent the corner, and with an empty seat where her butt should have been. There was nothing more to do than call home, but the office made sure to mention that Monika had been absent from each of her classes when her mother agreed to pick her up. She knew she was in trouble, and she waited, but no one came.

They assumed her mother was distracted when her car rolled into a lake. A car passed, and the driver saw Amara, drenched and alone, by the lake in the winter cold. She was 11. The driver could see no evidence of an accident, and the girl would not speak, so he took her to a convenience store and called the police.

When an officer arrived at the scene, he noticed debris and tire marks, and would later discover the woman whose hands still gripped the safety belt of the boy's car seat—both deceased.

Monika was never picked up from school, and ultimately walked home. When she arrived, the officer was there, her sister was shaken, hair soaked and knotted, and there was no sign of their mother or little brother.

Shattered, no one acknowledged the day Monika turned 14, and she dared not remind them. Monika saw her father's pain, and privately vowed to be his remedy. And the car ride that afternoon proved she had not kept her promise.

Bishop Dyer pulled into the parking lot of a fast-food drive thru and turned off the ignition.

He looked at his watch. "You're about 15 minutes late. I'm going inside here. Once I get out of the car, I want you to take the sidewalk down two blocks to the community center. Understood?"

A dove picked off by her hawkish father, Monika whispered, "Yes."

He caressed her chin. "We've all fallen short; but you have all the grace you need. I know you'll make me proud." He took his keys and exited the car.

His method worked each time. At any hint of rebellion, Bishop Dyer picked at the half-healed scabs of her mother's untimely demise and whipped Monika back into submission. For Monika, the lash of her father's words reopened painful wounds that were as unbearable as the thought of her father's agony. Her heart longed to right the wrongs of her short, guilt-ridden history.

Monika's late arrival landed her and Jabari in an immediate set of suicides, wall jumps, and pushups before they could rejoin the others. Jabari knew something was wrong when she avoided his eyes, or when she hurried along without him at points of transition. There was not a moment that his inquiry would go undetected, so the night continued without any exchange between the friends.

The following Saturday, Monika found herself begrudgingly in the middle of her sister's ballet recital in their father's absence. She steamed, inward of course, as she watched her sister's dedication to the craft reward the crowd with gracefully fluid movements, and the reminder that she had nothing of her own. It seemed Amara had the favor of Abel, but Monika was no Cain. She deeply loved her sister, but despised the inequity created by their father.

Jabari had volunteered to collect tickets at the door for community service hours and could steal glimpses of the night's performance between bathroom cleanliness checks or when he rushed to the entry to greet latecomers. He had no experience, nor did he like ballet, but he could gauge the essence of Amara's performance by the subtle gasps, smiles, and head-nods the audience made when she would glide across the stage. The only response that puzzled him was Monika's. With slumped shoulders and sad eyes, she was not moved by her sister's routine. Her hands resisted applause.

When it was over, Monika waited for Amara on the walkway outside. It was cold, but she could breathe better beyond the stuffy building and constant movements of the crowd.

"What's up?" Jabari asked when he approached her.

"Nothing."

"That's it?"

"I guess." She examined his attire. "Where's your jacket?"

"I'll be alright. What about you?"

"I have mine on."

"No. Are you alright?"

"That's what I said," she snapped.

She wanted to tell him—tell someone—but something contested within her. Monika believed she deserved the frustration, anger, and pain she endured. Any complaint could lure sympathy, and she was not entitled to it.

Amara bounced nearby with a grin stretched from ear to ear. She exited with the family of another dance student. "Daddy said for us to ride home with them," she said.

"You go ahead." Monika walked away.

"Where are you going?" Amara called.

"I'll meet you at home."

Amara had mere seconds of concern for her sister, but when she was pat on the back by a stranger from the audience, she instantly forgot what had given her pause, and gleefully continued down the sidewalk.

Monika's trek in the opposite direction began without a decent goodbye to Jabari.

"Are you walking home?" he asked as he followed.

"I think I'll teleport. Save some time."

"And you say nothing's wrong with you." He halted his pursuit. "Alright. I'll let you go."

Monika slowed her strides and turned to face him; others on the walkway were completely out of earshot. "She can do whatever she wants. I can't."

"You wanna dance too?" he asked.

"No. Run!"

"Then do it."

"Daddy's making me do this stupid after school training. He made me quit track."

Jabari drew near and consoled her with a single hand on her shoulder.

"It's alright. It's just track." He poorly gauged the depths of Monika's passion, and his words proved it.

She shoved his hand away and started to walk again.

"What? What I say?" He followed. "It's track. What's the big deal?"

"I knew you wouldn't understand. You're a quitter. They didn't stop making baseballs when your daddy died."

Before she reached the final syllable, she was confident the impact of her words would be lethal, but it was too late. It rolled from her tongue like flavorless chewing gum she wished she had swallowed instead. Jabari refused to waste another moment at her side and walked away with his cold hands tucked tightly into his pockets.

"Wait!" she called. "I'm sorry. I didn't mean it like that," she said, but her apology fell on deaf ears. Jabari moved further away. She walked alone in the dark.

While most students prepared for the week ahead, hung out with friends, or were at the dinner table with loved ones, Monika spent that Sunday after church alone in her room before she decided to take a walk. She grabbed her drawstring bag, tightened her shoestrings, and moved thoughtlessly out of her neighborhood — past the community pool, along a stretch of undeveloped land that awaited the construction of additional upper middle-class homes and, after a half hour, wandered through her school's parking lot.

Monika jogged to the top of the bleachers, looked out over the bare field, and felt just as empty. She sat there and longed for what seemed impossible for anyone to grasp. Although the void could not be ignored, no resolve was within reach.

Monika heard a car's engine as it pulled into the lot behind her. When she turned to look, Jabari stepped out of the driver's side.

"What you doing here?" she asked from a distance.

The metal steps creaked as he ascended the bleachers. "I went to your house. Amara said you weren't there."

"Soo…school on a Sunday is where you thought I'd be? I must be lame as hell."

"I didn't think of it like that, but I was right though." He chuckled.

"But I wasn't. What I said last night was wrong."

He shrugged. "It was true though."

"It wasn't fair."

"Sometimes what's real ain't fair — it's what my daddy used to say. All I know is that you were mad about getting pulled from track, and what I said made you think I didn't care. Didn't help with the long face or pouty mouth at all," he joked.

"I mean…is anything you *ever* say helpful?" she returned.

"Ha! Ha!"

"I'm just saying." She smiled and shrugged.

Jabari became serious again. "I'm sorry you don't get to stay on the team."

"Like you said, I'll be alright." She reached into her drawstring bag and pulled out a magazine with tattered corners and crinkled pages. *Track and Field News* had featured Marion Jones on the front cover of their September edition, and Monika had read every word within it dozens of times. "Guess this won't be me."

Jabari took the magazine from her hand and glanced over it. "You're right. This is her. You're you."

"Who is that?"

"You don't need the cover of a magazine to know how good you are."

Light flooded back into Monika's eyes when she looked at him.

"You don't need a huge audience, or a winner's t-shirt either." He flung the magazine onto the bench and grabbed Monika's hand. "Come on."

She did not resist, and followed him, step-by-step, onto the empty track.

"Sometimes you gotta use your imagination," he said. "It could be all you need to feel better. I'll be the audience."

Puzzled, she asked, "For what?"

"If you love to run as much as you say, you would do it even when no one is watching."

"Let me guess...your daddy told you that."

"Yeah. He did." Jabari smirked. "Lucky for you though, someone's watching. I'm here. So, let's get it." He clapped briskly.

Initially reluctant, Monika stepped onto the track. The autumn sun began to sink in the distance, but not before it lit the path in front of her. Jabari moved off to the side when he was confident Monika would go for it. Beyond gone, she was transported into the depths of her imagination.

As she positioned herself behind the white line of the third lane, Monika could hear the roar of the crowd's excitement, hands that clapped loudly to no particular rhythm, jaws exhausted with joy. She was not on the track alone. Her opponents, some from faraway places, stood, jumped, and stretched to the left and right of her. An assortment of numbers stretched across their backs — 24, 17, 85, 33. Each of them also wore a single, paper digit numbered one through eight, which hang from their fitted shorts. The sprinters were real; the crowd who cheered in the stands was real.

Jabari assumed a deeper voice, and announced, "Get in position!"

Monika jumped twice, brought her knees to her chest mid-air, and wiggled her limbs to loosen up.

"On your mark!" Jabari said. "Get set!"

Monika crouched down and pressed her feet against the imagined starting blocks.

"Go!" Jabari clapped his hands together with as much force as he could muster, and Monika took off like a cheetah unleashed on succulent prey.

She was careful to stay in her lane as she gained momentum and was fully upright. The unseen challengers were no longer there. The fire beneath her feet had torched them all.

At the finish line, Monika raised her head and struggled for air as Jabari jogged towards her.

"Congrats," he beamed and reached out to hug her. The two were locked in a firm embrace long enough for a bird to fly completely in and out of view before they let go.

"What's my time, Coach?" Monika inquired.

"Don't matter. You won."

Monika smiled and nodded her head; the imagined accomplishment flooded her with gratitude and delight.

Jabari reached into his pocket, "A winner should have an award."

"I thought you said I didn't."

"I said you didn't *need* it. And you don't to know how great you are. But we're here now."

He pulled from his pocket a gold-plated medal with "#1" engraved on the front; it dangled from the green ribbon between his fingers.

"This is yours."

She laughed nervously. "What?"

"It's not the same as Marion's, but you're just as much of a champion." He placed the ribbon around her neck. "Go for the gold—whatever makes you happy—and you'll always win. And yes, my daddy told me that too." He smiled.

Monika grabbed the medal and raised it close to her face. She was pleasantly overwhelmed by Jabari's actions. For the first time, someone had not only heard her words, but her heart, and delivered to her a ribbon-tied moment of bliss.

When he saw that the band was twisted around her neck, Jabari moved closer to adjust it. Although there were inches between them, their heightened magnetic energy made them feel closer than a wrestling spar ever had. Jabari's hand brushed against her neck as he gently tugged the medallion into place; the two were entranced in each other's gaze. Anything more was forbidden on every front.

"It's getting dark. Ma said I had to get her car back before it's pitch black out here." He observed the sky. "I can take you home, so you don't have to walk."

"Cool."

Monika floated to the top of the bleachers, grabbed the magazine and her bag, and met Jabari at the bottom. As they walked towards the car, she turned to the bleachers a final time. Jabari stalled and watched her. Her eyes glistened like sparklers, and her face glowed as she lifted a hand into the air and offered the invisible crowd a grand wave before she took an eloquent bow. She pressed her hand to her mouth and blew them a kiss goodbye.

Whatever developed between Monika and Jabari remained unspoken—even when they graduated high school and went on to college—but the moment on their high school track was never forgotten.

Their duty to train with TAAR, forced the young adults to enroll at a local university. It took only 30 minutes to get there. However, they were permitted to live in on-campus housing—a compromise for the sacrifice of many youth-stolen years.

TAAR assigned occupations to its soldiers based on strengths demonstrated during training or educational workshops. Because of his stature and fortitude, Jabari was on a fast-track to law enforcement; and although Monika was physically able to do well in such a role, TAAR recognized society's sexist limitations. They believed education would be a better route for her. She would not only teach whitewashed history in the public sector; she would teach future TAAR soldiers the truth of who they were.

Jabari and Monika were open to the idea of a romantic relationship—with *other* people, that is—but their schedules and secrecy hindered them. They had each other and, to them, it was enough. They had two common courses and always sat together, would meet in the student union at least twice each week for lunch, or borrowed snacks and supplies from each other almost daily when they visited the other's room. The pattern was beautifully established, and as rich as Joseph's coat. By the end of spring 2002, all of it would change.

Jabari threw what was left of his possessions into a duffle bag and paced the small room to ensure he had collected everything.

"I don't understand why you can't do two more years and get a bachelor's degree," Monika said as she folded his clothes from the drawer.

"Because it isn't required to enter the academy. The credits I have are enough."

The years added inches to Jabari's height, and boom to his voice. "

"They want me to go now."

"They! They! They! We don't ever get a say?"

"And you know why, Monika. But I applaud the little rhyme you did there, MC Moni."

Disappointed by her own protest, she drew back and refused to laugh. "Just hate to see you go."

"Awww...you gonna miss me." He formed an exaggerated frown.

"It's not funny." She tossed a pair of shorts at his face.

"I'm not going far. I'm not even leaving the city. I just won't be a student here anymore."

She lifted the painting of black boxing gloves from the dresser. "Just mess the whole thing up why don't you," Monika sulked.

Sentiment rose within Jabari's voice, "What whole thing?"

They looked at each other and knew.

"I guess I have to wish you the best."

"You guess? So, wait—you're taking back my painting now?"

She placed it on the bed. "Fine. You can keep it."

"Listen, we can hang on Sundays. Moms won't stop cooking Sunday dinners because I'm not in school anymore. Hell, she'll need to cook extra with all these workouts I'm about start." He drummed his belly playfully. "Just come over."

Monika rolled her eyes. The gesture was not enough to satisfy her need to be near him, but transition was inevitable.

She sucked it up, saw him off that May, and went on without him. She was proud to learn that his hard work paid off, and he was quickly accepted into the police academy. Yet, the void of his absence drove her to finish her academic program as quickly as she could. Against most recommendations, Monika enrolled in 15 credit hours that summer, and barely found time to sleep between class, studies, or her continued TAAR training. Even there, she was unable to see Jabari, whose duty ceased while he successfully completed the police academy. They seldom spoke or saw each other.

Monika even went to Jabari's home for a hot, home-cooked meal two Sundays in a row, but he did not show. By the third Sunday, Mrs. Rushing sensed that something was off kilter. As she chopped sweet potatoes and prepared them for the pot, she invited Monika into the kitchen.

"I appreciate you cooking dinner for me, Mrs. Rushing."

"It's nothing," she spoke, and the sound of Africa rang from her voice. "I know your father is not much of a cook."

They giggled.

"Not at all. I don't see how anyone can burn an egg. He does it every time."

There was a noise outside, and Monika's head whipped around for a look.

Mrs. Rushing put down the knife and offered her full attention to the young lady who sat at her kitchen island.

"Listen. He won't be coming."

"Ma'am?"

"Jabari. He usually keeps his word. His father taught him that. But the demand on him has kept him away." Her words did little to encourage Monika, and she noticed. "I miss him too."

"It's not that," Monika lied. "Just haven't seen him. Wanted to make sure he's okay."

Mrs. Rushing smirked. "If he wasn't, I wouldn't be here peeling potatoes."

Monika huffed at her own foolish statement. "You're right," she said.

"I don't mind your visits, but I'm afraid I'm not good company for a girl your age—and probably not much of a good cook to you either since you're usually done after a few bites." Mrs. Rushing cut to the chase. "I won't waste your time, and you won't waste my food, if you can rest assured that Jabari is okay."

"I'm sorry," Monika said.

"No need. We're all trying to figure it out. One thing you can be sure of: when I hear from him, I will let him know to call you."

Monika hopped down from her seat but could not conceal the injury of Mrs. Rushing's dismissal. The woman watched as Monika grabbed her purse and car keys, and her heart went out to her.

"Thank you, again," Monika said.

"Anytime, my sweet."

With her heavy workload, the switch from summer to fall caught Monika completely unaware. She could finally climb out from the cave of all her studies and return home for a peaceful, extended visit. It was the perfect time. Her father had planned a social gathering and wanted to ensure she would attend. With the ministry's success, and his purchase of a new building that could only be compared to a convention center planted in a major city, Monika was ready to celebrate him. In those years, his social functions could rival Gatsby's. Oddly, Dyer was of a more sinister kind.

Bishop Dyer rented a beautiful banquet center surrounded by lush gardens with black lanterns and candles that glowed in sunlight, which created the ambiance of an animated fairytale. No expense was spared on his soiree, and Monika was happy to take part in her father's excitement. It was all she could ever want—to witness his outward success coupled with genuine happiness.

Car still piled with clothes and the firefly painting from her dorm room, Monika arrived and handed her keys to the valet. She took the stairs up to the main room. Her black, knee-length dress formed perfectly around her curves and accentuated her toned calves as she stepped with confidence in a pair of red stilettos. She stopped to share a few hugs before she made her way into the grand room and was escorted to a seat at her family's table.

At least two hundred people joined her father's celebration, and were ready for the festivities to begin, but he was nowhere to be found.

As a crew worked the kinks from the lighting issue on stage, a large, white spotlight angled towards the audience flicked on and blinded her. Once she regained her ability to see, Monika's eyes darted through the crowd in search of her father and sister. Instead, she saw him—Jabari. He was clad in a suit and fresh haircut, but nervous—not as she remembered him. He noticed her too.

Monika went over to meet Jabari near the center of the room. They shared a friendly embrace, but neither displayed a speck of happiness.

"Where have you been, man?" Monika playfully slapped his arm.

Jabari looked around anxiously. "Monika, listen..." he started.

"What?" She grew concerned.

"When I left school in May, I didn't know..." Jabari whispered.

Monika smiled nervously. "Didn't know what?"

Jabari looked up, and a man signaled for him to come over.

"What, Jabari?"

"I'm sorry," was all he said, and he walked away.

Puzzled, Monika made her way back to her seat at the empty table. The wait was brief. The lights were raised on the platform, and immediately her father and sister stepped into the center. The crowd clapped, and Monika joined in.

"Ladies and gentlemen," Bishop Dyer spoke. "God has been a most gracious, incredible God."

"Amen" echoed through the room.

"This has been a tremendous year in ministry, and I cannot express how grateful I am to God who has given so abundantly, and for each of you who never fail to celebrate the significant moments of my life."

Bishop noticed Monika seated at the table.

"Monika is here." He smiled. "Come up here, baby."

As the crowd applauded, Monika walked to the edge of the platform. Before she could step onto the stage, she saw that Jabari was there. She slowed as they crossed paths and looked at him with deep suspicion.

"Some of us say we'll come when called, and don't really mean it; but Monika always does. If I call, she's there."

Monika smiled at her father's compliment and leaned in for a hug.

"After my wife passed, I knew that taking care of these girls, who have grown up to be such beautiful, intelligent young ladies, would not be easy."

Monika glanced in Jabari's direction.

"Monika is set to graduate college. I'm so proud of her. And as you know, Amara graduated high school this year and will enroll as well." He paused. "But there is something that you don't know." He blushed.

Amara became giddy and gripped her father's arm in excitement. Her white dress swung loosely mid-thigh and exposed the dancer's slender legs.

"There is another member of our family. I knew his father since before he was born, and I am proud to have watched him grow into the responsible young man he is today."

Bishop Dyer motioned to Jabari, who moved with haste up the steps and onto the platform. He stood next to Amara and smiled uncomfortably as he waved at onlookers.

"Again, I am proud of these young people—and overflowing with joy to soon call Jabari my son-in-law."

The crowd gasped and clapped excitedly. Monika's hands were as heavy as bricks, but she managed to join them together a short while to participate in the applause.

The noise settled before Bishop spoke again. "And when I say 'soon', I mean today. Welcome, one and all, to the nuptial ceremony of Mr. Jabari Rushing, and my daughter, Amara Dyer. Surprise!"

Monika's poker face melted behind her saddened expression. Her father's words, true to form, constricted her airway like a snake coiled around her throat.

"Settle in. Enjoy some refreshments while we prepare for the ceremony."

They all left the stage and walked in opposite directions. Monika grew faint and was helped to the bottom step by a male usher. She had drunk from the cup of Jabari's compassion and the contents were proven toxic.

"Is there somewhere I can sit down?" she asked the usher.

"Your table." He motioned towards it.

"No. Somewhere else."

"Sure. I think there are a few rooms not being used by the wedding party."

His words sickened her, but Monika maintained enough composure to grab her handbag from the table and follow him to a quiet room.

She flounced onto a crème-colored chaise and stared blankly at whatever object was before her. Nothing made sense; but everything hurt. She could not turn out the light of her father's joy and profess her love for Jabari or ruin her sister's moment and future. She was helpless.

Monika opened her handbag, unzipped the small side-pocket, and pulled from it the medallion Jabari gave her years before. She stashed it there when she packed her dorm room to return home; and it was a bitter reminder.

After a few light knocks, the door to the room opened, and Monika hopped to her feet.

"Yes?" she asked. "Mrs. Rushing, are you looking for something? Jabari's not in here."

The short, dark-skinned woman quietly shut the door. "I'm not looking for my son," she said, "but you."

"What can I help you with?" Monika offered.

Mrs. Rushing noticed the medallion in Monika's hands. "What is that?"

"Nothing."

"Let me see it." The woman reached out to receive the piece of metal. She immediately turned it over and rubbed her thumb along the surface. "I think I've discovered what I was looking for."

"The medal?"

"Where did you get it?"

"A friend."

"My son," Mrs. Rushing said. "It's his. The ridges on the back—it's from the time it scraped along the concrete when my husband accidentally ran over it in his car and dragged it to the end of the driveway. Jabari could hear the scraping sound, convinced him to stop the car. He didn't know it had fallen from his belongings when he returned home from the game the night before." She looked at the scratches again. "And he gave this to you?"

Monika nodded and plopped back onto the chaise.

Mrs. Rushing sat next to her. "You see, he received this his 8th grade year—for baseball. His team was undefeated—terrorized the boys on the other teams. His father and I were there when they placed it around his neck—the last game his father would see. He went off to jail after that, and then he died."

"I'm sorry, Mrs. Rushing. I didn't know. I wouldn't have let him give it to me. You can take it home with you."

The woman smiled. "I couldn't." The woman paused. "There's a reason Jabari gave it to you. Whether you understand it, or not, he saw you worthy enough to have it." She looked at the somber young woman next to her, and whispered, "I can see it too."

Mrs. Rushing wrapped her arms around Monika. She held her tightly and delivered a mother's embrace. Monika did not know how much she had missed such affection until the moment revealed it to her. She could not recall a comparable instance of deep connectedness. The bubble that housed her suppressed emotion ruptured suddenly and soaked a section of Mrs. Rushing's royal blue blouse.

CHAPTER TEN

THEY TELL US WE ARE WEAK

BY 6 a.m. on the third day of conflict, gunfire slowed and the stench of burned debris floated up and away but was replaced by the repulsive smell of decayed flesh. Many remained hidden, unaware of the officers' ploy to rescue them. It was difficult to decipher their movements amongst the misplaced cars that lined the roads, so they continued to wait it out—until they no longer could.

Monika and Jabari's position had been compromised by Wolves, who kept their eyes focused on the access door where the pair escaped the spray of bullets. For as long as TAAR's opponents were armed and presented a threat, their plan was to stay the course.

As the sun pierced the darkness, Jabari looked through the partly opened door as Monika crouched close by.

"There are two of them on one roof—only one on the other," he said.

The inside of her mouth was sore. "Have any gum?" she asked.

"No."

"Think you can take the shot?" she quickly refocused.

When Jabari looked from the door again, he was immediately blinded by the intense light of sunrise.

"Not from this position, and not without being seen," he said.

He released the door. When it slammed closed, he sat and pressed the back of his head against it. "Dammit."

"Waiting them out—I don't think that's even an option. They know where we are. All it would take is for them to get more of their men on these other roofs, and we're finished."

"That won't happen." Jabari spoke with closed eyes. "We can't go out there."

"You should rest a while. It's gotten quieter. I'll think of what to do next."

"Yeah," he mumbled. "You've always been a good partner."

"At least you think *that* much of me." Monika sat down on the floor and propped herself against the cold, brick wall.

Jabari opened his exhausted eyes and corrected her. "I thought a lot of you. I can't explain it."

"Or you don't *want* to?"

"Maybe both, Monika. None of it matters."

"I'm so sick of being told what should and shouldn't matter to me."

"How could whatever we felt all those years ago mean anything to you now?"

Monika spoke bitterly, "I'm here *because* of you. What I felt for you all those years ago, which you think should mean nothing now, landed me right here." She fought back her frustration and was left helpless. "Why didn't you just let me go?"

"What? Let you go? I never gave you cause to be here. It was your choice."

"You're wrong."

"How?"

"A week after you married Amara, you came to my father's house. I was in my car and ready to back out of the driveway when you knocked on the window."

"I remember that. Your dad asked me to stop by to pick up some things he had for my mom. It was the first time I'd seen you since the wedding."

"I had nothing to say to you. I felt betrayed. I was done—completely over all of it—and trying my hardest to get over you too. Your small talk was unfruitful, so you pushed harder. Do you remember what you told me?"

He squinted his eyes. "I can't."

"You'd reached the half-way mark in law enforcement training, had a better grip on your schedule, and you were coming back to the community center in the evenings. Perhaps you said it to soothe my torment after I watched you exchange vows with my little sister in a room full of people I believed loved me, but they were clueless to everything I felt. And it worked. It gave me hope."

"Me coming back to training?"

"That's all it took." Monika leaned forward. "You looked inside my car while we stood there. Do you remember?"

He lowered his gaze to the floor. "Yes. I do. It was filled with stuff. You said you hadn't unpacked all your things from the dorm."

"I was leaving, Jabari. The people I loved most— Daddy and Amara—even if they didn't know what I felt for you, they planned an entire surprise wedding, dropped not a single hint, and never thought to include me. It was *their* secret. Who did I have left?"

"Where were you going?"

"Where I was going is not as important as what pulled me back."

"I knew how much you'd given up. I would never want to be the reason for another sacrifice."

"That's not what you were. You were my hope—all that made me feel like something."

Jabari took in each of her words and felt remorse.

"Did you ever feel the same for me?" Monika asked.

Jabari desired nothing more than to be open with her, but his sentiment was swiftly cut down by the thought of his family—his wife and their children.

"Like I said: none of it matters." His words could frost the entire stairwell. "You have to let this go. I love Amara. Despite how we got to this point, it's right."

Monika sucked up whatever pride remained and refused to utter another word. Like Jabari, she also loved Amara, and was just as loyal.

When the room was silent, Jabari shut his eyes until he heard Monika's feet shuffle against the floor when she stood.

"Where are you going?"

"The window in the corner office could open. I remember seeing a latch along the frame. There has to be others like it in the building. I can fire from them if needed— at least until this whole thing is over."

"We shouldn't separate."

"We're only exposed on the roof. I don't need you to have my back in here…and neither do you." She removed the gun from her hip, detached the empty magazine, and examined the chamber. "I'm out. I'll need a clip."

Jabari pulled the bullets from deep within his pocket and tossed it over to her. "It's all I have. It won't be enough if you find yourself in trouble."

She nonchalantly loaded the weapon. "Guess we'll see, huh."

"Don't do this," he pleaded.

"I'm making moves. I've spent enough of my life waiting around."

Monika's feet pounded against the steps as she went away.

* * *

ALSO weary from the wait was Amara, and her frustration was deepened when she noticed uniformed officers rush others to safety from her 20th floor view.

"Come on, kids. It's time to go."

They sprang to their feet and followed her to the elevator. When they reached the lobby, the crowd she watched escorted away had disappeared, and the street was clear.

"Where'd they all go?" Amara said to herself.

"Are we leaving?" Shiloh asked when they halted at the entryway.

"Someone will come for us, baby. Just wait a minute."

"I want to eat," the girl said.

"I know. I know."

A path clear enough for Amara to move her car from the garage was visible, and the absence of Wolves and gunfire boosted Amara's confidence in a new plan.

"Listen. I want you both to hold my hands. When we go outside, I want you to run as fast as you can. Do not stop. You hear me? Don't stop."

Amara uttered a "help us, Lord" before she pushed the door open and took off with her children. The camera mounted at the garage's entry point—patient and peaceful—watched the children's hands clenched in their mother's grip as they scurried by.

In the shadows of the covered lot, she continued to run, and tried to remember where she had parked her car days before. When Amara realized she had already passed it, she turned around. The car doors unlocked automatically when she was within range, and she tossed her children into the backseat.

Relieved and excited, Amara cranked the car and put it in reverse. The black, rearing horse seemed to rise and greet her from the steering wheel's emblem. Before she could back out, she noticed a pair of shoes on the pavement. The shoes were filled by feet. Those feet had an owner, and that owner caused those feet to move down the ramp and in Amara's direction. She ducked down and thought to return the car to park and wait them out; but she knew they would soon hear the engine.

"Get all the way down," she said. Her children obeyed.

The men drew closer, but the late-modeled luxury car did not emit a sound loud enough to warrant their attention. It was not until Amara shoved her foot on the gas that they knew she was there.

"Hold on!"

She shifted quickly into drive and floored it as three Wolves fired at her vehicle.

"Stay down!" she yelled as they neared the cars scattered in front of the garage.

There was a gap almost large enough for her car to pass through, but her car would require at least another foot to avoid a collision. It was not enough to stop her, so she continued to press her foot on the gas.

As she braced herself for the thud of impact, the car suddenly stopped and flung them all backwards. The car's automatic brakes prevented her escape, and Amara feared the Wolves would soon catch up to them.

She pulled her children from the backseat and ran into the closest building—a bookstore—and hid amongst the shelves. She counted at least six others within the space, and quietly acknowledged them.

"Why do they want to hurt us?" Shiloh whispered between breaths.

"Not now." Amara watched the door and listened like a hawk suspicious of danger.

Suddenly, the bell that hung near the store's entry sounded, and Amara was certain they had been discovered. Then there was nothing. The room was quiet again. She needed clarity. If there was no threat, it would clear the headspace needed to concoct a new plan.

"Stay here."

She crawled along the crunchy carpet and looked towards the door. Two armed men, both in black, took cover in the room, and watched the street.

"Get out of here!" an elderly man demanded. "You can't be here." He stood, and his brown, wrinkled face was made known.

One soldier gripped his rifle and pointed it in the man's direction before his partner pressed his hand against it, which caused him to lower it.

"You can shoot me, but you can't stay here," the man boldly declared. A thin, blue ring encircled the iris of his intense eyes.

"Why not?" the TAAR soldier asked.

"The folks out there don't have enough bullets for all us. They savin' 'em all for you." He pointed. "You gone bring 'em this way."

The soldier scratched his temple with a pinky. "You don't think us being here means they don't get to *you?*"

"You don't think they know we in here? One looked me right in my eye and he went away. You done went and stirred up trouble. You ought to know better—shootin' at these folks."

"Come on," one of the soldiers said. "Let's go."

"I wanna hear this," his partner insisted. "I oughta know better than to shoot at the people who's been shootin' at you? Have you seen all the bodies out there? It's only a few specks of white on the concrete—a whole stretch of black."

"Come on!" his partner commanded. "Ain't no gettin' to him."

* * *

AFTER she assisted with evacuating as many people as she could call out of dark, improvised hideaways, Valerie returned to the station for rest and sustenance. She was confident her body would soon surrender to slumber against her will, and without a discerned end to the madness, decided to be more proactive.

Most of the precinct crowd from the night before had been bussed to the safe zone, and the officers' ability to move about was restored.

Valerie sat down in her chair and placed her head on the desk. She stared at a photo she and her husband took at a picnic the year before until her eyelids descended like a curtain of snow.

"It's nonsense if I ever heard it," a voice shook her from her sleep.

"Who would ever believe that? It's total bull," another man spoke. "This country's never seen it—black people organize in such a way, I mean."

Valerie sat up and twisted around in her chair to see the chatty officers.

She moaned as she stretched her arms into the air. "What you two talking about?"

"Got a real nutcase. Some guy we brought in from the drop-off site says—get this—the people up on the roof are a highly-skilled group of blacks who trained for war. *This* war. Can you believe that? Ninjas." He laughed, sat down in his chair and locked his fingers behind his head.

"And you brought the guy here?" Valerie asked.

"Yeah. He's in conference room D."

"What else did he tell you? Anything about Bishop Michael Dyer?"

"Wait... you know the guy?"

Valerie hesitated, and was forced to quickly decide how much of her discovery to release.

"No. Not at all. *If* it's the same guy, I ran into him right before we started to bus people away from the core." She chuckled to match their skepticism. "He said something along those lines—black people on the roof, training of some sort. Crazy. I put him on the bus to be taken away."

"Well, he managed to find his way back. Might've been better if he'd stayed put. Running his mouth won't do him any good."

"Especially if it's hogwash," the other man spoke. "I still can't believe he said he killed his kid."

"I can. Some people will do anything for attention. The guy was shady from the jump."

"I want to ask him some questions," Valerie said.

"A total waste of time." The officer smirked and rocked in his chair.

"There could be something there," she insisted.

"Well, well. Let's see—a Life Saving Award when you performed CPR on a woman with half her face burned off because her psycho husband torched her car; an Exceptional Service honor a few months ago... Let me guess: you're aiming for a Valor Award to add to the Purple Heart your husband got for his bum leg? Rackin' 'em up, I see."

Valerie did not respond to his petty assumptions but shifted, annoyed, in her seat.

"No, actually," he continued, "you definitely deserved recognition for bringing that woman back. She was ugly enough without the burns. Kissing Freddie Krueger couldn't have been easy. No, wait...the Crypt Keeper." He snickered.

When the other officer sensed the depth of Valerie's aggravation, he chimed in. "No one will stop you, but you'll get nowhere with that guy."

Valerie took the corridor down to conference room D, and haggardly brushed her shoulder against the wall as she went. Calvin sat in a dimly lit room and thought he could catch some sleep when Valerie walked in and wrecked his hope for rest.

"It's you," he said wearily.

She closed the door behind herself and took a seat across from him. "We're barely running on fumes here, so don't waste my time."

"I haven't. What I'm telling you—all of you—is true. Those other cops laughed in my face. I shouldn't say a damn thing. I'm not under arrest."

"Do you see me laughing?" Valerie leaned closer. "I believe you."

Calvin relaxed his shoulders and gave a subtle nod. "Good."

"You told me about Monika, and Officer Rushing," Valerie began.

"Yes, yes."

"And Amara Rushing, Bishop's other daughter, isn't involved?"

"No. We found out at the same time."

"How could you be sure?"

"Believe me, if *she* had known before now, this wouldn't be a surprise to any of us. She's a woman without a filter. Monika would say, 'she can't hold water'."

"Tell me about their father."

"I know about as much as anyone who watch him on TV every Sunday."

"No private meetings you know of? Suspicious gatherings? Anything?"

"No. Nothing." He considered her questions more deeply. "Wait. What do you think Bishop Dyer has to do with this? He wasn't there when it all went down."

Valerie sat quietly, reluctant to reveal the outcome of her probe to the weasel of a man, but he had an epiphany.

"Wait. He *wasn't* there." Calvin roughly brushed his beard with his hand. "He left right before it happened. It wasn't late, but he said he had to get ready for some event or something the next day." He leaned back in his chair. "You think he had some part in this? I didn't think he could—being in the church and all—but I wouldn't put it past anyone," he rambled.

"Besides the fact that he left early the other night, did you find anything else awkward about his behavior?"

"No. I can't say."

"Monika's?"

He sat quietly and pondered, and then snapped his fingers when a clue dropped into his conscious.

"The community center."

Valerie's eyes were sharp. "Where? What about it?"

"I don't know where it is. She never took me. Said she was volunteering with some program, but she was gone almost every night. At first, I thought it was a church thing, but when I tried to surprise her one night and take her out to dinner, she wasn't there. That's when she mentioned some community center." He shrugged.

"Did Bishop Dyer ever mention it?"

"No." More details flooded his thoughts. "She worked out a lot when she was pregnant—running and such. Didn't stop the volunteer work though, even at the end of her last trimester. After our son was born, she was obsessed with rebuilding her strength; she wasn't into competitive fitness or so out of shape that she would need it. She wasn't even the type of woman to put so much attention on her appearance. It makes sense now. She was training."

"The baby..." Valerie refocused his attention. "If Monika is on the roof, why would she run off with him? Where do you think he is?"

"He's up there with her for all I know. Nothing would surprise me now."

* * *

MONIKA exited the stairwell on the 19th floor and searched several rooms for a window that would open. As far as she could see, the floor was empty, which put her at ease. The danger prowled from rooftops, or passageways, where Wolves continued to withhold their surrender.

One by one, Monika swung open doors and glanced at the windows. When she pushed into a sixth room, a white woman and her young son, startled, were clung tightly to each other. Surprised by their presence, Monika reached for her gun.

"No! Please don't shoot us," the woman cried.

Monika asked, "It's just you two in here?"

The woman responded with a brisk nod of the head and pulled her son closer. "Please. Please. Don't shoot us."

Monika looked at the boy, head buried in his mother's bosom. He would only peek from the peripheral of one eye. She thought of her niece, Shiloh, who was about his age — how frightened the gun would make her, or how the girl would surely panic at the threat of her mother's death — and she knew the people in that room could only see a monster standing before them. She lowered her gun and holstered it.

"How long have you been in here?" Monika asked.

Before the woman could answer, the floor creaked behind Monika, and she turned to look. Instantly, a large man jumped from the closet and pounced on her. He wrapped his hands firmly around Monika's throat.

"Wait! Stop!" the woman called out, but the man refused to relent.

He gripped tighter. It was not because he hated Monika. He was afraid. Survival was instinctual, and his family was more important than the need to first discover Monika's intentions. Patience would not abound.

Monika tried to pry his fingers away from her neck but failed. She grabbed his shoulders to steady herself and forcefully shoved a knee into his groin. The pain drained power from his grip; but when she reached for her gun, he conjured strength from every corner of his being, and delivered a powerful blow to her face with the back of his hand. She landed on the floor; her legs wiggled before she clutched the gun and raised it towards the man whose vicious attack would not end until one of them was dead. Monika decided it would not be her and fired two shots as he charged towards her. His blood painted her face and clothes when he landed on top of her. With his hands pressed against the holes in his chest, she shoved him away.

"Brian?" His wife went to his side.

Monika coughed into the air.

"Why'd you do this?" the woman cried. "Don't die, honey. Please. You didn't have to shoot him."

The room spun around her. Monika's body was mush; her limbs lacked poise; her eyes rattled like shaken dice in their sockets. Vomit rose from her gut but stopped short of her throat.

"I'm sorry," Monika said as she aimed her weapon at the heartbroken woman and staggered backwards. "I'm sorry."

She moved into the hallway, and the door closed on the boy's view of the woman who took his father's life. The monster was real.

The rest of the corridor appeared empty but looks had already deceived her. Monika rushed into the restroom at the end of the hallway and quickly locked the door.

The mirror immediately caught her attention. The man's blood was smeared across a face she no longer recognized. She scrubbed it away with the hardness of her nails and cool water that flowed from the faucet; but nothing could quench the desert of her soul.

When she reemerged, Monika had no desire to conflict with another innocent person, so dashed for the elevator. Inside, she did not press a button to guide it to another floor but allowed the doors to close as she collected herself.

* * *

AT Wanderer's Refuge Temple, people continued to arrive as they had the day before, and men quickly helped them inside. Many sprinted through the large parking lot towards the front door where men stood guard, checked each bag they carried, and searched anyone who wanted access. They were given water and was rationed whatever could be spared from the kitchen, which was not much. Known diabetics were served communion grape juice to hold them over. Over 300 people who gathered there grew hungrier by the hour.

Bishop Dyer walked into his office, and Patrick extended the phone towards him.

"Who is it?" he asked.

"It's Monika."

He snatched the device from the man's hand and pressed it to his ear.

"How are you?" Bishop Dyer asked in a grim voice.

"Not good," she said. "Daddy, I killed someone—an innocent man."

Bishop Dyer knew the cost of war; it was not until then that Monika discovered it for herself.

"Are you hurt?"

"I'm okay."

He sighed. "Many will die," he said in a whisper, "but our cause will be undeniable."

Disappointedly, Monika listened to her father's words.

He turned his attention to the television screen that aired the chaos downtown and sat down in his chair. "They left Tulsa and Chicago out of history books, but the world will see the monster we've run from all these years. Even if we die destroying everything our ancestors died to build."

It was not the answer she expected. Monika was convinced she mirrored the monster of her father's nightmares. She was a lioness confined to a rabbit's cage— unless her father would lift the hatch. "End this now and go home" would have sufficed, but she could not petition him for an acceptable response because suddenly the elevator chimed and began to move. She frantically pressed buttons for it to stop. When it rebelled against her effort, she put the phone away and aimed her weapon towards the door. Someone was inside the building, and Monika would not know who until they were already face to face.

CHAPTER ELEVEN
ABANDON THE NOBLE STRUGGLE

"POLICE! Drop your weapon!" a female voice demanded as the elevator door glided open on the first floor. With her weapon aimed, Valerie's arms blocked full view of her face.

"You'll shoot me before this gun will touch the ground," Monika replied.

"You don't want that."

"Think so?"

The elevator prepared to close, and Valerie knew that a verbal order for the woman to come out would not yield her desired outcome, so she jumped onto the elevator and blocked Monika's escape into the lobby. Valerie tilted her head to look around her own steadied hands, and the barrel of Monika's gun, to the woman in black. She was familiar. The doors closed on their standoff, but the elevator did not move.

"What do you want?" Monika barked.

"It's obvious. Put down your weapon."

"That won't happen. So... what now?" Her jaw clenched.

Valerie searched Monika for a hint of fear, but there was none. She knew the feminine fighter was prepared to duel to the death—whatever it meant in that instance—and she would need a strategy that would lower Monika's defenses.

"I know who you are," Valerie said.

"That's it?"

"Just put down your weapon," Valerie said.

Monika would not budge an inch. The small elevator camera joined their intimate dance—private, purposed, a knotted three-strand cord—and captured the experience.

"Listen. I'll put mine down, and I want you to do the same."

"I wouldn't do that either—unless you have titanium where your skull should be. No deal."

"You wouldn't shoot me, Monika. We both know that."

When the officer spoke her name, Monika aimed the gun slightly lower and stared curiously at her. Initially, Valerie expected a venomous spider of a woman; but her experience proved Monika's bite only *appeared* deadly. There was more life in Monika's eyes than in the soldier's Valerie had encountered in the alley.

"That's right, Ms. Dyer," Valerie continued. "I know who you are; I also know you don't wanna shoot me. However, as an officer of the law, I can't stand around while you shoot someone else—black or white. So, I need you to put the gun down."

"In this moment, you can trust that I know more than you do."

"I wouldn't be so cocky. Here you are—ready to die for something you don't even understand."

"I understand. Believe me. I've understood for a long time."

"Understand that you won't get off this elevator with that gun in your hands. Let me help you."

Unexpectedly, Valerie's words shook Monika at her core. Her dreadful truth was in plain sight and, although she was judged for her position, she was offered help—a way out. Monika had wanted to hear those words for decades. To know that someone could bear witness to her warped reality, and still extend a hand, captivated her; but it was too late.

"You can't help any of us!" Monika yelled through sheltered emotion. "Now get out of my way."

"You have to know fact from fiction. Or do you enjoy putting your life on the line for a lie? Let me tell you, the story won't end well."

Monika stared at the officer. "I never expected it to. Now, move."

"Fact or fiction?" Valerie's shoulders bounced like a juggling act. "I'm trying to help you here."

Monika examined the officer—face free of makeup, but whose features created beautiful shadows and emphasized its flawlessness.

"Since you're into small talk, how could a woman with such a pretty face be on the force? Not afraid of being disfigured?"

"Let me guess—you're a lesbian?" slipped randomly from Valerie's lips.

"Never bet on a guess."

"The truth is that the gruesomeness of the job couldn't keep me away. I'm a peace-lover. Didn't have a single fight as a kid. Something drew me back to this. Purpose, I guess. Possibly why I have a gun to your face."

"That's quite purposeless actually. Someone afraid of the gun would be more fitting—may better justify your journey."

"Harold Francis Washington," Valerie blurted out. "Does the name ring any bells, Monika?"

"How the hell should I know?" She shrugged.

"It's your father's name," Valerie said.

Monika smirked at Valerie's outrageous assumption. "I think we both know who my father is," she scoffed.

"I guarantee the men are one in the same."

"So, what? Get out of my way. I may not kill you, but I'll shoot if I have to."

It was a challenge for Valerie to not execute her duty to society and justifiably take Monika, a known participant in a deadly organization, down with a single shot. Yet, the longer they stood there, she became increasingly confident as Monika failed to fire first.

"Before your father was Michael Dyer, Harold was his legal name. He ever mention what happened in Alabama where he grew up? I have good reason to believe that this is all his doing—revenge for what happened back then."

"Try harder," Monika said with the upmost reluctance.

"Where are your grandparents? Ever meet them? The bishop ever share childhood stories with you? Talk about his first car? School dances?"

"Who gives a damn?"

"He's lied to you. I'm sure in more ways than one. I know it. You know it too. Don't go down for this. That's exactly what will happen when the smoke clears."

Monika contemplated Valerie's words. "I think I have enough reasons of my own to be here, and to fight on this side. You stand here with a gun and badge, a black woman. It's clear you don't know what it's like to deal with what black people in this country are forced to accept as some twisted standard of living. Their screams of injustice are like dog whistles to the privileged—even some black folks."

"And you think you know their pain? You've lived well, sheltered even, since you were born. Whoever's behind this forced you to see all the ugly in the world. You didn't see that on your own."

"It doesn't make it any less real. Their pain is my pain."

"And this badge doesn't make me any less black. My brother got 22 years in prison for dope small enough to fit in my palm. My sister was arrested for taking a belt to her son's backside after he stuffed snacks he'd stolen from a corner store into his book bag. They took all three of her children. You assume I think that's just? Or that I never considered that her being a black woman made it easy for the system to punish her that way? Yes, I'm an officer of the law. I'm passed over, looked over, seldom taken seriously. I watch my tone, lower my head at times. So, yes, I know. I became the law in order to impact how law is enforced. But *this* isn't the right way to handle it, Monika. Despite how I'm treated, no one can deny the work I do. A single 'job well done' will outweigh 100 criticisms when you're moved by passion."

"You have your methods. We have ours. Kindness and patience are long exhausted. They have to know that we're ready."

Valerie was curious about her statement.

"Ready for what?" she asked. "What will happen?"

Monika was silent.

Valerie looked at the woman with fire in her eyes. "Monika, please. Listen to me. Your father's not well. And he hasn't been for a very long time. I know you want to do right by him, but this is not the way. He's using you—all of you. Think it a coincidence that you were all gathered down here the other night? And after a last-minute venue change only four days before? That your weapons were readily available to you? Or that Darius Jones, the man whose sons were murdered last week, wore the same boots as you are right now when he shot and killed a police officer and sparked this whole thing?"

Valerie paused to let her words penetrate and soften the soldier's stubbornness as Monika glanced down at the boots on her tired feet.

"There could be details of his plan that he's not telling you," Valerie continued. "What more could he be keeping from you? The fighting has to end. End it now, or when this is all over, there will be nothing but prison for you both."

"This is not my father's doing." Monika spoke with passionate conviction. "He's as much of the leader of this organization as you are president of this nation."

"You will die trying to protect him, Monika. Come with me now, and I promise things will go better for you. I can't say how all of this will work out, but you deserve to be safe, and out of this situation."

They stood in a breath of silence.

"Come on. What's it gonna be? Your allies are dropping like flies. It's only a matter of time before they're all dead or in cuffs."

Again, Monika refused to budge; but Valerie continued to unearth the facts of her findings.

"Think! What powerful, Black man would marry off his 17-year-old daughter? For men like him, daughters are their pride and joy. Tell me: was it to keep her blinded within the organization? That's why your sister is not geared up with you, right?"

Monika sensed the gun-wielding officer had knowledge of more than she initially accepted and was reminded of her father's deception—the arranged marriage of Amara to the man she once loved intensely.

"As cruel as it sounds, he protected your sister." Valerie could see a shift in Monika's eyes. "But what about you?" she said gently. "Who protects you?"

Suddenly, a powerful explosion shook the elevator and tossed the women around. Monika delivered a swift, roundhouse kick to Valerie's head, and she flew against the wall. Monika pressed the button to open the elevator door before pushing the button for the 15th floor. She quickly backed away.

Valerie sensed the pain rising in her face yet aimed at the hurried woman as the doors closed.

When Monika reached the entryway, another bomb exploded and rattled the building. Plumes of smoke and dust quickly saturated the air and decreased the roadway's visibility. She watched the formerly hidden people scatter into the streets in a lethargic frenzy. Interestingly, no Wolves were present. They had not caused the blasts, and it was made clear when Monika noticed the presence of law enforcement.

And then she saw him and was distracted from her initial observation and thought. Jabari sprang from the building across the street, rushed down the walkway, and entered another door. Focused and determined, Jabari did not notice Monika as she watched from the window.

Without warning, there was an eruption of debris accompanied by a deafening boom. Monika winced as rubble pelted against the glass. Fire and smoke rose from the building Jabari entered just a flash before.

"Jabari," Monika whispered and pressed her palm to the glass.

To her amazement, a short, thin man emerged from the wreckage a human fireball. He ran out into the street to quench the flames but failed.

Monika had no time to reflect upon her partner because the elevator chimed, and the possibility of another encounter with the female officer was more than likely guaranteed. Urgently, Monika pushed open the door and took off in the direction opposite the fire. Had she gone towards it instead, she would have noticed Amara as she helped her children from the bookstore's shattered window.

In her rush to escape the smoke, Amara left everything behind, which included her cell phone; but she carried her son and held firmly to her daughter's hand. People ran by from all directions, and without knowledge of a safe place to hide, or knowing who they could trust to help.

Amara hopped on a sprained ankle when she spotted a bus that made its way down a crowded cross street. City bus drivers were commissioned to pick up those who sought refuge and took them to designated safe zones. As the bus slowly chugged by, and dodged one runner after another, dozens of white faces gleamed from its large windows. A few Blacks were sprinkled here and there, which was ironic since the march itself was comprised primarily of Blacks.

"Hey! Wait!" Amara yelled. "Please!"

She released Shiloh's hand and pounded her fist against the rear of the bus as she hobbled towards the front. When he saw her, the white driver squared his shoulders and looked ahead. Perhaps it was Amara's unconcealable color that initially gave him pause, but the presence of her children softened him. He placed his foot on the brake and moved his hand towards the lever to open the door. Another woman leaped wildly in front of the bus as the driver motioned to open the door. She violently shoved Amara, son in tow, for a seat on the bus. Her behavior frightened the already cautious driver.

"Get back!" He locked the lever into position.

"Let me on!" the woman said frantically. "Open this door!"

The driver shook his head and refused. The woman backed a few feet away from the bus when it started to move again.

Amara grabbed Shiloh's hand, and made a second attempt to get on board. "Sir, please. Help me," she pleaded from behind the glass.

Again, he shook his head.

"But I'm not with her! I swear!" Amara yelled.

An explosion roared in the distance; Amara's body jolted with fear.

"Please! Please! I'll give you money!"

When she realized her ego falsely assumed that she was easily recognized—known throughout the city and beyond—she relied on a trusty representative.

The driver refused to glance in her direction, and soon found enough clearance to accelerate. She was appalled by his lack of compassion, but Amara's determination to escape could not end there. She regrouped and took in her surroundings. The woman who hindered Amara's shuttle-ride to safety stood nearby with the ghastliest stare Amara had ever seen.

Annoyed by the woman's gaze, Amara asked, "What?"

"Even with money, you still a nigger," she said, and ran away.

CHAPTER TWELVE

GUIDED BY THE LAMP OF EXPERIENCE

1967

THE summer of 1967 was intense for young Harold Washington. Years earlier, the relentless efforts of civil rights workers held Jim Crow in a chokehold and had finally convinced political figures to force it into the grave with the Civil Rights Act of 1964; but for years to come, its memory would haunt the people who once celebrated the victory.

Riots spread across the North American landscape— 34 states to be exact. Many Whites had not embraced the fresh integration of Black people, nor had the government created a solid structure to ensure economic progress or safety. The removal of signs above water fountains, bathrooms, or waiting areas would not guarantee Blacks the same future afforded by other citizens. They were not separate, but still unequal.

Without access to proper housing, continued racial injustice, unemployment, and consistent violence at the hands of police, it was impossible for those who suffered to hold their peace, or for civil rights leaders to have a moment's rest. On one side of the 1967 soundtrack was "The Long, Hot Summer"; and on B-side was "The Summer of Love". The side that played in an individual's experience was determined by geographical location. Rock 'n' roll and psychedelics were never amongst pastimes held by the browbeaten people of Birmingham, Alabama.

Harold was twelve years old. Beyond his studies, he was most devoted to his father, Jeremiah. Like other Black leaders of the time, Jeremiah was a pastor-turned-civil-rights-activist who did not hesitate to join the alliance that challenged inequity. Of course, doing so came at the expense of his freedom, and he found himself in jail 16 times over the course of three years. Despite his trials, Jeremiah remained committed to nonviolence and the vision of Dr. King, who had twice as many stints in jail. Amid the catastrophic climate of Birmingham, many searched for moments of peace and normalcy that would make the fight easier to endure.

It was late June, and Jeremiah spent most days and nights in talks with national leaders and members of the community. However, he was conscious of his loved one's needs, and the impact the consistent demand of his time could have on those he cherished. Jeremiah's efforts were not always received well by his wife, but there was some redemption in his son's appreciation of his efforts.

"Get your shoes on, Harold. We're going down Bessemer," Jeremiah announced when he walked into the house one Friday night.

"What for?" Harold squinted at the book, and then lowered *The Outsiders* to his bed.

"You coming or not?"

"Ma coming too?"

"I don't think she'd want to. She don't care much for picture shows."

Harold smiled to know he would catch a movie with his father.

"Throw on your shoes and let's go. And I saw you when I walked in. What I tell you about straining your eyes? Use your glasses, son."

"Yes, sir."

It was a quiet ride to the theater as Jeremiah revisited the day's conversations and plans. His desire to decompress and release the voices in his head surrendered to the sound of duty.

When they pulled into the theater's lot, nearly every parking space was taken. As they approached the ticket booth, Harold was intrigued by the new release posters plastered on the wall. The red and green figures armed with deadly weapons, with a damsel in a red dress plopped into the center, captivated the boy. "Train them! Excite them! Arm them! Then turn them loose on the Nazis!" was sprawled across "The Dirty Dozen" poster.

"Can I help you?" asked the pimple-faced teen in the booth.

"Two for 'The Dirty Dozen' please." Jeremiah removed his wallet for the two dollars and change he would need for the tickets, and Harold was immediately giddy to know he would see the film.

"It's already full."

"You sure?" Jeremiah asked.

"I'm afraid so."

Jeremiah watched the light go out in his son's eyes.

"Alright then."

The pair proceeded towards the car as a white couple passed them.

Jeremiah stopped and looked to Harold. "Maybe we can try again tomorrow—an early show. Let's grab a burger."

Jeremiah overheard the white couple's request for "The Dirty Dozen" and, to his dismay, they were granted seats after the patron handed over a few dollar bills. A young, Black man and his girlfriend walked past Harold and Jeremiah on the walkway, but Jeremiah sped ahead of them to address the boy in the ticket booth.

"Did I see that right?"

"Excuse me?"

"You just told us you were out of seats in there. We got around the corner a little ways and you let in those folks."

"I don't know what you're talking about," the boy denied.

Jeremiah quieted the frustration that boiled within him and took a deep breath. "I saw it with my own eyes."

"They were already here."

"I saw him give you the money."

The Black couple watched intently as Jeremiah addressed the boy.

"You know what—get your manager. Think I'd like to see him." He propped his hands on his waist. "Right now, please."

The boy left, and returned with a heavyset, middle-aged white man. His glasses rested near the tip of his nose.

"What can I do for you?"

"I'm not trying anything funny here. I swear. But he told us there was no more seats. We walked away, and then somehow the people come after us got seats inside."

"A customer can reserve a seat and come back if they wish. It's our policy."

"No. They paid him—just now. Saw it myself."

A few more Blacks drew near and, unaware, anticipated a seat in the theater.

"How could you know what you saw?"

Jeremiah blushed through his inescapable anger. In the most serene voice, he said, "You've been open a few months. Blacks and Whites patronize this place. You may have a theater full of white faces tonight, but oh boy, I'd hate to see what comes of it when Black bucks ain't in that register. That's exactly what'll happen when I tell 'em stay away from here."

The man listened to Jeremiah's annoyed display, noticed the mocha-skinned spectators who stood nearby with furrowed brows, and looked at his employee disappointedly.

"Did you check what was available before you turned away these people, boy?"

"But sir, you said to—."

"Never mind what I said." He cut him off, and then looked at the ledger on the desk. "Looks like we may have a few open if you give me a minute to double-check."

The manager positioned himself to collect the ticket money. In all, eight patrons stepped to the booth and paid for a seat. The man disappeared into the brightly lit theater and did not reemerge until it was a dark room and the film had already begun to play. He ushered the group inside and showed them an empty row of seats in the back of the theater. Distracted by the long-awaited attraction, the others were unaware of their presence.

Jeremiah had not won, but Harold saw his father's boldness as heroic. He could have backed down, walked away just as others had before them, which was evidenced by the absence of other Black faces in the room. Jeremiah was never compliant in the face of inequity, and his example made his son proud.

* * *

HAROLD could gauge the emotional atmosphere of his home by what he heard spinning on his father's record player. Most mornings brought the sound of Sam and Dave's "Hold On, I'm Coming" as he prepared for the day, or packed for a trip. Some evenings, Harold could hear his father belt out Marvin Gaye's verse on "Your Precious Love"; he knew dinnertime would be enjoyable, and his mother's smile would take up its own seat at the table. On the contrary, the tune of Solomon Burke's "Cry to Me" was Jeremiah's go-to when his wife was less agreeable or had distanced herself for whatever reason.

One evening, it was the melody of Sam Cooke's B-side that floated through Harold's dream as clouds of cotton candy and woke him from his sleep. He drifted into the living room where his father relaxed in his favorite chair.

He sang and took a sip of whisky.

"Daddy," Harold said as he rubbed the flakes from his eyes.

"Too loud?"

The Sears Silverstone record player was his father's most prized possession. It had a hardwood veneer and was amongst only four pieces of furniture in their living room. His father moved over to the open console and adjusted the volume.

"Get on back to bed now." He pulled the loose, beige tie from his collar.

Harold started back to his room before his father called to him.

"Come here, boy," he said. "Sit down."

He took a seat on the sofa next to his father's chair. "Sir?"

Jeremiah returned to the relaxed position in his chair. "Came in a little late. What time your mama get to bed?"

"I don't know. Maybe 9."

"Was she alright?"

"Yes, sir." He shrugged. "I guess."

"Okay." He breathed deeply and took a swig from his glass. Jeremiah reached for his pack of cigarettes on the table, lit a match, and took a slow pull.

"I love Sula. Love her, I do," he belted and then wrapped his lips around the cigarette with a chuckle.

"How old are you?" He slurred and batted his eyes as though he would see a word cloud of his son's reply.

"Twelve," Harold responded gently.

"That's right. Then it's been a little over 13 years since I met your mama." He drank from his glass. "A pretty little thing. Long hair, a smile I couldn't get around."

"How you meet her, Daddy?" Harold asked solely for kicks. It was a story his father shared many times when they were alone.

Jeremiah sat back and postured himself to reminisce. He blew out the cigarette smoke and stared at the wall beyond his blurred vision.

"Went to Palm Bay in '54 to speak at a conference. Your mother was there. You know me, son. The woman couldn't say 'no'." He smiled at the memory, but it faded quickly. He had a splash of whisky. "I was young. Graduated Stillman the year before. Wasn't thinking about a wife—but there she was. Brought her back here, and before long, here you come."

He reached over to the console and reset the record player to spin the tune again. He listened. Although Harold found his father's behavior strange, he dared not dismiss himself, or ask to return to his room for rest. He sat with him and watched—his head would nod to the lyrics, his clean-shaven jaw became more defined, square, each time he would grit his teeth.

"Yep. She made me a father," he said as he reflected. "But would only let me have one."

Harold was puzzled.

"Wouldn't give me more—not as long as I give more to the work I'm doing than to her—so she says." He held smoke in his mouth and pointed as he spoke. "I know what it is. She don't wanna be widowed with a gang of children to care for. Can't argue with that." He shrugged. "Actually, I think that couple that was killed near where she lived as a little girl just planted fear in her. Moore—I think was the name—started that NAACP chapter to sign up voters in Florida. They killed both of 'em for it. No one tried for the crime either. Sula's scared. That's gotta be it."

Jeremiah lifted the glass to his face and mumbled to himself. "Think I can't hear her banging around the washroom after we been together. I keep watch of the Lysol. I know she do more than clean the toilet with it." He grew quiet again.

"Mama said she only got enough strength to worry about me, and that's it. Said she don't want to happen to me what happened to that boy in Mississippi—the one in the magazine she keeps in that box under the bed."

"Talking about the boy they pulled out the Tallahatchie River some years back? The Till boy."

He nodded. "Mama said he wasn't much older than me."

"He wasn't. But don't worry yourself with that. Your mama does enough for all of us. You gonna live to be a nice, old age. I'mma see to it."

"Why they do it, though? Kill him, I mean."

"Because they can." Ribbons of smoke streamed from his lips. "They don't need a reason to do what they *free* to do. But listen, son...I'm home. I talk about these things all day. I just want some quiet when I'm here. It ain't the hour for anger. It'll wake itself up again tomorrow."

"Yes, sir." Harold lowered his head.

Jeremiah leaned forward and held out his glass. "Here. Take this."

Harold politely received it and held it in his hands.

"Drink it. Just a little."

The boy took a gulp, and a little dripped onto his grey, striped pajamas. He instantly released a series of coughs as it travelled down his throat. When Harold handed the glass back to his father, he resumed the conversation and confided in the boy as he would a close friend.

"It's hard to understand how a woman can know all I'm made of—see it from the start—and won't make peace with it. She don't have any issue making peace with the white man though." He released a puff of smoke. "Rather keep quiet than stir up the water."

Jeremiah's observation of his wife was part true. Sula was a descendent of the Black Seminoles. While she appeared to quietly accept the harmful circumstances of black people, she had not fully experienced their struggle. Her ancestors had more freedom than slaves held by southern Whites, so she was conditioned to see the contents of a half-full glass and teetered on Booker T. Washington's side of the debate.

Sadly, Jeremiah's excessive passion for the movement caused Sula to draw distance between them, and he suffered on the home front.

"Trying to find that peace somewhere, son." His words were tinged with pain.

Harold offered a subtle bounce of the head.

"Plan to get married, boy?"

Harold shrugged.

Jeremiah's finger fluttered at his son to emphasize his words. "Son, a woman that's truly for you, will honor what's within you—even if it's not also in her—but *never* abandon your passion. It's what keeps you moving—makes life mean something to you. The ones meant for the journey will take the ride with you. The others will get off and make room for someone else to have a seat. But watch the ones willing to stand the whole ride. They're anxious to get off, and probably won't go the whole way. You see..."

Suddenly, the record started to skip in the player and "come" echoed through the room. Jeremiah sprang from his seat and sprinkled ashes onto the chair's upholstery as he stopped the needle. He blew on the vinyl and examined it closely.

"Look alright to me," he said. "Guess it's due a break."

He turned off the equipment and placed the record into its sleeve.

"Alright. It's time for you to head on back to bed. Important rally at the church tomorrow. I need you sharp."

"Yes, sir." He stood.

"And son..."

"Sir?"

"Do right by your mama. You only get one in this life."

"Yes, sir," he said, and went away.

He was not snuggled in his sheets five minutes before he heard the evidence of his father's broken promise. The record player started to play the tune he had heard all evening, but more quietly, so Harold soon went off to sleep.

* * *

WITH heightened tension, black communities that held firmly to peaceful streets tightened their grip. Thousands were sent to hospitals or lie dead in the grave because of nationwide riots. Although the standard was for people of color to travel together and never go out alone, Jeremiah had his son; and he was certain the other organizers would soon meet him at church that September Saturday.

The group often met secretly no more than three miles from the Washington home. It stood at the end of a dirt road lined with trees, which stretched a quarter mile. Behind it was a wooded area too dense to determine its end. When Harold and his father approached the building, no other cars were outside.

"We'll get things ready before everyone else gets here," Jeremiah said as he shifted his car into park.

The air inside the church was stale, so he propped the door open with a piece of plywood left over from the recently refurbished steps that led to the front door. Jeremiah flipped on the lights and evidence of their previous rally was made clear. They had not cleaned afterwards. Crumpled paper, dirt carried in the crevices of shoes and empty paper cups polluted the space.

"Look at this," Jeremiah said. "We can't have it look like this for service tomorrow." He bent down to pick up a cup and a few pieces of paper. "Go to the closet and grab a broom. Help get this cleaned up."

Harold went to the rear of the church and looked inside the supply closet. He moved the mop aside, and a few trash bags that hung from a metal bar, but there was no broom. He knew he could not return without what he had been sent for, so he searched the four-foot space a little longer.

Jeremiah, with an arm stuffed with collected garbage, noticed two cars speeding in their direction and were kicking up giant plumes of dirt.

"Why they coming so fast?" he wondered. He looked a little closer. None of the faces were familiar, or black.

He dropped the garbage to the ground and made a dash for his son, who was caught off-guard when his father violently shoved him into the closet.

"Don't come out of here. I mean it. Keep quiet."

When he closed the door, the space went dark and silent.

Jeremiah knew the only way to avoid the caravan of trouble that travelled quickly down the roadway was to get into the car and drive off, but he was certain they would not make it to his vehicle in time.

He saw the handle of the broom sticking out from beneath one of the pews. Jeremiah grabbed it and swept the floor as four white men walked into the sanctuary. They all wore slacks and white collared shirts which varied in degrees of dinginess.

"Can I help you?" Jeremiah asked.

"What you doing out here?" a man with a balding head and gray beard asked.

"This is my church. I'm Pastor Jeremiah Washington. Name is on the door there."

"I know who you are. Hard to overlook a man with a record long as yours."

"How you know what's on my record?" Jeremiah asked curiously but did not receive an answer.

Another man, short in stature, looked around. "I don't see anyone here, so what you doing?"

"Just getting ready for tomorrow's service. Cleaning."

Alone, Jeremiah was forced to play nice, or altogether pretend.

"No one else on your Saturday cleaning committee?" asked the bearded man.

"No. Just me."

"Not what I heard."

"No, sir. Just me." He continued to push the broom across the floor.

"I heard there are forty or fifty of you. Come here to plan your marches and bullshit boycotts."

"Not here, sir."

One of the men picked up a piece of paper from the ground and ran his eyes over the words. He rushed over to the short one and handed it to him.

"Says here your little group plans to take on city hall."

"I don't know where that came from. Maybe a church visitor. Got new faces in these parts every week."

The older man picked up a piece from the floor for himself. "Says it here too."

The one closest to Jeremiah had not spoken but stepped within a foot of him and snatched the broom from his hands. He pressed the top of the handle against his chin. "You keep lying to us, boy, the rest of your meals will be sucked through a straw. Got it?"

Jeremiah was outnumbered. He imagined that at any moment someone would pull up to the church; but *that* moment was better than *any*.

"I guess you can't teach a nigger new tricks. Plottin', schemin', destroyin' everything we built—it's all his nature."

The man with the gray beard stepped forward, stopped two rows from where Jeremiah stood, and took a seat. "Had a dog when I was a boy. Big ol' Rottweiler. Loved 'em. But his mischief couldn't be broken. Somehow, he would get over the fence into the neighbor's yard and go digging up all Ms. Hardeman's herbs. Would chase a car coming up the road, squirrels—anything that moved would send him over the fence. My folks would have to wrangle him back in every time.

"We fed him good, gave him room to run the yard, but what he wanted was over the fence. He couldn't be satisfied otherwise. But when he got there, he left a mess for everyone else to clean up. Jumped over that fence for the last time and clawed a pretty little girl playing in her front yard. The old man was fed up and shot my dog. He told me, 'An animal can never own its master. If they don't know their place, they'll know the grave.'"

As the man spoke, Jeremiah heard the floor creak behind him, and turned his head slightly towards the closet. Harold needed air; the warmth of his breath made the lenses he wore dewy. He opened the door and breathed through a small gap when he noticed his father, the slight tremble of his body, his face that glistened with sweat—and knew he was afraid. Harold had never seen his father that way.

The short guy went to the door, removed the plywood that propped it open and closed it shut. He carried the piece of wood towards Jeremiah and, with a swift motion, whacked him in the head. When he did not fall, the man hit him a second time in the belly, and then aimed again for his head. When Jeremiah fell to the floor, Harold gasped from his hideaway.

"Get up, boy," the man taunted, and then hit him again.

Jeremiah crawled by the inch to get away, but he was surrounded. One placed his foot to Jeremiah's back and pinned him to the floor while another aimed consecutive blows at his head. Harold could no longer watch his father's anguish, and when he thought to move away from the door, he removed his glasses instead. Colors and figures were completely distorted, but the men were undeniably there.

After a few more blows, Jeremiah was unconscious, and no longer moved.

"Get the rope," the bearded man ordered. "And let's get out of here."

One of the men rushed to the car while two others dragged Jeremiah to the entryway, out the door, and onto the walkup. He started to mumble from his swollen, bloodied lips as they drew a tight knot around both feet and tied the other end to a log inside the trunk of the late-modelled sedan. One man sat on the trunk to ensure it remained closed.

"Mind the paint, boy," the bearded man said before he climbed into the passenger side and started the car. "And don't fall off." The man readied himself for the deadly adventure.

Their movements were like an elegantly synchronized ballet, and they were indeed experts in the craft. The driver shifted the car into gear and pressed the gas with enough ease to ensure his comrade would not plunge from the trunk; but with enough weight that Jeremiah would fly from the walkup, bypass the steps, and bash his head against the ground with enough force to produce a gut-wrenching *crack*. His head drew a clear line in the earth and was outlined by his blood. His body flailed about as they set out towards the oak tree nearest the main road. Once there, they removed the rope from his ankles, threw one end over a sturdy branch, tied the other to Jeremiah's neck, and strung him up like a pig over a fire pit. He was blinded by the blood that dripped into his eyes as his feet tap danced in the air. To hurry the finale, the short man took his pistol and fired two shots into Jeremiah's head.

Before they drove away, the second car's driver lit a stick of dynamite, and tossed it onto the stoop outside the church. The explosion frightened Harold and, as the flames consumed the wooden frame, he emerged. The boy ran full speed behind the pulpit and out the back door.

The woods were only a few yards from the back of the church, so he made his way around the side to get out into an open space. To clear the haze from his vision, he placed his frames on his face. What became clear was the ghastliest visual he would never escape. His father's bloody figure dangled in the distance like a brown, low-hanging peapod amid emerald-green leaves.

Harold raced down the road to his father. On the way, he resisted the urge to bat an eyelid as soot from the fire flew near and caressed his face.

When he was within reach, he wheezed loudly and extended his hand to nudge his father's shoes. He waited, but nothing happened. He tugged harder. Still, nothing—which was exactly what Harold felt inside.

When a car approached the scene, the driver slowed and came to a halt at the sight of the lynched man. The passenger noticed Harold, jumped from the car and went over to the boy whose glasses were steamy with tears.

"You shouldn't be here," the man said with urgency. "Come with us."

"No," Harold said.

"He ain't coming down from there, boy. Come on." The man wrapped his arm firmly around Harold and moved him towards the car. They drove away, and left Jeremiah's corpse to swing in the morning sun.

Within the hour, several men who planned to attend that day's meeting lowered Jeremiah to the ground. They removed his suit jacket and used it to cover his face until the coroner came to take him away. Afterwards, the men decided to converge at the Washington home to express sympathy for the fallen man. Surprisingly, they were not welcomed.

"Get away from here!" Sula yelled desperately from the porch and shooed them away. "Go on now! Leave here!"

The men backed away without a chance to get out of their cars, or to embrace her.

Inside the house, a rattled Harold shuddered on the couch as Sula paced the floor.

"We don't need the attention, you hear?" she barked at her son. "It's best we stay here. No company. We don't want them coming this way." She looked from the window curtains.

Harold's mother was gripped more by fear than grief of her husband's death.

"We'll go someplace. Hightail it out here." She continued to pace. "I just have to get to your father's car. Or get somebody to bring it this way. Shoot. I should have told one of them to do it—make 'em useful." She bit her thumb nail. "Won't know where he put the keys though."

"When will be bury him?" Harold asked solemnly.

"That's right." Sula sat next to him. Her leg shook as she thought. "Soon. I'll go down to the coroner's office first thing tomorrow. Get it all done." She looked at her son. "Listen, don't you say nothing to nobody. You weren't there—didn't see nothing—you understand me?"

"Yes, ma'am."

"Go on back there. Clean yourself up."

She took a cigarette from the pack on the table and noticed Harold had not moved.

"You heard me. Get to it."

He stood up, but still did not do as he was told. Instead, he went into his bedroom and laid in bed. He thought of many scenarios—alternatives for his father's demise. He knew that if he had left the closet, he would have joined his father on the rope; but his present pain made the idea bearable, preferable even. His thoughts ran rampant all evening and hindered his sleep.

Days later, a crowd gathered at the cemetery after a somber funeral service in a Birmingham church. Jeremiah's body was mostly intact, so many walked past the open casket to offer their final goodbyes before it was lowered into the ground. As they paraded around the wooden box and back to their vehicles, two police cars pulled into the lot. Four uniformed officers stepped out and gathered near the hood.

"What they here for?" a woman asked.

"Can't go nowhere without them showing up," another answered. "Not even to bury the dead."

Soon, the casket was closed shut and was lowered into the freshly dug earth. Sula and Harold were the last to leave the grave, but others were scattered here and there.

Sula reached beneath her black, lace veil and wiped her face with a small handkerchief.

"Let's go," she said as she reached for her son's hand. "We're done here."

They watched their steps and respectfully maneuvered around the headstones. Those who were curious about the police presence stood by and waited to ensure everyone was safely on their way.

When Harold reached the end of the headstones, he raised his head. He looked curiously at the men in uniform, and quickly recognized them. Fear had stopped him in his tracks the day his father died. He made no attempt to save him, but Harold resisted the urge to feel the guilt fully. He opened his mouth, and "they did it" shot from his lips like a lightning bolt as he pointed. His words were loud enough for those nearby to hear and alerted two of the officers who had watched them at the grave.

Sula grabbed his shoulders and shook him. "Hush, foolish boy. Don't say another word."

"Is there a problem here?" one of the officers asked as he approached.

"No, sir," Sula responded. "Afternoon to you."

He looked to Harold. "And you, boy?"

"He's just fine," Sula assured him.

"I'm talking to the boy," he said. "You know me, child?"

Harold shook his head.

"You sure about that?"

The boy nodded.

"Sad what happened to your daddy. If I were you, son, I'd do what I could to hold on to mama kitty here." He smiled. "She's a pretty lady. Seems just as nice. Understand me?"

"Sure, he does. We'll be on our way now." Sula grabbed Harold's hand and yanked him through the lot. They rushed into a friend's car and climbed inside.

His mother slammed the door, and the driver pulled away. As soon as she was out of the officers' view, tears spouted from her eyes—more than they had all afternoon as they laid her husband to rest.

"What the hell were you thinking?" she screamed.

"I don't know. I'm sorry. But it was them. I swear. It was."

"Would you shut your mouth! I don't want to hear another word. Never say it again."

He cried. "I watched them beat daddy in the head. I saw his blood. And they was right there."

"You just don't listen—and probably won't until you're lying right next to your father."

"I don't care!"

Sula turned towards the backseat to look at her son. "And that's what makes us different. I want my life, but I can't want yours enough to keep your mouth shut. So, go ahead. Keep talking. Hopefully, when they're done with you, they'll leave behind something worth burying."

She turned back around and stared from the windshield the entire drive home.

Sula stood guard through the night with a baseball bat and a knife at her side. She could not sleep, so watched and listened for any movement in the yard. Behind the closed door, Harold also had a view of the yard from his bedroom window. The two remained awake beyond the early morning hours. The house was quiet, but Harold could hear his mother's sobs break up the silence.

With puffy, red eyes and pressure in his head, Harold dressed for a day at school and moved quickly towards the front door to make it there in time.

"Wait," his mother called. She held up a small paper bag. "Your lunch."

Harold walked into the kitchen and retrieved his ham and mustard sandwich and crème-filled cookies. "Thank you."

Sula grabbed him gently and pulled him in for a hug. "You be good. Get your lesson."

"Yes, ma'am. I will."

Harold knew the loss of his father had caused tremendous pain, so the tear that she quickly wiped away was easily understood.

He went to the front door and turned to his mother again.

"Bye," she whispered with the wave of a hand. And then he left.

Because of their exchange in the kitchen that morning, Harold was certain that all was forgiven, and that he would return home to his loving mother that afternoon.

He powered through the day on a salt grain of strength and made it back home to rest. The aroma of that evening's dinner did not greet him at the door as it normally had, but it did not matter. He was desperate for rest. Fully clothed, he climbed into bed and was soon asleep.

When he awoke, the sun took its final nod and disappeared into the west. Harold walked past his parents' quiet bedroom and into the living room. Empty—and so was the kitchen. His mother was not at home. She had not left a note or the evening's dinner as she had done in the past.

The fridge was bare, but he grabbed the only hot dog left in the package and two eggs from the half-dozen that remained. He chopped the meat into a hot pan, and then whisked the eggs on top of them until the dish was fully cooked.

He ate alone at the table and savored each bite of his meal. As he chewed, he noticed something strange. His mother's keys were on the placemat next to him. Suspicious, he shoved another forkful of the hotdog concoction into his mouth and went to his parents' bedroom. He flipped on the light switch as he chewed and looked around. Initially, nothing was out of place; but something nudged him to peek into the closet.

When Harold cracked it open, his father's clothes, mostly suits and ties, were as neatly organized as they always were. He looked further and saw that none of his mother's clothes were there. He yanked open each of her drawers in the chest, looked under the bed, checked the bathroom — all her things were gone.

Harold went into the living room and sat in his father's chair to connect the dots. Although he could not fully wrap his mind around her reason, he was certain his mother was gone.

Within days, a family friend put Harold Washington on a bus to Montgomery to live with his father's close friend. On occasion, he hummed the melody of Sam Cooke's song; but for him, change would not come soon enough. At the close of the "long, hot summer of 1967" 83 were dead, there were millions of dollars in damages throughout the states, and entire communities had been demolished. Yet, no one assessed the damage of young Harold's heart, nor counted his father among the dead. He blotted out the stain of the painful memory and, as a young man, became the Michael Dyer many would come to know as an impactful minister of the gospel.

CHAPTER THIRTEEN
NO RETREAT

EVERY major television network was interrupted to display the gruesome death scene in the American city. No one could estimate the number of people impacted, innocent or criminal. No one could stand still long enough to count them. They were too afraid to aid those who had not yet succumb to their injuries. And they would suffer most; to watch others step over them was as painful as their injuries.

Although most TAAR soldiers had shifted from rooftops, the media looped previously captured footage that displayed their involvement in the chaos that plagued the city. "Terrorists", "radicals", "extremists" spewed from the lips of news reporters. To them, the real culprit had been revealed, and all would be well if they were just "taken out", as one reporter suggested.

Police officers moved about the core. Some chose to help as many people hidden there as possible; others were driven by the thrill to find and execute the perpetrators. The scales were almost balanced with the number of officers represented on either side, but woe be unto those who encountered a trigger-happy officer who had recently received the green light to fire at will.

Mayor Oakley watched the scene from her home office in utter dismay. For a while, gunfire had almost ceased completely, but had since become more rampant than at the onset of violence.

"What the hell are they doing?" she said.

The mayor stood from the ottoman and walked closer to the television screen; but even there, it was still impossible to determine who was responsible for the steady streams of gunfire. One thing was for sure; bullets that exploded on impact was nothing less than an automatic grenade launcher—the kind used by the National Guard.

"Hand me the phone," she ordered her assistant.

After dialing, she pressed the phone to her ear and waited. When there was no answer, she ended the call and dialed again.

"Hello?" steamed from her lips.

"What do you have for us, Sharon?" Governor Spalding responded.

"A better question is: what have you done? Did you order the National Guard to use this amount of force? What I'm watching has to be a scene from Vietnam. Unreal."

"Yes. It's very real," he said casually. "I did whatever I could to regain control."

"But it's not what we discussed."

"The National Guard moves by my power, not yours. I gave you time to end it. If I don't take charge, it would also be out of *my* hands, and I won't stand for it."

"We were doing just that."

"And how many arrests have you made of real perpetrators?"

She paced the floor. "It's not arrests you want. With this strategy, you want body bags."

"That would suffice as well. Listen, this keeps going if there is no surrender, or if they're not cut off. Get with it! There is no way you can stand behind terrorists as an officer of this state."

"That's not who I'm defending. You can't deny there are innocent people down there, and there are real bullets being fired at them. How the hell can officers tell them apart?

Some are hiding because they're afraid to come out. Not because they're terrorists. Tell me: how could anyone tell one from the other?" She pleaded like Abraham for Sodom and Gomorrah.

"Well, I guess the dust may have to settle first."

"Wow." Flustered, Mayor Oakley did the most unlikely thing—struggled to find her words.

"We're putting out fires all over this state in response to what's going on there. Even with state-wide curfews in place, we're responding to arson, vandalism, and looting at a rate we did not expect." He paused. "We're geared up for a fight that will make news anchors resign before they describe horror they see on screen. Believe me. Either they'll surrender or be shot down—unless they've prayed for God's angels to protect them. It's done. There will be peace."

Mayor Oakley halted her movements and spoke slowly. "When it's all said and done—when they find out you had the power to help but senselessly murdered their loved ones instead—there will never again be peace."

"History has shown that the threat of 'no peace' is nothing more than a fruitless war cry that's quickly extinguished when the fire's been put out. Just call me the fire chief."

Mayor Oakley imagined the loss of innocent people—executed without cause—and delivered her final plea. "Governor, there has to be another way."

"This isn't high school, Sharon. You can't submit your solutions past the deadline—if you even have one to give. It's over. In front of your TV screen is the safest place for you right now. Had those imbeciles known as much, and not shown up for a pointless protest, we wouldn't be in this mess."

"Those people had the right to assemble—understand it or not. I hope you can wrap your head around this little nugget of truth: the people will hear every word you've said. We'll let them decide the fate of your future even if it costs my own. Extinguish that, Chief. Goodbye."

"What? Hello?"

Mayor Oakley ended the recorded call without another word. Her plan to expose the man in the governor's seat could possibly make an impact but was not an immediate solution to spare innocent lives. There was no *win* in the cards for her, or those who would soon experience great loss.

* * *

THE local news station was on mute to give his ears a much-needed break, but Bishop Dyer watched intensely. Each hour, the developments were increasingly devastating, and to Bishop, it was not because many were left dead. It was the fact that the work of TAAR had gone mostly unacknowledged. The monster appeared yet remained faceless.

He waited for reporters to recognize the unsightly revolution sprawled across the nation's front lawn, but it was not as apparent as he intended. The organization had no spokesperson, no voice to guide the people's thoughts, or deliver an "aha!" when the message eluded the masses. Instead, TAAR's presence merely perpetuated prejudices they carried as Blacks in America—violent, animalistic, unworthy of empathy—but it was not yet over, so Bishop Dyer remained hopeful.

The sanctuary buzzed with both celebration and worry as people continued to sprinkle in and escape the nearby madness. Nearly 400 bodies were in the room. Weary lips spoke of deadly adventure from their chairs, or they lie on the floor for rest, or paced around and worried for lost loved ones. For most, safety was the most precious gift afforded to them, but others grew more concerned about what was to come. Their present conflict offered no warning before it rushed in with the power of a thousand tsunamis and took them unaware; and there was no end in sight.

Bishop Dyer's men busied themselves with their guests, so when a woman lingered on the executive hall, she easily slipped past them and towards Bishop's door. She knocked.

"Yes?" he called from within his office.

He heard a woman's voice speak from the other side.

"Bishop, I want to say thank you. Thank you for opening your doors to us." The haggard, middle-aged woman pressed her ear to the door for his response. She could barely hear over her own wheezing, brought on by smoke that polluted the core.

The gesture took him by surprise, and he responded with, "However I can help, Miss. God bless you." And then he returned his attention to the caption at the bottom of the television screen.

"You see, that's just it. I was wondering," she stalled, "if you can pray for me—I mean, for us. I lost my son in all the confusion. He's 23 years old. I don't know much about prayer, but I heard you had a way of getting God's attention. There are others out here—all in need of comfort."

Bishop Dyer was so consumed by TAAR's false persona that he lost sight of his role as a well-respected religious figure—or perhaps, he no longer believed that he was. Nothing within him desired to leave his office, but the future was saturated with too many "what ifs" to stand at the kerosene-soaked bridge with a lit match.

He pressed the power button on the remote and opened the door. She was thin, and just as tall as Bishop, but her voice—shrunken by fear—made him assume she was much smaller in stature. Her skin was dark with soot, and the stench of dried urine and perspiration expanded a 3-foot radius in the hallway. Bishop knew people were in the building, but he had not seen one up close.

"I don't mean to bother," she said and, conscious of the smell, took a step backwards.

"No-no. It's okay." He clasped her hands within his. "What else would I be good for if not the work of the Lord?" he said.

The woman was immediately comforted. "Will you come into the sanctuary?"

"I will, but I'll pray for you right here first. The courage to knock on a strange man's door for prayer should have its reward."

"I don't think you're strange," she wheezed. "We just never met before now."

"Precisely. You have no clue who I am."

She smirked. "Thank you."

"Agree with me," Bishop began. "Heavenly Father: Many are broken. Many are without answers. Many are powerless. But we come to you, God, our source of strength, our healer, the One with all answers and power in His hands, and we declare that the victory is already ours, that our hearts are mended, and that we are reunited with the lost. Touch this sister's body right now. I speak to her lungs and her airways, and I demand them to be cleared in Jesus' name. Hold up her head. Bring her comfort and peace as she waits with patience for her son's return and trusts that all is made well through you. In the mighty name of Jesus, we pray. Amen."

"Amen. Thank you, again."

"Glory be to God. Go and rest in the sanctuary. I will come see about the others."

"Yes. Okay." She nodded and went away.

After he changed into a less-wrinkled shirt, Bishop Dyer walked into the sanctuary for the first time in two days. The air was foul, and the people were scattered—high, low, seated, standing, stretched out, stoic, or unable to keep still. He was not accustomed to such disarray in the house of worship but remembered that ministry leaders were not on duty.

One of his men, Sam, saw the bishop walk deeper into the sanctuary, and immediately went to his side.

"Bishop, what's going on? What you doing down here? Something you need?"

"Didn't take my office for a prison. My name is on the deed. I'm just moving about."

"It's not what I meant. This place is chaos. It isn't necessary for you to be down here. If you need something, one of us can bring it for you."

"No. This is where I should be."

Bishop walked the floor and prayed under his breath like a lion amongst a devastated pride and touched those he passed. Some would stall him, and cause him to pray longer if they stood, lifted their hands, and prayed aloud with him. When others noticed the commotion in the room, they made a beeline for the prayer section.

He was amongst only four others whose attire was intact, and who did not reek of bodily fluids, so his presence alone encouraged them. Yet, it was not enough to satisfy their severe hunger, or remedy the ongoing tragedy they faced.

When he reached the front of the church, he took the seven steps up to the pulpit and grabbed the microphone. Once in his Sunday-sermon stance, Patrick rushed over to the sound booth and fired it up. However, Bishop did not reach for the metal frames beneath the podium as he always had before he ministered to the people of God.

"God is still good," he said. "The goodness of God is not determined by our condition. He is, and always will be, a great God. I won't preach to you. That's not what you're here for. Some of you may not have ever been inside a church before today. I'm not here to be your pastor, but to reassure you that all is well.

"You wonder how I could stand here and declare that everything is okay when it appears to be a war zone right outside these doors. Hear me. God don't make mistakes. He reveals possibilities when you see dead ends—can help you tap into joy in the midst of your pain. He's a great God."

A few hands applauded Bishop's message, but exhaustion and a lack of hope weighed heavily on them.

"I can see it in your faces. You believe we've reached the end of time. And I can't deny that we've reached the end of something—if it be life or an old way of living, something must perish."

There was an obvious shift. People adjusted in their chairs and stared. Just as blank were the properly positioned cameras within the room that were not powered on—its vision cut off.

"Why are we so afraid? We were conditioned to fear the most predictable promise we all possess—death. Two things we have in common is that we are marked by a date of birth and will all transition on our day of death.

"So, why are we afraid? Has anyone come back to tell you how hard it is on the other side? Let go."

Bishop Dyer rambled another ten minutes about how a surrender to death would free people from fear. Though his presentation was ominous, Bishop Dyer had the conviction of the three Hebrew boys. In this instance, King Nebuchadnezzar's image was America; Bishop Dyer refused to worship it and stood firm in his beliefs. It made little sense to those who barely survived the ordeal downtown and was not expected from the mouth of such a prominent pastor. He had packaged hope so nicely but failed to deliver with his words. If they had been first-time visitors of the ministry, it was not likely any of them would ever return. That was fine with Bishop Dyer; he was more focused on his plan to never let them leave.

* * *

THOSE who remained in the core were safe if they came from their hideouts and ran speedily with raised arms to nearby officers who would shuttle them away from the scene. However, for every person lured into the open by a spray of bullets or explosions, three others were trapped, injured, or gave up the ghost. Tragically, the ill-fated souls fell victim to the absence of a real method to rescue them. The governor's orders were a costly scare tactic that had no end, and no one could guess how many would die before it was all over.

Some held their positions within high rises if they had been fortunate enough to gain access to them and escape the madness. On the edge of the conflict, others fell, jumped from or was shoved from short viaducts that meant the difference between death and freedom. Some remained hidden in alleyways and old vestiges that, even with the sun's radiance, were shadowy and grim. The fearsome glow of their eyes pierced the darkness.

Valerie yelled for people to surface as she moved from building to building, but they were not her focus. Monika had slipped easily from her grip, and her ego wrestled with all the niceties and extensions of grace she offered her. Somehow,

Valerie's duty to uphold the law and protect American citizens was overshadowed by empathy for a desperate people who would fight to the death for their cause. However, the Valerie that emerged from the Liberty Centre was without her gloves of compassion; her knuckles were bare, and she was ready for a fight—one that would prove her position of power. And she was eager to release her fury on Monika.

"Everybody out!" she yelled as she sprang past a short alleyway where several were concealed behind dumpsters.

"Get your hands up and move!" she ordered loudly and pointed her weapon. At once, they all went towards her, hands raised. "Head out! Let's go! To the right! Move it!"

She ordered them with her words, but kept her eyes peeled for her target.

A group of eight decided to make a collective run for safety, and startled Valerie as they flew from beneath a breezeway that connected two buildings.

"Put your hands up and move!"

As they paraded by, two men dressed in black captured her attention. On a quiet side-street, the men raised the metal gate of an abandoned garage and ducked down to crawl inside. Valerie ran full speed to catch up to them before they vanished; and like a true limbo champion, she contorted her body to fit beneath the barely opened gate.

"Police! Freeze! Throw down your weapons and get your hands up now."

The men were barely visible in the shadows of the cool structure. They turned slowly but held tight to their weapons. The garage was void an alternate exit. Valerie stood unflinchingly between them and freedom.

"I won't tell you again." Rage rose within her. "I said 'now'!"

With the evacuation underway, the soldiers' plan was to wait it out in the darkness of the dilapidated garage until they could transition to the next phase and avoid detection. It could no longer work. The only way out was through Valerie. One of the men took a deep breath and charged towards her; he hoped to intimidate her to move. The plan was flawed.

Valerie shot him instead—twice in the leg. Her only mercy was to not aim directly at his head.

His partner watched with a gaze of compassion as he fell and squealed in pain.

"Don't move!" Valerie warned.

He ignored her command and stepped in her direction with his pistol at his side.

"I said 'stop'!"

He refused, and approached with the common countenance of man, but with zombie-like persistence. Valerie fired again, and a bullet caught him in the shoulder. His response was minimal. He could not be provoked. He did not raise his gun to Valerie. The soldier kept it at his side as he drew near his partner. The officer thought to fire again but did not sense any threat; yet she was incredibly angered by his defiance.

Their movements were unnaturally controlled. The pair was completely detached from reality, but not each other. The man moved casually towards his partner, who sat upright on the ground, and slightly extended the arm that carried his weapon. Before Valerie could grasp what would happen, he fired a single shot into his partner's head, and then placed the smoking barrel between his teeth and pulled the trigger.

As his body collided with the pavement, so did Valerie's. She had no strength to stand, to think, to move, to process whatever created the level of loyalty the men and women in their organization possessed. She thought of rogue groups that existed before; highly structured, militant activists who consistently walked their talk; bigots who terrorized others for over a century, and none of her knowledge could compare to what she witnessed in that moment.

Valerie searched herself. She wondered if their sacrifice was worth what they petitioned for and was disappointed at the audacity of her reflection. Was she black enough? Compassionate enough? Brave enough to bear the bloodline of those who died to prove their worth to a society that undervalued them?

Her days were long, and everything within her had been spent. There was nothing left, and she went numb.

* * *

THE streets started to clear, but the sound of gunfire remained. There was but one place in the core where Monika would feel safe enough to take refuge—the basement of her father's old church.

She was right. No one was there. The space was cluttered with clothes left by TAAR soldiers who changed quickly to report to duty. Their cubbyholes were mostly emptied of its contents, and there was not a single sound—not the tug of boot strings or the cock-back of pistols. It was bare.

Monika searched for weapons left behind or stashed away but had no luck. The arsenal that would enable her to fight was as depleted as the energy she had to do so. At minimum, she would gather bullets for the gun she still carried. After she tossed a few boxes around, she went for her own—the one marked "18".

She flung the garment she wore nights before onto the floor. Unlike the others, she had neatly folded it and placed it inside the box, but thoughtfulness no longer mattered. She reached inside and removed a small, plastic container.

Monika shoved a pile of clothes and mismatched shoes onto the floor and took a seat on the bench. She opened the box, and her eyes beamed when she spotted a fresh gun clip on the very top. As she removed it, she heard a *clank*. Monika pushed aside the gold bangle she wore to the ball; it had collided with the never-forgotten medallion Jabari gave her years before.

As if the piece were poison, Monika did not touch it, but examined it within the box. She was reminded that he was no longer there. Protocol was for TAAR partners to avoid separation at all costs. Cuffs or grave, they were in it until the end; but nothing prepared Monika for what would become of Jabari. The chance to go down with her partner escaped her, and she sought comfort for each question she knew would never be answered. As much as she could assume, Jabari entered the building to rescue his family, and they were all dead. The pill did not go down well and was lodged in her shrunken throat.

For TAAR, surrender was death. The chance of survival once activated was zero. Although they remained ready to battle the enemy, none of them hoped it would happen. There would be no jail time. Historically, a plea "for less" would require the captured to expose others, and result in long years of enslavement. It was a fight to the death, or death to end the fight, but nothing else.

Monika pulled her weapon from the holster and laid the box aside. It was time she faced the reality of her situation and finally surrendered. Beyond sorrow, she was angry. There was no solution, resolve, or closure to any aspect of her life, yet she took a final bow and was prepared to make her exit.

She wrapped her hands around the steel and pulled it close to her; they bonded. The ducts of her eyes were overused, emptied, and drought made them unfruitful. Monika pressed the gun against her scalp and counted her breaths quietly. The third would be her last.

"Two," she counted in her head as her chest expanded.

She released the breath slowly but had not made it clear if she would pull the trigger as she inhaled or exhaled. "Exhale," she thought. "Three."

Suddenly, the sound of a metal box and dozens of tools clattered against the floor and distracted her. Monika aimed the gun in the sound's direction and stood up.

It was 42, and he was also alone.

"Don't shoot. It's me," he said.

Monika lowered the gun. "If you came looking for weapons, you won't find any."

"No. Told my partner to meet me here."

"There's no one but me."

"Where is your partner?"

Monika hesitated. "I can't say for sure."

"Wherever he is, find him quick and get to the church."

"Why?"

"We got word they're bringing in more enforcement. Ready to shoot anything that moves at this point."

"Okay." Monika holstered her weapon.

"Walk north—twelve blocks. Someone will be there." He walked out as abruptly as he had entered.

The interruption gave Monika hope—and life altogether. She was not what many would call a devout Christian; her father had strangled every breath from her beliefs, but she believed in God. She still had her head— certain it was Divine intervention, a clear message from the Holy One. Alive and grateful, Monika still could not know how long the delight would last.

CHAPTER FOURTEEN
THE CRY FOR PEACE

PROTESTS that swept across the nation raised eyebrows and provoked the media and political leaders to speak out against the aggressive measure officers took to gain control. Videos surfaced that displayed their use of batons, rubber bullets, and tear gas and was met with outrage. It fanned the embers of fear that conditions would worsen before they improved.

As people expressed their constitutional right to assemble, citizens demanded their safety, and called for the brutal response to end. However, conflict of that caliber had never been seen, and pepper spray would prove ineffective to gain control over semi-automatic weapons in the hands of crazed civilians. It was no longer a protest; an outright war was underway. Methods that were once viewed in a harsh light paled in comparison to the officers' current measure of force.

The 5 o'clock news gave viewers a front row seat to the fight—Wolves against Blacks, TAAR against Wolves, police against everyone—as drones consistently flew overhead. Persistent.

The freedom to fire at will enabled officers to approach without confidence of a person's innocence or desire to surrender, and many were immediately shot—sometimes with rubber, sometimes steel. The behavior caused them to reassess the risk. Although law enforcement was not initially a threat to innocent protestors, they would later become a promise of death.

Police made over 300 arrests throughout the city since the onset of violence. Most of the apprehended were locals who violated curfew or were caught looting; but those captured in the core were not easily labelled agitators, or innocent. It remained impossible to tell them apart. So, it was the threat perceived by officers that signaled a suitable, or unsuitable, response.

Sleep spread as thin as melted butter on warm toast, Mayor Oakley was seemingly strapped to the television screen. Her fury over the officers' actions, or isolation from higher-ups, was not as disheartening as the community's ability to bear witness to it all.

Her channel toggled between local and national coverage of the scene downtown, Desmond and Dante Jones' mother's pleas to end the violence, and the public's rebuke of her ex-husband's actions—which they believed fed the beast of continued calamity.

When she switched back to the national network, Mayor Oakley was surprised to see the governor's face. His home-office bookshelf was the backdrop of the remote interview.

She raised the volume.

"Governor Spalding, can you tell the public about a proposed process as you endeavor to end the fighting in downtown Atlanta?" the young, Black anchor petitioned.

"Honestly, the process has been revised numerous times since our initial response. As of now, we want to make sure American citizens are safe, and officers, firefighters, and volunteers return home to their families."

"Can you tell us how many officers have been wounded or killed at this point?"

"We don't have those numbers as of right now."

The anchor nodded and glanced down at the desk before he responded. "Sources in nearby hospitals and those very close to the deadliest zones have reported that officers are not being treated for injuries. It appears they are not being injured. Is that true?"

"I can't say what's happening in that area. What I *can* say is that even if they are not the target, their lives are still at risk when as they put out fires or rescue people who are trapped in them. Regardless, a bullet doesn't bear a name."

"What's clearer is the number of people we see being shot by officers."

Footage from the frontlines was displayed on a split-screen next to the governor.

"We're dealing with terrorists here. Those who refuse to follow orders, or surrender, pose a great threat."

"It appears law enforcement is more of a threat than the men and women shown here."

"That's not the case."

"Listen, I don't condone any act that result in the death—especially of those who've sworn to serve within or beyond this country. That said, we must consider all options to minimize the number of casualties amongst these innocent protestors as well."

"Who's to say these people are innocent? They are given one specific order: to come out with their hands up."

"I'm sure these people have endured the most dreadful three days of their lives—possibly in shock as they trample over each other to get to a line of officers that are literally gunning for them. In essence, you're telling them to remain hidden."

"No, I must correct you. These officers preserve the lives of innocent citizens."

"You mean, the citizens not presently hiding downtown—those who didn't attend the protest? Wouldn't it show the American public that silence and inaction, neglecting their First Amendment rights, are the prerequisite for protection by law enforcement?"

Mayor Oakley, arms folded snug across her chest, whispered from her position near the television, "That's exactly what he's saying."

"No," the governor responded. "It is every citizen's duty to ensure that our nation moves peaceably forward. Protests, though permitted, have been counterproductive with upholding that obligation."

"And they deserve to be shot?"

"No. They must understand that our nation has zero tolerance for terrorism, and the unfortunate truth is that their decision to participate in the protest landed them exactly where they are. Let's not forget that I also gave orders to move them out of the core."

Mayor Oakley was appalled by the lie.

"So, your initial plan was to evacuate them?"

"Yes."

The mayor's head shook in disbelief.

The reporter continued, "We have footage as they were loaded onto vans and busses and taken to the now overcrowded safe zone. At that point, we hoped to see the end of it, but that's not the case."

"Exactly. We received intel that the shooters we observed firing from rooftops are a part of a terrorist organization."

"The ones dressed in black?"

"Yes."

"They're all Black as well. Correct?"

Spalding swallowed the saliva in his mouth. "Unfortunately, which made it difficult to tell them apart when rescue efforts began."

"So, they would apprehend perpetrators before they were transported to safety?"

"Yes."

The reporter's forehead tightened. "It still does not justify the amount of force being used against people who have not proven to have any involvement beyond their participation at the protest."

Mayor Oakley cringed as she observed the governor's flawed response to the questions.

"My thoughts and prayers go out to each of them, but what's beyond the camera's view are those who are on foot, armed, and continue to terrorize these people."

"Let me ask you this: How would you assess Mayor Oakley's ability to control the violence in her city? How much has she weighed in on the measures taken to restore order?"

"The mayor has consistently been a part of the conversation and plans for peace. None of us have the experience to deescalate an event as catastrophic as this. Considering, she's done a pretty stand-up job."

More lies. The truth was at the press of a button, and Mayor Oakley's only dilemma was which finger to use. Governor Sterling's public praises of the mayor went unbroken long enough for producers to prepare her call-in, and to connect her to the interview in progress.

The anchor pressed his earpiece and listened intently. "I'm sorry—one moment Governor Spalding. It seems Mayor Sharon Oakley has been added to this interview. There should be audio, if I'm not mistaken. Mayor Oakley? Are you there?"

The governor sat back in his chair and commenced the most impeccable poker face.

"I am," she said.

"Obviously, you've been viewing the governor's response. Tell us, where do you believe this is all going? Will we see the end of it soon?"

"That is definitely my prayer, but it's not why I called in."

The reporter was puzzled. "Then why did you?"

Governor Spalding interjected, "What's most important right now, Sharon—Mayor Oakley—is that we put the people at ease by giving them the facts."

"And that's the exact opposite of what you're doing. First, I have not been in on the conversation between the governor and President Couper. I was not aware of the order to descend upon innocent people until officers were in place and bombs were already exploding."

"We took the mayor's initial tactics into consideration. We did," Governor Spalding said in his defense.

"Don't interrupt me. You've had enough time to lie to the people."

He continued anyway, "As I was saying, it was slow and did not respond on a scale such heinous, criminal acts warranted."

"What was that plan exactly?" the interviewer asked.

"The part about sending in vehicles to pick these people up and take them to safety," the Governor admitted.

"So, that was *your* doing, Mayor?"

She clapped her hands together dramatically. "Kudos for one truth, Governor. Yes, it was. But he conveniently fell short of saying that there is law enforcement in the safe zone. It is completely enclosed and guarded by over 100 officers. Every exit point is manned by police and Guardsmen. No one is able to leave. Our plan was to identify individuals who are part of this disruption, or who could be a potential threat, *before* they are released into the public. In no way are these people just free to go home and cannot easily disappear. They are secured from pick-up to drop-off, and while in holding."

"Wow," the reporter responded, "We have video of the scene at the safe zone. Take us there now."

Drone footage of thousands rescued from the core and seated in the old Turner Field popped up on the screen.

Mayor Oakley continued, "These people are frisked at pick-up and monitored in the stadium. What's most ironic is that anyone who would have conspired in any way to carry out these acts would naturally resist the drop-off, but they all went willingly, and there has been no report of violence on any level in the safe zone. They're provided with food and medical attention as they wait this out."

"Well, this is my point exactly," Spalding added. "Those who remain in the core are more likely to have had a hand in the attack. It more than justifies our need to push in, and the amount of force we must use."

The reporter said, "What we see unfolding is quite reminiscent of Waco and the Branch Davidians who were killed by federal agents in the 90s."

Mayor Oakley huffed. "However, that siege lasted 6 weeks; the governor here barely allowed 6 hours to get innocent protestors out of harm's way and identify the actual agitators before he moved to destroy them all."

"These are not agitators. They're murderers. And there is no representative to discuss these people's intent. As much as we'd like to think we're superheroes, there is no language that can stop a moving bullet, and that has been their only means of communication. There's no way possible to better understand what we're up against, and why we're up against it. And that is completely unlike the Branch Davidians in Waco who had an incredibly vocal David Koresh; and who, might I add, was *not* shooting American civilians. This is terrorism, not an isolated raid."

"But it still begs the question: how to know who's who, Governor?" the correspondent asked.

Mayor Oakley boldly interrupted. "I'll tell you. Actually, I'll let him speak for himself."

"Who's that?"

"The beloved governor."

"Sharon, that's unnecessary and you know it," Spalding said.

Without warning, the audio of her conversation with the governor was heard through every television tuned to the interview. The anchor listened intently to the conversation, and when it ended, he looked to the monitor for the governor's response.

"Any words, Governor?" he asked.

"Why would there be?"

"For one, the notion of smoke clearing before you can assess the amount of damage caused by your decision to push in and use deadly force."

"What's taking place in Atlanta is a direct threat to national security. As a result, minimal force won't do. What the American public wants is smoke and mirrors, but that's not what the men and women in uniform see every day. There is no illusion. Bullets are real. The stench of a decaying body is real. Most people will never experience either—and would never choose to. How can I tell officers to enter peacefully with clubs and pepper spray when hundreds of bodies are already in the street? Would *you* do it?"

"Sir, what we need to understand is…"

"Answer the question: would you risk *your* life to help these people, carrying pepper spray and a nightstick, after you've seen the bodies?" There was silence. "I thought so. I stand on my decision to protect these men and women, and to lead the state of Georgia back to a place of peace by any means."

"At the expense of innocent lives, Governor?" Mayor Oakley asked.

"Come on! Are officers not just as innocent?"

"Innocent, but under oath. They entered the force with full understanding of the risks involved—the possibility that they may someday face injury or death."

"So, their lives should matter less?" he snapped back.

"No, but self-preservation should not drive their actions."

"It is impossible to completely defy the first law of nature."

"Then why take the oath if it means that when a situation escalates beyond the ability to ensure safety on both sides, it's civilians who face a tragic end more than the officers meant to protect them? Make sense of that," she said.

"If you think about it, that argument landed us in this very position—and not just the threat of danger sensed by officers, but their need to preserve their own lives above others," the anchor clarified. "The situation perpetuates the Black perspective of officers who consistently resort to violence for a quick solution to altercations that involve them. I must say, if it was not evident before, it's crystal clear now."

"Exactly," the mayor co-signed.

"Governor, can you share with viewers what they can expect to happen next? It's hard to imagine the conflict becoming worse than it is; but honestly, how much worse can it get down there?"

"It's not just Atlanta. This nation is in a state of emergency. With all the violence and looting springing up across the American landscape, the National Guard is spread thin. President Couper could potentially deploy the U.S. military. I cannot speak on what happens at that point. Just pray we can bring it to an end before it escalates."

∗ ∗ ∗

CONDITIONS had not improved the slightest in the seat of turmoil. While many experienced it through the combined pixels of their devices, others feared imminent death that could come from any direction. There was no time to consider government—its decisions, fairness or policies. Strategies for survival extinguished all other thoughts; and without a true sense of direction, all that remained were plumes of panic and desperation. Not even the fittest could survive—even a wrong turn could prove fatal.

Amara, trapped between slow-moving traffic and consistent gunfire, crouched behind a city bus stop with her children. She was excited to see the red Pegasus of a popular fuel station, but joy faded quickly when she saw smoke rise from the rubble where the store once stood.

The children were feverish. Their eyes were barely open, and their mouths were dry with crusty, peeled lips. Amara drew James closer to her, and his body flailed like a ragdoll pulled violently from a shelf. Hunger and exhaustion took its ugly toll. She hugged him and, like the ram caught in the thicket, she noticed a food mart amongst a line of other businesses across the street. People pushed against anyone in their way as they moved in and out of the looted store.

Amara pulled Shiloh close to her and looked at her children.

"Listen guys. We're going over here to see if there's food. Stay close to me."

Amara hobbled barefoot on the injured ankle as they shuffled across the street and attempted to break through the crowd without breaking their physical bond.

Completely ransacked, the convenience store was littered with broken glass and debris. Amara gripped both of her children's hands within one of hers as she sorted through the mess and took inventory of the consumables. Only liquor was fully stocked, and some household goods—laundry detergent, dish soap, toilet paper. Water, juice, and milk were all gone. There were no chips, pastries, nuts, crackers or bread. She continued her search for cookies, granola bars—anything to satiate the hunger. There was nothing more than crumbs and wrappers scattered along the polluted floor.

Amara noticed the small, deep freezer that was shoved to the rear of the store during the shuffle.

"Come on," she said to her children.

She paused when she noticed her reflection in the glass. Her makeup was mostly gone, smeared around her eyes. Discontent over her appearance took a backseat to the goldmine that opened to them. The freezer was at least half-full of melted treats—novelties overlooked by the famished crowd. Amara reached inside for the two pints of leftover ice cream—cookies and cream and plain vanilla—and ripped open the packages.

"Here." She placed a container before James' frowned face. "No spoon. Just drink it. It's like a milkshake."

Amara handed the other to Shiloh, who drank it down without hesitation, and then she turned to search for something for herself. A softened Neapolitan ice cream sandwich rested on top of the pile. With her love for variety, the treat had been a childhood favorite; but she knew she would not delight in its consumption as she had in the distant past.

Suddenly, the crowd shifted within the raided mini-mart, and most of them were gone. Their movements made Shiloh nervous, and she tugged on her mother's dingy dress.

"Let's go, Ma," she said.

Amara turned towards them as she opened the wrapper of the liquefied decadence, but did not notice the thinning crowd, the leveled commotion, or the crackle of gunfire that steadily approached.

"Okay. I have something. We can go."

The vigilant surveillance camera watched as she raised the molten goodness to her lips with swan-like elegance to suck down the sweet sustenance.

Suddenly, she heard a man yell, "Run!"

Before she could observe any need for caution, she heard a series of gunshots nearby. She dropped the ice cream, grabbed her children's hands, and made a run for the exit. She reached the entryway, and in an instant, an explosive was detonated within an attached storefront. The blast tossed Amara's body backwards. Her head bounced against an immovable, steel receptacle outside the store before her body hit the ground.

The force of the blast parted them, and Shiloh and James suffered numerous scratches, a few cuts made by specks of glass that pricked their skin—or remained and painfully protruded from their flesh—but they were alive. Upon first glance, that was more than what could be said for their mother whose posture resembled those they had seen from the 20th-floor window.

Shiloh's arm bled from glass that sliced through it. Her brother was far from her; and when she noticed, she was immediately distracted from the pain. When she approached him, she examined the wound on his forehead, the fresh lines carved across his cheek, and knuckles that had been scraped against the concrete and bled. His wails could not be contained.

"Shh. Shh. It's okay," Shiloh pacified him. "Don't cry."

Shiloh helped her brother over to where their mother remained motionless on the ground, and they were instantly elated to see that there was no blood or obvious injury. However, the iceberg of her injury rivaled Mount Everest beneath the surface.

Shiloh pulled the shredded red dress covered in smut over her mother's bare thighs. She nudged her mother as James cried incessantly at her side.

"Wake up," the girl said. "Get up." She grew discouraged by the moment. "Please," she whined.

Soon, Amara's fingers tapped against the harsh concrete and her eyes opened. She heard her son's cries, but he was a blur. Cheek against the pavement, she extended her arm and pat his shoulder to soothe him.

"Ma, come on. We have to leave," Shiloh said excitedly.

Amara gave a subtle nod to agree and slowly lifted herself, incredibly dizzy, from the ground. Dazed, she placed her hands against her head, and was barely in an upright position before she surrendered to her injuries and collapsed to the hard surface again.

* * *

AS the dust settled in the fiery core of chaos, officers combed through each building and sought out rooftop shooters to take into custody—but only if they were compliant enough to avoid a bullet. One by one, they ambushed pods of Wolves—still in position and armed, but mostly without ammunition. Their weapons had been their greatest threat, and many found themselves without it.

They were lured from their quiet caves with the officers' "it's over" declaration, and most of them believed it. However, there were others who saw their continued freedom as a sign to further the fight. Terror branched into new methods as they discovered ways to more evenly distribute devastation.

Unlike the people of TAAR, there was no specific attire that unified the Wolves. Some wore khakis or denim; some wore polo shirts, and others were in plain tees. There were several with tattoos or biker's jackets, and others with peace-making countenances that were as clean cut as Mike Brady. Without a weapon, or discovery in a surveilled area of gunfire, it was easy for them to slip into the crowd, escape on foot or onto one of many vehicles commissioned for "safe zone" drop-offs.

Valerie, ready to end her unconventional work shift and return home to rest, called for people to move out and head towards officers with raised hands. Steam diminished, her limbs rejected her will to move through the streets or raise her gun into the air. She passed each building and set her sights on the barricade where she expected to have relief.

As she walked, eyes peeled, she noticed commotion a few yards down a side street. At least a dozen protestors stepped onto a tan-colored van as a white man at the passenger door gestured for them to move quickly aboard. Someone ran past Valerie, and the wind of their swift strides brushed against her cheek. For those desiring to avoid officers, any means of transportation was as enticing as Jonah's whale when the biblical figure was tossed into the violent ocean.

"Everything alright over here?" Valerie asked the man.

"Yes, it is," he said eagerly.

"You're a volunteer?" she inquired.

"What does it look like, lady? Yes. We'll get them where they need to go."

Another person stepped onto the van as Valerie looked to the driver, another White man who stared straight ahead. "Okay," she said.

With each seat filled, the man attempted to roll the door shut, but Valerie's curiosity deepened. "Wait." She stopped him.

Three white men sat on the first row of the 15-passenger van and, like the driver, kept their eyes focused on the windshield. She examined them closely. Complexion was not all that set them apart from the vehicle's other passengers. In contrast to the heavily soiled, tattered clothes the Blacks wore after three days in various hideouts, these men were clean—shirts tucked, buttons attached, shoes tied.

"You three being picked up?"

Only one was emboldened to speak. "Yes."

"Been together this whole time?" she asked.

"Yes."

Valerie quickly raised her gun and backed away to ensure each of them was in range. "Get out now! On the ground!" she ordered.

Immediately, the unarmed man outside the van dropped to the floor, but his companions would not relent so gracefully. Valerie fired two shots into the front of the van and stopped the driver's movements, but a shot from one of the three passengers behind him struck Valerie's vest. She pushed through the burn as she landed on the ground and fired into the open door until all of her bullets were spent, and they were no longer a threat.

Officers had overlooked the Wolves who lured dozens of protestors to an abandoned warehouse beyond the border and executed them. Cunning, they successfully impersonated good Samaritans, and desperate men and women were eager to believe they had come to their rescue.

Valerie got back to her feet as the others poured hastily from the van and away from the scene. She pulled a magazine from her gear belt and loaded it into her gun.

"Get up!" she ordered the fifth man.

He stood just as he was told, and Valerie escorted him towards officers who waited two blocks ahead. Without handcuffs or zip ties, he marched with his hands behind his head. If he should deter an inch from the white line marked along the road, she promised to shoot. It was the closest she had come to the pack of hatemongers. Questions for the group stacked liked dominos, just as those she had set aside for the brown-skinned bunch.

"Who are you?" she asked from behind. "Your name—what is it?"

"Dustin."

Valerie sensed a lie. "How many others are there?" she continued.

"I don't know."

"Why not?"

"How could I know everything?"

"Then who's in charge?"

"Seriously? You won't find out that easily." He smirked. "Looks like someone has a little homework to do. But I hear niggers never been too fond of books."

He stumbled over a large, round piece of cement, uprooted from an explosion and tossed into the road. He extended his arms to avoid a fall. He quickly regained composure but did not relock his hands behind his head.

Valerie had a good chuckle. "God don't like ugly. Let's see what else comes down the pipe when you're rotting in prison."

"You will…" he started, but the sound of gunfire rang in Valerie's ears.

As the man went down, she saw the uniformed National Guardsman whose weapon remained pointed in her direction. She jogged over to the dark-skinned man who was shocked by her approach. She raised her gun to his face.

"Explain, officer. Now! What did you shoot him for?"

Another guardsman stepped closer to them from a position Valerie had not noticed.

"Shoot me, or get the hell out of my face," the shooter said with a calm gaze.

Sickened by the officer's actions, she contemplated the fulfillment of his wish and inched the gun close to his brow.

"Kemp!" a voice called out. Her superior officer approached quickly; gun raised. "Put it down."

The officer on the dreadful end of Valerie's gun spoke in a low tone, "It takes balls to pull the trigger, I know. Especially on someone who doesn't give a shit if you do."

She lowered her weapon and stepped back at Sergeant's orders. The officer who lurked nearby joined him. Her glistening wide eyes locked firmly on them.

Valerie whispered, "You're one of *them*."

The shooter smirked and the other officer gave him a friendly pat on the back. The men were partners, but their partnership extended the bounds of their commitment to the U.S. government.

Sergeant caught up to her and snatched the gun from her hand. "What's going on with you, Kemp?"

229

"But Serge, you don't understand," she contested.

"Now won't be the time to make me. Get back to the station. Now! And you better wait there. Don't make me look for you."

Valerie locked eyes with the shooter who took out the unarmed captive, and her understanding of the Black vigilante group expanded.

She backed away and watched her superior officer converse calmly with the guardsmen, and she pondered his possible involvement—but he was White. In an instant, she flashed to a history lesson from some forgotten source, and recalled the legacy of John Brown, the White abolitionist who led the raid in defense of Blacks and their freedom. He was ultimately hanged in 1859, but his daring deathblow to end slavery was the catalyst for the dawning Civil War. Each breadcrumb that fed Valerie's suspicions had already taken her by surprise and, if proven true, the Sergeant's participation would be no different.

Nonetheless, one thing was certain: those devoted to the cause made it clear that the threat of death was too weak to solicit a change in action; and it was obvious that the concept of imprisonment was far from mind. They were a breed of people Valerie would bear witness to for the first time as an officer of the law; and she hoped, for the sake of all, it would be her last. A pair, or a single soldier, with that level of commitment was enough; but there was possibly an entire army of them. No one wavered. No one surrendered. No one cared for anything beyond their cause—which was not fully understood.

CHAPTER FIFTEEN
UNWILLING TO BE RECONCILED

THE Wolves may have been taken into custody, or quietly surrendered and were shipped off on borrowed, yellow school busses, but the handmade bombs they left behind—a finale of sorts—boomed through downtown. The core purged itself of those who found asylum in its dark crevices, but at least 5,000 souls, severely wounded or too scared to surface, remained. Over 2,000 men and women had already perished from their injuries.

As violence in the core curved downward again, Monika began her twelve-block trek to vehicles that were arranged to transport TAAR fighters to the church. There were at least a hundred others who scurried nearby. She passed through the shadow of Liberty Centre, what remained of Fatima Shamoon, the rubble from the explosion where she last saw Jabari, her sister's vehicle with custom, white rims— stuck between two other vehicles In the road—and the memory of days past. If there was anything in her belly, it was enough to vomit.

Monika looked up at a traffic camera in the intersection as she passed. Once persecuted for its use, it faithfully captured lawbreakers, and judged them. Monika would not escape its grasp.

A random explosion forced her to quicken her pace and take cover on a cross street as her heart rate settled. Before Monika could move again, her phone rang.

"Daddy?" she answered.

"It's time to head this way," he said.

"I've been told, and I'm in transition."

"Good girl." He sighed. "Where is Amara? Still holed up in Liberty or did Jabari take her elsewhere?"

Monika hesitated to break the news to her father, so the call went quiet.

"Hello," Bishop Dyer said.

"Daddy, I don't know where she is."

"What do you mean?"

"She wasn't on 20 when I came down from the roof."

"Would Jabari know?"

"Maybe...if he was able to tell us."

"What do you mean?"

"There was an explosion. I saw him go inside. I also saw Amara's car, but she wasn't there—or the kids."

The tide had turned, and the other end was silent.

"Daddy?"

"Just get here as fast as you can."

Suddenly, Monika's phone powered off.

She moved towards the heavily guarded barrier where dozens of people waited for pardon into the promised land. Officers and medics pushed in and moved a block further into the core every half hour as the risk lessened. Emergency vehicles were still unable to break through cars scattered in the roadway. Rescues were made on foot. So, with time, they would significantly shorten the distance for the injured to receive assistance.

As Monika moved with the crowd—hands locked behind her head—she heard a single voice above the chatter, coupled with the wails of a child.

"Excuse me, Miss."

Initially, Monika ignored whoever it was that remained polite in the valley of Armageddon.

"Miss. Miss. Excuse me." The voice drew nearer.

Someone touched her, and Monika immediately turned to mush.

"Yes?" she said, nervously.

"They said you were injured. Why don't you step over here so that I can take a look at you," he said as others watched their interaction.

Initially, Monika wanted to deny the notion that she complained of ailments to anyone, but the man, dressed in EMT attire, nudged her towards a makeshift trauma unit.

"Don't worry. I'll take a look, and you should be fine," he spoke as they passed onlookers.

Once beneath the tent, the paramedic pulled a chair near and motioned for her to sit. He pulled out a metal box large enough to house two bowling balls and opened it up on the floor next to her as he kneeled. He gripped her right calf muscle and massaged it. Monika watched him curiously.

He checked their surroundings. "I need your gun," he said. "Drop it in the box."

Monika reached for the weapon concealed at her back.

"Careful," he said. "Put it in quietly."

She did as she was told, but the weapon clanked against the bottom of the box. They both looked to see if anyone heard.

"You wouldn't be able to get past the next checkpoint with it." He switched to her other leg and squeezed it gently. "They'll frisk you, but you're good. Look for the black van," he whispered.

"Got it."

He raised his voice loud enough for others to hear, and said, "You should be able to make it to the safe zone. Just take it easy, Miss."

Monika stood, and was on the move again. As promised, over thirty officers, heavily armed, created a second barrier. They patted, searched, and briefly questioned anyone wanting to pass through. She briefly locked eyes with an officer—black behind his mask—but broke her stare quickly. She knew eyes that lingered did not signify a planted ally.

She took another step. Her heart pounded as she approached an officer whose gloved hands were eager to frisk her, although she knew he would find nothing.

"You're good," he said when he was done.

The sound of the crying child rang in Monika's ears — an endless chime of bells. There were other voices; many wept, but the sound of the child's sobs resonated with Monika. It was special.

As she moved from the body search and towards an American Red Cross agent ready to record her name and contact information, she raised her head in meerkat manner and canvassed the area for the child. When she spotted him, others moved around him as if they were deaf and completely blind to the child. He was completely ignored. It was James — her nephew.

Monika turned swiftly to move opposite the crowd's direction. She drew suspicion.

"This way. Move this way, lady," the Red Cross representative called out. "Excuse me! You can't go back in there!"

Monika gave no attention to the woman's command.

The officer, whose eyes she had avoided, turned to see the disruption, and noticed Monika's backward movement.

"Turn around," he ordered.

"No." She attempted to pass him, but he shoved her back with his rifle.

"Turn around now!"

"That's my nephew over there. I just want to get to him. Now, get the hell out of my way." She shoved back. Monika's toughness was never attributed to a weapon she carried; she was bold without it.

The officer watched her jog desperately to the boy on the sidewalk.

"James! James!" she called frantically.

The children heard James' name through the commotion but could not place it. As the area cleared, Shiloh noticed her aunt. The girl could not move as quickly as she imagined she would but hobbled over to greet her. James' wails ceased at the sight of her.

"My God! Are you okay?" Monika asked when they embraced.

"She won't wake up." Shiloh pointed to her mother.

Monika sprang for her sister, who was motionless on the pavement and in a small pool of vomit. She examined her closely but was careful to touch. She placed an ear close to Amara's mouth and took inventory of her breaths. The tips of Monika's fingers moved gently along her sister's cheek.

"Come on now. Get up, Amara. Come on. Come on. Come on."

Amara did not budge.

"You have to wake up. Wake up!"

Monika's sense of loss had been premature. Now that she could feel the warmth of her sister's breath grace her ear and lay eyes upon her body, she was not ready to lose her. Amara's condition could not rival Monika's faith that improvement was at hand. The children watched their aunt struggle to bring their mother back to life; and the absence of tears would denote their hope in her ability to do so.

"Somebody help me! Help me!" Monika shouted, but help was already on the way.

The aggressive officer had already alerted the medic who confiscated her gun, and within seconds, they were both at her side. To Monika, their alliance was clear.

"I got her," the medic said.

He checked Amara's airway, crossed her legs at the ankle, and supported her head as the officer helped to maneuver her onto her belly. The medic tilted her head back to improve the airway.

"She'll need a hospital."

The armed officer raised a dense eyebrow to Monika before he hurried back to his post. And after a minute, Amara faintly opened her eyes, and mumbled. Her children gasped in relief, but Monika's response could not be articulated by words or actions.

"Welcome back," the EMT said to Amara, and then spoke candidly to her sister. "Listen, she needs immediate attention. We can't get a vehicle beyond the checkpoint. I'll have to help you to the van. Only a handful has passed this way all day, so I'm sure it's there."

Monika was distracted from her sister's condition by the man's statement.

"Where's everyone else?" she asked.

He did not respond with words, but offered a slow, backwards nod until his chin jut far from his throat. It was not a good sign, and almost impossible to know how many, or which of them, were left.

"Let's get her up," he said.

They lifted Amara from the ground and draped her limp arms across their shoulders.

"Come on, kids," Monika called.

Shiloh helped her brother to his feet, took his hand in hers, and followed slowly behind.

"Where we going?" Amara spoke faintly as her head drooped close to Monika's.

"We're taking you to the hospital," she said.

"Good," she whispered. "The kids—where are they?"

Monika turned to see. "They're right here. Don't worry. They're fine."

"Okay." Amara's head flopped to the other side.

The officer commanded the crowd to clear as Monika and the kids passed through with Amara. "Move aside people."

Once they were through, the severity of Amara's injuries enabled them to bypass agents with clipboards and walk another hundred feet to the parked van. They laid Amara across the front row of seats, and the children climbed in behind them.

"You got it from here," the medic said, and closed the door shut.

"Take us to the closest hospital," Monika told the driver.

"It's a zoo in there. It's a task getting through the parking lot," the husky driver responded.

"We don't have a choice. We have to try."

He looked at Monika curiously from the rearview mirror and spoke at a slow pace. "We've been told to get to the church."

"Yes, I know."

He was cautious with his words. "You know — the next phase."

"So, what?" Monika retorted.

"Maybe we should head straight there. A hospital can't mean much now."

Monika looked at her sister whose eyes were delicately closed.

"Get us to the hospital." Monika said with undying compassion, "She's not one of us."

"I'm on it."

Monika watched her sister fade in and out of consciousness. It was the most helpless Amara had ever been, and her condition caused something to break within Monika. There were no snappy comebacks, or finger-wagging, neck-rolling sass to light up the commute — just quiet acceptance of what was.

The stench of Amara's vomit overtook the entire van and was a pest to Monika's nostrils. Amara's hair was matted together with puke glue and dangled stiffly near her chest. Monika lifted the hair and pulled it into a knot, but the odor remained. She tugged a little more and noticed that her sister's wig was easy to remove, so she did, and tossed it from the passenger-side window. She sat next to her sister, loosened the braids that were tucked beneath the wig, and combed through the lovely, natural strands with her fingers while her sister rested.

With numerous barricades, cars that cluttered the streets, and pedestrians who escaped the core on foot, the van was forced to travel at the steady pace of an outdated riding mower. The four-mile distance could easily take over a half hour, and Amara had already slept through half of it when she came to again. The children slept peacefully in the back. Even Monika had drifted off in the serenity of safety until she felt something brush against her arm. She lurched forward.

"It's me," Amara said.

Relieved, Monika sat back again. "Try to relax. We should be at the hospital soon."

"Where's Jabari?"

Monika was ill-prepared to respond. "What?"

"He still there?"

"I can't say for sure."

Amara tried to sit up.

"You should really relax."

"How do you not know?" She paused.

"I don't know, Amara. Now lay back."

She placed her head against the seat's itchy fabric and touched her wigless head without complaint. As she rested her palm on her forehead, she said, "I texted him. I know I did. Told him me and the kids were in the bookstore across from Liberty. Called him a little after, and he didn't answer."

"Don't worry. You need to rest," Monika insisted.

"Call him." Amara suggested.

Monika lifted her device and waved it. "Dead. Let's call once we're at the hospital."

For a moment, Amara did not speak. Her eyes opened and closed softly and would widen abruptly as she avoided the urge to fall asleep again.

"Monika," she said.

"Yeah?"

"When did you see him last?"

The answer was already at the edge of her lips, but she prolonged the truth. "The roof."

"When?"

"Not long after you left us there." It was a moment Monika had no desire to rehash.

Amara's thoughts were a swift spokes-wheel, and she desired to poke a finger between the rods and bring them all to a halt; but feared the pain.

"If you knew something," she huffed, "would you tell me?"

Monika was initially quiet. "I don't think you would let me keep it from you."

She giggled to engage the blinders of her deception. However, Amara was queen of the craft, and could see straight through her, so said nothing more.

"Hey driver, have any chewing gum up there?" Monika asked.

He removed a pack from the compartment inside the door and handed it over to her. Monika grabbed a handful and returned the pack half-empty before she popped a fresh piece into her mouth.

"Where's your stash?" Amara asked.

"Couldn't fit it in the purse I wore with my gown the other night."

"Practical, but no common sense, huh. Didn't the dress have pockets?"

Monika laughed. "Damn."

A pair of metal, folding chairs in the rear of the van clanked together as they travelled along a bumpy road. When the driver pulled into the lot, he removed one of them and offered it to Monika.

"I'm sure there is nowhere in there for her sit down."

"But I can't help her inside *and* carry it. The floor may have to do, if necessary," Monika said as she helped Amara to her feet.

Shiloh and James woke from their slumber and, when they saw Monika's movements, climbed out of the van as well. They expected to trek a while longer, but sensed they were finally out of harm's way.

"One of the kids can carry it in for you," the driver suggested and attempted to hand it over to Shiloh.

They had slept so peacefully in the back, their presence had almost slipped Monika's mind. "No. They're not coming," she told him.

They heard, but the children were too exhausted to protest.

"They have to go with you," Monika said. "Just take them on to the church."

Though they were accomplices, Monika was a stranger.

"I can't be responsible for them."

"Nothing will happen. Trust me. Tell them 27 was—is—their father."

The man was hesitant. "Look, I want to help, but I can't get involved when it comes to kids." He started to wobble away.

"These are Bishop Dyer's grandchildren," she said. "Can you take them to him? Please."

He was puzzled by Monika's suggestion since she knew what awaited them at the church. However, her insistence to take the youngsters to the bishop could also mean she was fully committed.

He widened the door's opening. "Get in. Put on your seatbelts."

"But we want to stay with you and Mama," Shiloh said.

"This man will take you to Pop Pop. He has a place for you to sleep until we come."

Amara, with an arm fastened around her sister's neck, overheard her daughter's plea and called her. Shiloh embraced her mother, and James followed suit.

"Be good. I have to see the doctor, and when I'm done, I'll come there."

The girl assumed her mother would cave to her silent resistance, so she stared at her and awaited the break.

"Okay?" Amara said to reinforce her previous statement.

A heavy weight fell into Shiloh's shoulders at her mother's orders.

"Okay," the girl said, and then turned away.

"Shiloh," Amara called.

"Huh?"

"Don't forget to take your brother to the restroom. And if Pop Pop has snacks, don't just give him the ones you don't like."

"Okay." She moved to a seat.

"Wonder where she got that from," Monika joked.

"Be quiet. Let's go."

"Thank you," Monika said to the driver.

He shook his head and mumbled under his breath as he closed the door shut, "From one danger to another."

A bright orange butterfly nestled delicately on a beautiful bed of white gardenias along the walkway. Amara smiled at its vibrancy, and moved with ease towards the entry, but the peace of their transition was shattered by mayhem within the hospital's emergency room.

The hallways bustled with victims and there was no way to keep order. It was as if they had evacuated a Midwest city and taken refuge in a storm shelter underground. Those who made peace with the conditions lined the floors; some stretched out completely while others nursed their wounds and waited for no appointed time.

On the contrary, those who were confident they could convince others to move on their behalf created discord. If there was a chandelier mounted from the ceiling, people would have struggled for a seat upon its thin arms and hoped for a fraction of relief before it collapsed. No one stood watch. No one engaged them with a check-in process. Even there, they could only hope for help.

"This is crazy," Monika said.

A man moved from his seat in one of the waiting areas, and Monika pounced on it.

"Come on. Quick."

She lowered her sister into the seat next to a woman whose arm was severely wounded and wrapped in one of the free car dealer ads found on street corners. Blood saturated the once white Acura near her elbow; yet she did not appear to be in pain, or had grown numb to it.

"Wait here," Monika said.

"Like she has a choice," the woman said to herself, but they heard.

Monika journeyed towards the floor's reception desk and stepped over one person after another to get there, but it was void an informed employee. A family of four was huddled together and overwhelmed with concern about the deep gash on the side of the man's head. His wife and children watched helplessly as blood from his wound dripped onto his white, skull and bones patterned tee shirt, so did not notice Monika when she stood nearby.

Nothing divided the waiting area from patient rooms; there was no triage to determine whose condition would be prioritized. Monika could only observe. She thought if she poked her head into one of the rooms, she could confirm that people were receiving help. It was not the case. Three people sat on a single bed within the room she entered, and another was asleep, or so it seemed, on the floor. She pulled back quickly. The staff had jumped ship and left them to lick their wounds.

When Monika was on her way back to Amara, she spotted a nurse who bandaged a man's head with gauze and office tape.

"Ma'am. Excuse me, nurse. Is it possible for...?"

The nurse stood and started to walk away. "No requests please. We'll get to whoever we can."

Monika followed her into a bare supply closet. "Broken leg. Broken leg," she said as she searched each shelf.

"My sister has a head injury. It's not good. She needs help."

"Aspirin. Here." She dropped two into Monika's hand as she passed.

The camera angled towards them in the supply room righteously recorded the exchange.

"It's not a damn tension headache." She continued to follow. "I'm afraid that if she falls asleep—she won't wake up again."

"Then don't let her. And stop following me."

"There has to be something you can do."

"Take it all in, lady," the nurse said with agitated laughter. "What do you need? CT Scan? X-ray? When you go to the fifth floor, find someone who's still here and actually knows how to use the machine, shove over the dozen bodies of people who also didn't come in with complaints of a tension headache, and make room for your sister to hop on." She shrugged as she could barely cling to the residue of hope.

"Half of these people just landed in a place proper enough to die in."

There was nothing Monika could say, but she remained vigilant as she traipsed back to her sister in the waiting room. Before she passed the reception desk, a figure to her right caught her attention. He kneeled on the floor and placed a final stitch along a woman's upper abdomen. Her bare breasts hang from beneath her shirt but enticed no one enough to give it much attention.

"Doctor," Monika spoke as she approached him from behind.

He turned, and her assumption was accurate. "My God! George."

"What's wrong, Monika?"

"It's Amara. I need your help."

"I know. I know." He gestured somberly. "But so do they."

Monika snapped, "You won't even ask me what's wrong with her?"

"Why would it matter if I can't help?"

"But you're obviously helping *someone*. Why not her?"

"There is no way for me to keep tabs on these people's needs. I pass and do whatever I can as I go or will double-back if I've found something to make them more comfortable. That's all I can do."

Amara observed the people in the area. Those who were bandaged, stitched, hooked up to IVs, or whose limbs bore improvised casts, had one thing in common—they were not Black. It was not an appropriate time to argue race, so Monika pulled her potential remarks inward and swallowed them.

"If you so happen to pass the woman you've engaged in a 3-year-affair with, maybe stop to see how she's doing."

Monika was mortified. The doctor's refusal to look in on her was the slap in the face Monika consistently warned Amara would someday transpire. She had only become privy to the affair between George and Amara eight months earlier.

Monika was in her final stage of pregnancy and wanted to enjoy the privilege of spontaneity before the baby arrived. When she surprised her sister with a midday office visit to invite her to lunch, she received a surprise herself. The sexually adventurous pair had forgotten to lock the office door, which was as open as Amara's legs. She had no choice but to fully confide in Monika, who delivered threats to expose the truth to an undeserving Jabari.

George was already a divorcee, and Monika was convinced that he would not be fully satisfied until Amara joined him on that side of the tracks. Openness and availability would quench the thrill of selfish deception and forbidden, passionate sex. George's fling with Amara was fueled by the cost of her suffering had they been discovered but would ultimately cost him nothing.

When George showed his face at the gala, Monika was stunned by her sister's audacious behavior—both men within the same room—but the tables had turned. Her "I told you so", or the perfect plot to leak the secret to Jabari while she somehow remained anonymous, was not worth the condition she watched her sister endure. She chose to save Amara the embarrassment and pretend the moment between her and George never happened.

Before she reached the waiting area, Monika grabbed a clean, white bed sheet from an abandoned cart of linens.

"Someone coming?" Amara asked with low eyes; her head rested against the yellow upholstered sofa.

Monika used the sheet to cover what was left of her sister's gown. "They will come this way momentarily."

"Liar." She pulled the sheet around and wore it like a cape.

"What?"

Amara gave a faint snort. "Whenever you lie, you turn into this proper-speaking, high-pitched white girl."

Monika smiled. "Whatever. Your English is more eloquent than mine."

"I don't have the pitch though—to have an entire conversation like I'm in absolute amazement." They chuckled. "Really. It's like someone's playing A7 on the violin."

"Unreal. Total exaggeration," Monika said.

"See, what sister uses 'total'?"

"Obviously yours."

"Our relation may be questionable."

"Whatever. I'm surprised you remembered though," Monika said.

"What?"

"Violin. I haven't held one in my hands since we were kids."

"Yeah. That was the one thing I had to let go of when Ma left here."

"Just one thing, huh?"

Amara looked to her sister and was prepared to inquire about her comment, but when Monika spotted George in the walkway, she jumped from her seat to block her sister's view of George.

"What's going on?" Amara asked.

"This is pointless," Monika said. "We should have gone to the church."

"Really?"

"I don't know. Almost anything would be better than here."

"Maybe not the grave."

"You know what I mean. Tell me, how do you feel?"

"Tired. Weak. A haze when I look towards light."

"It could be because you've been awake three days straight, or because you haven't eaten a solid meal in as much time. You probably also have a concussion."

Monika knew that injuries invisible to the naked eye would not be treated in that environment and, even if it were possible, her skin color would push her farther down the list. However, she concealed the details.

"What should we do?"

"Where would you rather be?" Monika asked, and then turned to see George leave the area.

"With Daddy—the kids—Jabari."

"It could be forever before you're seen here. Maybe there's a doctor at the church. The medics at church keep their supplies in the building. We can probably find anything you need there."

"Okay." Amara nodded subtly.

"I'll just use the phone over there to call for a ride."

"Okay." Amara paused. "Liar." She smiled.

Monika watched her sister and dialed the number to their father's office. They had not experienced that moment's energy since they stuffed their bras with socks and washcloths, and it was a beautiful spark after three dark days. Monika knew the tiny flicker could never evolve into the flame she desired; the battle was not over. The soldiers had merely positioned themselves for a different course of attack, and the church was the new battleground for those dedicated to TAAR's mission.

After Monika confirmed the safe arrival of her niece and nephew, she received promise of a pickup within the hour. The time allotted would have to do. Her heart was determined to savor every second she could with her sister.

CHAPTER SIXTEEN
LET US NOT DECEIVE OURSELVES

AS the sun prepared to clock out from a day's labor, the black van returned for the women. The smell of vinegar and the rip in the back of the passenger's seat were both there—but the drivers had been exchanged. A short man with a baseball cap and sunglasses maneuvered the vehicle through the madness of misaligned cars and wounded foot traffic, and they were on their way—or so it seemed.

At the edge of the hospital's parking lot, officers were assembled to monitor people's movements since unrest had infiltrated the entire city. As they regained control in the areas of severe conflict, they were able to better focus on containing the spread. Of course, that was not what Monika sensed when their vehicle was waved over near the makeshift exit point, and her nerves immediately sent needle-like shocks through her limbs.

"Looks like they're stopping us from leaving," the driver said.

"Were they here when you came in?" Monika asked.

"No. They must have just set up a checkpoint."

The driver pulled up near the armed officers and lowered his window. "Yeah?" he said and removed the shades that blocked the blinding rays of the descending sun.

"Where you heading?" one asked. The other walked around the vehicle.

"We're going to the church."

"We're telling everyone to stay put. We don't need people joyriding right now."

"No joyride, officer. It's only a few miles from here."

The longer their interaction, the more aggressive the tremble in Monika's right leg became. When she noticed, Amara pressed her hand to her sister's thigh.

"Shhh...," Amara whispered.

Suddenly, the door rolled open and the man eyed the women, who boldly returned his gaze. He glanced at the empty seats in the rear. The third eye of his vest, a camera, would be a great vindicator and giver of truth if it was ever required, but there was nothing to see. Pleased, he lifted his rifle to his shoulder, slammed the door shut, and moved around the vehicle towards the other officer.

"Which church is that?" the policeman questioned.

"Wanderer's Refuge Temple on Dunbar Street."

"I know of it. Quite a few people there already."

His partner returned to his side and gave him a nod.

"Go straight there. Watch out for the unmanned vehicles in the road. Good luck."

As they pulled away, air flooded back into Monika's lungs.

"You may look like GI Jane, but you got the balls of Barbie," Amara poked at her through fatigued eyes. "Still don't know why you didn't bring me with you all those years. I can fight too. I could have been your sidekick or something—Wonder Girl, or Robin, but with a 'y'."

"Yeah right. You can't flight." Monika laughed faintly. "Like the time Gina Kennedy pulled your ponytail and you went running to Mama like she'd stomped your face in."

"That's not the best example." Amara contemplated. "More like when we pretended to be X-Men. Remember how you would never let me be Rogue?"

"That's because I wanted to be her." Monika chuckled at the memory.

"Storm was better."

"Then why'd you always argue to be Rogue?"

"Because I knew that if you wanted to be her, she had to be the best," Amara shared.

A sentimental silence saturated the small space between them.

After a brief reflection, Monika said, "I wanted to be many things I never became, but I watched you achieve exactly what you planned."

"I guess they *would* be easier to achieve if I wasn't Daddy's puppet."

"What's that supposed to mean?"

"Monika, I'm not the only one carrying the burden of Mama's death. You are too. I've felt it for a long time."

"Not true. I let it go."

"You wish you believed that." Amara pressed her head against the window. "I remember that Wednesday. We had Bible study that night. Daddy told her to get to the church early and unlock the doors because Pastor Moss was away. We waited for you to come home. School was over, but you didn't come in. Mama watched the road for a while after your bus dropped off the other kids. And then you called. She knew you had cut school, otherwise you would have made the bus."

"Yeah, yeah. I know. I messed up." The guilt-inducing memory was lodged in Monika's jugular.

"Even if I'm not passing blame, that's exactly what you feel. You see, you weren't always a daddy's girl—at least you weren't before she died. There is nothing wrong with remorse, but it made you Daddy's puppet. You don't know who you are. But you're not *this*." Her eyes slowly moved up her sister's frame.

Amara's words lifted from the pages of Monika's thoughts and became three-dimensional. Memories of the history she shared with their father seemed to confirm what was spoken, yet there was nothing Monika could do to remedy times past, nor could she bring herself to feel anything but love for her father. Platters of truth were on the table, and she partook in a few, but those she deemed indigestible remained untouched.

"It's time we both let it go," Monika said.

"How could you? Look at you." Amara paused and reflected. "One Saturday—you had to be in 10th grade—you came home after riding the city bus to the art store and spending all your lil' allowance on a new canvas, brushes, and paint. You said you were going to enter the art contest at the museum."

Monika looked from the corner of her eyes. "Yeah. I remember."

"Do you remember how you vowed to spend all weekend on the perfect painting? Told me to leave you alone and make my own lunch so you could focus?"

"Yeah. I did, huh? It was a long while back, but I remember."

"Then Daddy came home and told you to help with tutoring at church that afternoon. You couldn't tell him 'no'. You were gone all day Saturday, had services all day Sunday, and then we went to a dinner to celebrate one of the pastors' birthdays, so you had nothing left in you—not even time."

Monika remembered. The pain became real to her again, and she faced the darkness.

"I went into your room to borrow your hairbrush, but you were asleep. Drained, uninspired—there was just a pencil sketch of a butterfly on the canvas. I guess it had emerged colorless from its cocoon."

"I didn't care anymore," Monika said in a gruff tone.

"You're really gonna lie to me? Your excitement that Saturday was genuine. You just couldn't make the deadline."

"I should have gotten my materials sooner."

"Or you should have told Daddy how important it was to you. That probably wouldn't have even mattered. Either way, I felt sorry for you. But if you didn't want to speak your mind, I wasn't going to make it my business."

Monika came to grips with the trap she found herself unable to escape. "I know," she said hopelessly. "And I'm sorry Daddy controlled you too. Marrying Jabari kept you under his thumb."

"Yeah." Pleasant thoughts of the past flooded into Amara's mind. "To some degree, that may have been the best manipulation I've ever been victim to. Jabari's a good guy."

"Yeah. But I'm sorry it happened the way it did," Monika said.

"Be honest. You wanna know what you missed?" Amara spoke candidly, but Monika feigned indifference. "Well, he's consistently been there for me and the kids—kind, generous—but there was always something missing. It was like being in a beautiful dream but never able to see the faces of the people around you. You know they're there, but the thing that could bring you closer just isn't—some missing element." Amara shrugged. "Maybe he loved me out of duty and honor, and nothing else."

"I won't let you believe that."

"Prove me wrong. I don't know if it's this training thing y'all were up to all these years, but he's not like you, Monika. Perhaps it all rewired his brain, and he's just not himself. Nothing can excite him—make him laugh or cry. He's an empty shell most days."

As nausea set in, Amara sat up to ease the queasiness in her belly.

"Ever wonder why women initiate more divorces than men?" Amara asked. "Marriage seems like a fantasy but, for many women, it's more of a cautionary tale." She exhaled and her lips did not connect again.

"Are you okay?" Monika asked.

"Feeling sick." She huffed twice and then sat back before she continued. "After I had James, I wanted to find a life for myself and, right or wrong, I didn't make any apologies for it. I love my children *and* Jabari, but freedom— it's the sizzle of a hot, juicy steak after years of bologna sandwiches."

"Don't talk about food. I'm so hungry," Monika said.

"Speaking of bologna, do you smell that?"

Monika sniffed the air. "Smells like a spilt bottle of vinegar—or someone's funky feet."

"No. That's not it."

Monika pondered the shift in Amara's comfort level. Although she was not well-versed on her sister's condition, she knew that Amara had suffered a head injury, and that her senses could be impaired as a result.

"Anything else change since the hospital?"

"No," Amara said, but it was not true.

Amara's hands grew weaker by the minute and her fingers could barely make a fist. Occasionally, she glanced from the window to gauge the level of dizziness she experienced; on a scale of 1 to 10, it was an 8, and climbing. The pain of what felt like a baseball colliding with the head was consistent. An understatement would be that she did not feel like herself, but that is exactly what she offered Monika.

Despite her condition, Amara engaged in conversation to distract from her ailments. The woman whose exaggerations were easily perceived by those closest to her, finally held back. Amara knew full disclosure would only deepen her sister's worry and helplessness. Rest and recovery in the presence of her family became Amara's deepest desire, so she split her energy between time shared with her sister, and the hope of reuniting with the others.

"If you want, I can move to the other row, and you can lay across here."

"And lose my pillow?" Amara shifted her legs towards the window and laid her head on Monika's lap. She closed her eyes as she spoke. "What about you? How do *you* feel?"

Monika caressed the edge of her sister's hairline. "I feel everything at once. Pain, fear, sadness, anger, grief—all equally."

Amara's eyes opened at the sound of her sister's suffering. "Little Michael had an amazing mother. And I'm sorry for what I said. I can't imagine what it was like to leave him there."

"Wish I could tell you." Monika had grown numb to the loss, and her brain desired to block out whatever it could to refocus on what was at hand—just as she had been trained to do.

"What about Calvin?"

"What about him? Michael was the loose stitch that kept us attached."

"So, there's nothing there for him anymore?"

"There hasn't been for a while."

Amara's energy hit a high in the ebb and flow of her injuries. "His proposal was so hard to watch. I mean—why the hell would he drag all of us to the mountains knowing the risk of getting a 'no'."

"But I didn't say 'no'," Monika clarified.

"Maybe not with your mouth. But you weren't excited. You smiled a little, yes, but I don't remember you ever looking down at the ring."

"That's a thing?"

"For most women. At least women who are thrilled to receive a proposal. They check out the bling—flash it around. Oh wait! That's it! It wasn't much to look at, huh?" Amara joked. "A teacher's budget has a bling ceiling—a low one."

Monika giggled. "That's not it. But you're right about the other part. He wasn't the one. I enjoyed our time together. We had some common interests. He's brilliant, caring, liked to keep the peace, drama-free, but there was never a spark between us that made me think I couldn't be without him."

Jabari's face flashed vividly across Monika's inner eye, and she tried to think of what to say next regarding her relationship with Calvin. Nothing would come to her. However, a quick redirect was no longer necessary. She did not have an audience. Monika looked down at her lap and saw that Amara had fallen asleep—lips parted, eyes closed gracefully. She pressed her head against the cushion and hoped to rest until their arrival at church—which they could only inch towards as they navigated unending obstacles in the road.

"Eh hem," Amara spoke from her sleep.

Monika looked down at her. "What?"

"You—chewing like a cow on that damn gum. Give it to me." She held out her hand.

"You can't be serious."

"I'd rather you tear up the inside of your jaw than to wreck my ears with your smacking. It's making the headache worse!" Amara moved her hand closer.

"You're just like Ma," Monika said, and placed the gum in her sister's hand.

"Call me whatever you like." Amara closed her fist and fell sound asleep.

* * *

CIVILIANS who inhabited the police station had been bussed to the safe zone. And since officers were busy lining the coffin in anticipation for the 3-day debacle's end, the office was bare. The streets were mostly quiet as they took advantage of the sun's final hours to carry those who remained to safety. People were marched from stores, garages, business centers, alleyways, or from within residential areas where tenants were kind enough to welcome the runaways into their homes.

Lost in thought, Valerie sat at her desk and twirled left to right—right to left—in her chair as she thumbed through her husband's concerned text messages without reading a single word. The snap of a gun into a holster signaled someone's presence, and she turned to see.

"You want to explain what you were doing out there, Kemp?" Sergeant said as he approached her. "Holding a gun to an officer... What's gotten into you?"

"I don't know, sir. Maybe I'm exhausted. Wasn't thinking straight." She shrugged.

"Then you should have gone home."

"I know. I was trying to do the right thing."

"The *right* thing is to follow orders."

"I did."

"After I pried the gun from your hands. Why'd you point it at him in the first place?"

"I don't know," she pouted. The verdict of Valerie's trust in the sergeant was still out.

The gun clanked against the desk when he dropped it in front of her and covered it with his hand. "Give me the answers I need, or this is mine permanently—and your badge."

"I thought I saw something. Maybe I didn't."

"It's a war zone outside these walls—I know—but nothing should elicit that response from one of my officers—especially one as heavily decorated as you. I can't understand how someone as rebellious as yourself could gather the accolades you have," he scolded. "I say go right; you go left. What is it with you?"

A group of uniforms, prepared to retire after 16 hours in the core, walked into the room and light chatter filled the air.

"I go however I'm led, I guess." Valerie shrugged again.

He gave her the grim stare of a parent who reached the bottom of a defiant child's lies and stumbled upon a silly truth.

"But like I said, sir, I thought I saw something. I'm very tired, so it was probably nothing."

"Hey—turn that up." An officer's demand flew across the room as he pointed at the screen mounted on the wall. The volume was increased, and they all watched the newsflash.

The station released footage of those who were rescued and dropped off at the safe zone, those who flocked to hospitals, and finally, a massive crowd who entered the doors of Wanderer's Refuge Temple on the distant edge of the crime-riddled city blocks. Fellow officers were relieved to have a sense of resolve after days of combat, sleeplessness, hunger, and fatigue; but something did not sit well with Valerie.

She picked through her thoughts like Halloween goodies. "Why organize but never make yourself known?" She spoke to herself. "To avoid being infiltrated by spies is one thing—but even after you've surfaced, and everyone already know you exist?" It still did not make sense. "What is it Dyer? What's your plan?"

The network plastered visuals of heavily armed Blacks positioned on rooftops across the viewers' screens.

"Dozens of arrests were made," the reporter spoke, "but the people we see in this footage are not amongst them. We would still like to know who they are, their role in the attack and, of course, would like to see this mysterious terrorist group brought to justice as well."

Through recent observation and experience, Valerie knew the men and women of that group would never willingly surrender. She feared the sense of relief officers reveled in was signaled by a disoriented rooster's crow, and premature.

"I don't think there's anything there," the sergeant responded to the reporter's comments. "At least not the idea that they're an organized group. People's wheels are spinning in the wrong direction."

"Why not?" Valerie asked, and the two continued to talk among themselves.

"It's impossible for a group to organize in this way."

"You mean—for Blacks to unify?"

He hesitated. "Yes. That too."

The truth was clear, and Valerie's palate was cleansed. Sergeant was more than likely uninvolved, and blindly unaware of the group's abilities.

"I wouldn't underestimate them," Valerie said.

"You know who they are?" he asked.

"Not exactly, but they are very skilled and most definitely organized."

"How do you know?"

"I came face to face with a few. One pair even killed themselves—right in front of me."

"Pair?"

"Yes. They're partnered up. Look at the screen." She pointed. "Always in twos."

Sergeant spoke as he stared at the television. "It still doesn't answer the most important questions. Who are they? Who's the leader? Never in history has any group of this kind existed. There's always someone in the forefront."

The screen flashed back to an image of the church.

"The man in there." Valerie pointed again.

Although Valerie understood the mission of the dark-pigmented group, and their reach for equality, she could not excuse their methods. An eye for an eye had forced more into the dark than before the onset of conflict. The truth, and any revelation that could remedy the continued ache of one community, and the deep curiosity and panic of another, was all she had to give.

"He may not be the face of this group, but I can bet he has more answers than we do."

"Bishop Michael Dyer? What could he have to do with any of this? His church has been a part of this city for decades. He's had no run-ins with the law from my knowledge. Or been under any suspicion."

"It makes him the perfect candidate to lead a unit of sleeper cells."

"That's almost funny. Sleeper cells, Kemp? Are we dealing with Black Russians now?"

"No. But they are definitely Black. I told you I encountered a few. One was a shooter on the roof. She's his daughter."

"A coincidence, maybe?"

"Can't be. I'm convinced there's something we're missing."

They both stared at the screen again. "It's only a matter of time before it's found out," Sergeant said. "For now, it looks like we're heading towards peace."

"Peace for you and the force maybe. If we don't find out what moves these people, it could be a short time before we're here again."

"Whoever they are, I think they've made their point."

"Not if we still don't know their identity. There *is* no message without a voice to speak it."

"The bodies on the ground are singing! Anyone would think that's enough."

"Never mind what the news says. They're not responsible for those bodies," Valerie said with passion. "What good would it be to slaughter Black protestors? What message would that send?"

Sergeant thought silently and returned with engaging eyes but no response.

Curiously, Valerie moved closer to the television. "I can't believe it." She pinched her narrow chin.

Sergeant joined her. "What is it?"

"Look." She pointed. "These people here." She circled random clusters of men and a few women dressed in all black and boots as they were ushered into the church. "It's them."

"The people on the rooftops?"

"Exactly. What are they doing there?" She looked to the sergeant. "They could go anywhere at all — get the hell out of town. Who *wouldn't* run as far away as they could? But they're not. Why would they gather there?" She contemplated.

"Who knows." Sergeant shrugged. "But listen, at least we know where they are. They may be there for some time while everything is restored. It could be another day or two before displaced people are able to return home. For now, we need as many officers as possible to manage the outbreak of crime that's radiated from the core. Once you get some rest, I can use you there."

Valerie heard him, but the wind of her mind's swiftly spinning wheels drowned him out. "You're right. We know where they are." She lifted her finger towards the screen again. "They're not hiding. There is no backdoor drop-offs or any attempt to blend with the others. They know we can see them."

"What are you saying?"

"Maybe this is their final stop." A light flashed through Valerie's eyes. "We have to go there." She rushed back over to her desk and fastened her gun to her belt.

"Where you going, Kemp?"

"The other day the man said he accidentally smothered his son — ," she started.

"The looney who insisted there was a Black vigilante group?" Sergeant's initial skepticism surfaced and spit kindly in his face.

"Not so hard to believe now, right? He also said his son died, and that Dyer's daughter ran away with the dead baby in tow?"

"Okay. So what?"

"Where would she take him?"

"Why would that matter? The man wanted to save his own ass by pointing the finger at someone else—possibly even lead you to a prominent figure like Dyer."

"Think about it: Where is the kid's body? Have we discovered any dead infants?"

"Not to my knowledge. Not yet."

"She buried him."

"Where could she have done that?"

"Let's agree that she did it—regardless of where."

"Okay."

"It's the tying of a loose end. He was not in her arms when I encountered her after the fact—alone on the elevator in Liberty Centre."

"And?"

"A grieving mother can see the potential of tomorrow—the possibility of giving her child a proper burial. She could have let the father run away with the baby, but she didn't. She needed immediate closure. The baby was not supposed to die. She improvised."

"Now bring it all home for me, Kemp. I don't follow."

"Why would the men in the garage kill themselves, or Monika hide her dead baby instead of letting someone arrange a proper burial?" she asked. "Tomorrow."

"What?"

"To these people, there is none. No tomorrow. They only have today; they don't expect to see another day."

"And you believe they plan to die today?"

Valerie nodded her head with pulsating eyes.

Sergeant looked to the screen again. "At the church? What about all the others inside?"

"They must be clueless."

"Why would a religious leader like Dyer bring harm to so many people?"

"It's nothing new. 1978. The People's Temple. Jim Jones, also a once-respected, prominent spiritual leader, claimed the lives of nearly a thousand men, women, and children. And they were not all willing to die."

Valerie's words resonated with Sergeant, but his inability to fathom the existence of such a radical group of Blacks limited his will to move with haste.

"Unless you want to see a repeat of what happened in Guyana, we need to get officers in there now," Valerie commanded.

"Wait a minute. You don't give orders. Besides, if what you're saying is remotely true, and we tip them off, who's to say they won't execute whatever plans they have sooner than later."

"Sir, there could already be no *later*."

CHAPTER SEVENTEEN
THE STRONG, THE VIGILANT, THE ACTIVE, THE BRAVE

THE short distance between the church and hospital demanded an unusually significant amount of time, but they finally arrived. The air was calm. The threat of violence was minimal, and survivors walked leisurely to their destinations once they were beyond the center of chaos—or perhaps the injuries they suffered hindered hurried movements. Whatever the case, those who escaped with their lives—however traumatized and broken—were grateful.

Monika opened her eyes once she heard the gear stick click the van into park. She blinked the haze from her vision, and noticed others pass the vehicle and enter the church. It was a bittersweet homecoming.

Amara's head lie delicately in her sister's lap, and she was still sound asleep.

Monika nudged her shoulder. "Hey. Wake up," she said.

Nothing happened. The driver opened the sliding door and looked in on the passengers.

"Wake up, Amara." She nudged a second time, and then a third. Still, nothing.

She cautiously waved a hand over her Amara's face, and felt a gentle stream of air from her nostrils. Her fear was silenced.

"Can I give you a hand?" the driver offered.

Suddenly, Amara awoke and dry heaved uncontrollably. If there was anything in Amara's belly, Monika would have worn it on her pants, but there was nothing left. She had concealed the severity of her injuries, but her abrupt cries spoke the truth. Tears streamed from tightly closed eyes as she found the throbbing pain in her head unbearable.

"It's okay, Amara. We're here," Monika said, and the sobs dwindled down.

For a moment, Amara opened her eyes and Monika caught a glimpse of her dilated pupils.

"Help me with her," she told the driver.

He stepped onto the van and lifted Amara's weak body by the shoulders. Her legs dangled within her tattered dress and nearly hit the ground. Monika caught them and helped to maneuver her from the van as she draped the white sheet around her sister's frame.

Seeing them, two other men moved quickly to assist, and the tallest of the three lifted her with both arms and cradled her like a baby. Monika could hear her sister's disoriented mumble and noticed her arm swinging at her side. She had taken a turn for the worst, but not all was lost.

The men took Amara to a dimly lit counseling suite and laid her on the sofa. Monika watched in dismay as the woman who recently reminisced and joked with her lie motionless. The men, having done as much as they could, backed away somberly.

"Bishop is in his office. I'll get him," one of the men said and pressed his hand firmly to Monika's shoulder. The room was instantly silent.

When he was gone, Monika kneeled next to Amara and grabbed her hand. "It's just a headache."

She pulled the throw blanket from the back of the couch and placed it over her.

"I've seen you fall on your face in ballet and hop right back to your feet. This is nothing."

There was commotion outside the door. Panicked voices seemed to pass each other and echo down the hallway. While Monika expected her father's quick arrival, it was not his voice she heard.

"Amara?" a deep, masculine voice called. With the severe burns of his left arm bandaged from shoulder to fingertips, Jabari stood tall in the doorway.

Monika's butt collided with the floor at the sight of him.

He rushed over. "What happened to her?"

"An explosion, I think." She stared at him. "What happened to you? I thought—."

"Amara. Wake up for me." He grabbed her chin and nudged her face towards him.

Amara's eyes blinked delicately.

"Stay up for me, baby. Come on."

Bishop Dyer stormed into the room and was followed by Patrick and Sam. "Where is she?" Unable to bear the sight of his beloved, he stopped short a few feet of her. "My God!"

Amara started to mumble again, but no one could make out a single word.

"Sshh...," Monika said. "Maybe someone in the church can help her, Daddy."

"The lady who wrapped my arm is a retired nurse," Jabari said.

"I'll send for her," Bishop said as he rushed from the room.

While hope quickly faded in one situation, it had risen in another, and Monika was without any sense of direction.

Amara's subtle murmurs continued.

"How long has she been like this?" Jabari asked.

"It's the worst I've seen her. The way she talked on the way over was almost normal. She didn't complain much."

"When did you find her?"

"Maybe 3 or 4 hours ago, but who knows how long she'd been there."

"The kids said she was taken to the hospital. What happened?"

"Nothing. No one would see her."

"How long did you wait?" he asked desperately. "You didn't wait long enough."

"It was impossible, Jabari. Believe me. I tried to get help for her."

The tension could not be ignored, and neither could Amara's diminishing condition. It was the quietest room the three of them would share. Soon, the void was filled with the nurse's assessment of Amara's ailments. After Monika described each of her sister's complaints, the woman checked Amara's nose, ears, and eyes.

"Eyes dilated—fluids from her nose and ears. If she was involved in an explosion, it's plausible that she's suffered trauma to her brain. There could be fluid on her brain— internal bleeding and such."

"So, is she going to be alright?" Jabari asked. "Tell me."

With a sharp gaze, the woman shook her head.

"Maybe you should go back into the sanctuary," Bishop told her. "I'll lead you out."

Monika lifted Amara's hand to take in its warmth, and her fingers stumbled upon the sticky chewing gum wrapped in her fist. She recalled the moments on the van when her sister could respond to her; but she no longer could. Realization of the sudden, dramatic shift overwhelmed her. As much as she did not want to leave her sister's side, she knew she had already received the best part of Amara's final moments. She wiped the rolling tears from her cheek as she rose to her feet. Jabari would have whatever was left of the woman she had known, loved, and protected all her life.

It was not until the door closed behind her that sorrow became a boulder on her chest; but there was no time for sadness. Her niece and nephew walked the corridor and neared the counseling room.

"Aunt Monika, what's wrong?" Shiloh asked with genuine concern.

"Nothing baby. I'm fine." She wiped her face and dried her hands against her pants.

"Pop Pop said my mama's here."

"She is."

"In there?" The girl pointed.

"Yes. Go see her." Monika opened the door and let them in before she closed it again and waited alone in the hallway.

Once inside, their father's mournful energy and the unlikely calm of their mother's countenance, catapulted them into immediate distress.

"What's wrong with her, Daddy?" Shiloh asked as she boldly drew near. James, on the other hand, refused to step into the room another foot.

"She needs rest—maybe a doctor."

"But I thought she already went to see one."

"No. She didn't."

"Well, did she talk to you?"

"No, Shiloh. She can't talk."

"Why not? Will she talk to us later?" she asked.

"No," he said disappointedly. "You can talk to her, Shiloh. She hears you."

She gulped and rattled the ball of sadness in her throat.

"Mama," she started, but she had no clue what words to speak to her sleeping mother.

The girl looked to her father. "Daddy, Aunt Monika woke her up before. If you try, you can help her wake up too," she declared with a voice saturated with hope.

"No. It won't work."

Her optimism was not fully shattered. "But Aunt Monika is outside. She can just do it again. Mama will wake up. I saw her do it."

"I said, 'no', Shiloh. Do what I said." He grew irritated by the girl's naïve insistence.

As his daughter searched for the words to say, Jabari felt that, as painful as it would be, he owed it to his children to be direct.

"Tell her goodbye, Shiloh."

"What? Goodbye for what?"

"She'll die soon."

The girl was mortified. "Don't say that, Daddy. She won't."

"It's true." He swatted away surfacing emotions with the speed and force of nunchakus in the hands of a black belt. "Now say goodbye before you have to leave."

"I don't want to go."

"Say it, Shiloh. I won't let you stay here," her father said firmly.

Her lips quivered. She cried as she pressed her small hand against her mother's warm face. She leaned close and whispered into her ear. "I promise to give James the good snacks." She kissed her cheek. "I love you," she said with as much composure as she could muster.

"Okay. Now I want you and James to wait in Pop Pop's office."

"No, please." She delivered a tearful protest.

Jabari stood and picked her up.

"Mama please! Don't die!" she screamed.

Jabari opened the door and planted the girl's feet near her aunt. James followed behind.

"It's okay. I got them," Monika assured as she embraced the girl tightly.

He went back inside and closed the door.

"I want my mama."

"Ssshh... I know," Monika whispered.

Inside the room, Jabari's pleas for Amara to hold on were ceaseless, but she offered no response. The occasional mutters ended. Her eyes no longer flashed any level of responsiveness. To the unaware, the woman was merely asleep.

"You aren't supposed to be here." He tightened his grip of her hand as if the firmness could wake her.

Amara's body burst into violent convulsions, and he tried to hold her down on the sofa without calling the attention of those who waited outside.

"Come on. Please stop. Don't do this."

Thirty seconds seemed like an hour before her body no longer flailed around like a wild bird caught in a cage. Jabari held tightly to his wife, fearing a surrender. She took a few shallow breaths, and in the next minute, they were completely depleted. Amara was peacefully at rest. If it were not for the monstrous wails that announced her departure from the other side of the door, no one else would have known.

After they escorted the children into their grandfather's office, and distracted them with cartoons and broken crayons, the adults gathered in the counseling room where Amara's lifeless body lie upon the couch. Jabari had covered all but her face with the blanket so that her tattered dress would not distract from the resting beauty.

There could be no funeral. The full execution of their plan would not allow it. Instead, people entered and exited one after another to pay their respects to her family. Jabari was closest and had pulled up a chair next to her. Othello could not hold a candle to Jabari's grief. The sound of sniffles was continuous, but those who passed through were forced to shake their grief at the door.

Bishop Dyer sat at a desolate table across the room and mourned his beloved child from a distance. When visitations slowed, and only Jabari and Monika remained, Bishop opened his mouth to speak.

"She was our miracle, but you couldn't tell by looking at her," he said.

He grabbed their full attention, and they watched him earnestly for insight.

"She had surgery when she was seven months old, wore a cast for another six to fix her little hips. Your mother worried she wouldn't be a normal child—thought she would walk with a limp. But the girl could dance, and better than those who didn't have her medical history."

"I don't remember that," Monika said.

"You wouldn't. You were young. And your mother refused to take pictures of her. She would say, 'who would wanna remember going through this?' I understood. Honestly, we never spoke of it, so Amara didn't even know what she endured as an infant. We thought talking about it would give her a crutch to underperform. She was better off not knowing."

"Anything from *my* past you want to shed light on, Daddy?" Monika asked resentfully.

"No. You had your mother's strength—physically and mentally. You reached a level of independence sooner than your sister had. I guess we took advantage of it because we released you to figure out many things on your own."

She snarled, "While Amara was protected from everything—including her own truth."

The men sensed the tension in Monika's voice, but before it could be addressed, one of Bishop's aides stuck his head in the doorway.

"Bishop, the busses are refueled. The guys are ready to head out again to pick up anyone who wants to come back here."

The group was reminded of the task at hand. It was not over.

"How many busses are there?" Dyer asked.

"Three in all."

"I want to be on one of them," Jabari said, short of a wagging tail.

"No, son. It's best you stay here to deal with this."

"What good would it do?"

"Shiloh and James need you," Monika interjected.

"It's best I keep my distance."

"Okay then. Take one of the busses out, Jabari. If they're willing, let them on—no matter who they are."

Monika was astonished by the ease with which the men handled the tragedy as it literally laid before them. What gave her the most pause was how adamant her father was to carry out the plan to the letter without noticing how different things were. Amara was gone, and the well-being of the children preoccupied in the other room was never mentioned. She thought it was within reason to expect an altered trajectory of that day's events.

The men continued to discuss the evening's plans. The more Monika listened, the more nauseous she became. She eventually went into the hallway for air. Her son was gone, and so was her sister, but not a single beat had been missed. Perhaps Amara was right—Jabari's training had impacted him in ways that she did not experience herself. He was not heartless but had the intense focus of sleepwalkers in the dead of night.

Monika took the walkway towards her father's office and went inside. James' head rested on his sister's lap as they drearily watched an outdated animated film from their grandfather's collection.

"You two okay?" Monika asked, but neither would respond. She sat on the sofa next to them, and noticed a tear melting like butter down Shiloh's warm cheek. Monika wiped it away. "It's gonna be okay."

"I don't have a mama anymore," the girl said as she stared at the screen.

"But you know that she loved you."

She nodded her head. "Where's Daddy?" she asked.

Monika considered how she would word her response. "He's going out to help other people."

"Like the other day? With the guns?"

"No. Not like that."

Monika realized the kids' experiences that week could not be undone. They were helpless, undeserving of the torment they endured, and it was only the beginning of their suffering.

"Auntie Moni," James spoke. "Can we go home?"

The office door opened, and Bishop Dyer walked into the room accompanied by his aide.

"Hey guys, Patrick will take you down to the kitchen for something to eat. Heard they had a few eggs to scramble. Go on. Put something on your stomachs."

They rose to their feet and shuffled past Monika.

"Will you be here when we come back?" Shiloh asked.

"I'm not going anywhere," Monika replied.

When the door was closed and the kids were gone, Monika moved towards her father who stood distraught behind his desk.

"Daddy, what will happen to them?"

"Shiloh and James?"

"Yes."

"It's their father's decision."

"Jabari?"

"He was their father last I checked."

"But he's not thinking straight, Daddy. Who will make sure the kids get out of here?"

His eyes narrowed on his daughter. "Or is it you who's not thinking straight? This isn't done until it's done, Monika. You haven't forgotten that." He spoke with chilling authority.

"No. But losing Amara changes things. She wouldn't want this for them just as much as you didn't want that for her."

"Yet here I am still pressing on. You have to do the same."

Whenever Monika expected a reasonable Jekyll, a Mr. Hyde always emerged.

"These are innocent casualties. You have a choice. They're your own grandchildren." Monika took a second to breathe. "Look, we made our point. They know. The world can recognize that there are people who won't bow to injustice. It can be over if you say it is."

"This is bigger than you and me. It's not so simple. The blood that's shed will be my own, and possibly anyone connected to me. I've prepared myself."

Monika thought a moment, "But not without first protecting those you care for. Amara is not in that room because you intended for her to die. Your plan to protect her failed, but there is still time to draft a new one for her children."

"It's out of my hands, Monika."

He reached into the bottom cabinet of his desk and removed a sealed bottle of whisky and a metal box. He placed them on the desk and took a seat. He grabbed a glass, half-filled with water, and dumped the contents onto the floor before he opened the whisky's seal and poured himself a taste.

"What *is* within your reach, Daddy? Was it just happenstance the venue was changed to Liberty Centre? And on the night Darius Jones would shoot down a police officer? Or that the Wolves would show up? What part did you have in all of this?"

He sipped. "It was only a matter of time before injustice hit close enough to home for peace to no longer be an option." The toad-ish energy seeped from his pores.

"You used him to lure them out, didn't you?"

"No. Wolves never hid. Jones sacrificed himself. A spark in an ocean of ether. It was a noble choice."

"So, you knew the Wolves would be downtown that night."

"Does it matter? They were. So were we."

Monika's head shook with depths of doubt. "Why you doing this, Daddy?"

"Don't get all whiny. You know why."

"For Harold?"

Her father looked at her with repugnance and spoke slowly. "Harold died the last time I saw my mother."

"When you were a boy?" she asked.

He placed the top back onto the liquor bottle. "No, no. In a shopping mall—1976." He leaned back in his chair with his glass in hand. "I was 21. Had lived in Montgomery with my father's friend through graduation and came here for college when I was 19. And that's when I saw her."

He took a swig from his cup. "I wasn't very personable—got lost in books mostly. Landed a custodian job at Rich's downtown. It was Thanksgiving, and I had to work, but it didn't matter much to me. What did I have to go home to? Besides, the Great Tree lighting ceremony was that night, and the place was packed with people from all over.

"There were thousands of lights on that tree. I hadn't seen anything like it. The ornaments were larger than soccer balls, and there was a huge snowflake on top of it. If the kids weren't jumping on Santa's lap to pose for a picture, they waited in line to ride on the Pink Pig. That thing carried them from the toy section inside the store to the Christmas tree outside.

"The weather was cool—60 maybe. I spotted a woman. She carried a small handbag—poised and beautiful. I toted a sack of trash in my hands, and placed it in a large bin, but I couldn't take my eyes from her. I grabbed the broom and followed the woman at a far enough distance to not be noticed. It was her—my mama.

"I went up to the rooftop where she met a man who stood at the Pink Pig. Two children, girls about 7 and 8 years old, stepped off the ride and got a sticker from the attendant. I knew they were hers. Had her nose, cheekbones, eyes, hair. I assumed she was married again soon after she left Birmingham. I tried, but I couldn't remember the lines I rehearsed—the ones I would say if I ever saw her again. They didn't come back to me.

"There was a break in the crowd, and I swore she could see me watching her. She stared back for a few seconds. They counted down, and the Christmas tree lit up. The lights were so bright I had to take my glasses off to see clearly. When I put them back on, she was gone.

"A week later, I changed my name. My daddy was dead. Why would I be associated with the one person who wanted nothing to do with me?" He took another gulp of his drink and emptied the glass. "Fear can make a woman leave an innocent kid in the dust. Not me. I was determined to choose the life I would lead—and the lives you and Amara would have."

Monika soaked up her father's word like a fresh sponge, and the puzzle was near complete. Her father was a poster child for the broken man. Unfortunately for those in his path, his need for healing caused tremendous suffering. Even with Monika's ability to understand her father's tormented history, it was too insufficient to justify what he had shrewdly taken from her.

"It wasn't enough for us to admire you and go ignored, or for the thousands who came through here and tried to mold their lives by your bogus example. You had to control us too—me, Amara, and Jabari—just pawns in your warped scheme."

"You're right. It wasn't enough."

"Breaking my heart to marry Amara off to Jabari, that didn't suffice either?"

He sat up high in his chair. "What? It broke your heart?"

"You know it did. Was it always your intention to do whatever you could to hurt me—to destroy anything that made me feel loved?"

"If that's what Jabari made you feel, Monika, I couldn't have known. You never told me. The arrangement was about the cause; it wasn't done to spite you."

Upon hearing his words, the old man redeemed a speck of sympathy from his daughter, but not enough to restore the many sacrifices she had made for her father's personal convictions—those that placed her consistently on the losing end.

Bishop continued, "I wanted my life to mean something, and then I discovered that in death it would mean a whole lot more. I choose immortality over legacy—one can be forgotten in time, the other never will." He opened the case on the desk and revealed the gun inside.

"You don't have to be a martyr, Daddy. You can stop here. There are people in there who don't share the pain you've carried since childhood, or your hate for White people. They just want to go home," she said.

"Is that what you think this is—that I hate White people? I hate the system they have the power to dismantle but won't. I can't, Monika." He paused. "And I'm sorry."

"Don't be. End this."

"No. Not that. I'm sorry about your mother."

Monika looked at him with intense eyes. "What about her?"

"She left to get you from school and was supposed to rush over to the church. The road was all marked up by the tires as she tried to brake, so officers were certain she was speeding and just could not avoid crashing into the lake."

"I know that."

His eyes glistened. "It was my fault, Monika. Not yours."

It was the first time her father admitted his role in her mother's demise, but she was not immediately set free from the burden of guilt. She broke to think of all the times her wounds were salted by his words, and the moments he refused a chance to console her and blamed her instead.

"It's crazy how *you're* the martyr, but you've destroyed the lives of everyone else around you instead."

The reach of his vengeful tentacles was powerful enough to sink seven ships at once. He removed the gun from the box and placed it on the desk.

"There was always something in you that gave me so much joy. The love you had for other people was unlike any other child's I'd seen. I'm grateful to have had you as my daughter." He examined the gun in his hands. "I hoped to die an old man in my bed, but I was prepared to sacrifice so that future generations could die peacefully in theirs."

She felt no sympathy for him, and all belief in his cause melted like sugar in hot tea—but was bitter. The strings were snapped, and Monika was released from the bondage of his possible disappointment; but she still loved him deeply.

"Please. We can get out of here. Go as far away as money can take us."

"Nothing will be far enough. Even if I change my mind, others were trained to not change theirs, and are downstairs at this very moment preparing the building to burn."

In some compassioned observers' eyes, Bishop Dyer meant well, but his deeply injured soul failed to bear fruit sweet enough to satiate the hunger pangs of a starving nation. Instead, his tactics left a sour taste in the mouths of those who trusted him to nourish them with truth, and a nation more famished and barren than before. For Monika, the lines between compassioned activism, martyrdom and terrorism had been significantly blurred, and his lethal initiative was as purposeless as a swarm of gnats.

Bishop Dyer's mind had been fully made. There was no room to convince him to deviate, but Monika was torn between continued last-ditch efforts to sway him, or to make use of a chance to get away before the building went up in flames.

She rushed over to her father, still seated in his chair, and bent down to hug him. He embraced her tightly.

"I love you," he said.

"I love you too, Daddy," Monika whispered. "Goodbye."

Monika noticed the glasses on his desk and was certain that his final glimpse of her would be behind the haze of his distortion.

She went back over the couch and lifted the remote to power off the television. Her father, eyes planted on the desk's surface, said nothing as she flipped the light switch on the wall. The room went black. She opened the door, and light flooded into the room a final time. Monika clicked the knob into locked position, and closed it shut.

CHAPTER EIGHTEEN
LIBERTY OR DEATH

THE sky was splattered with the pinks and purples of a summer sunset. Over 700 people were sprinkled about Wanderer's Refuge Temple that evening—mostly stoic in posture and dazed—but there was no service. If they were fortunate enough to have escaped with loved ones, they embraced them. If they were concerned about those they left behind, they prayed for them. If they were overcome with gratitude for the life they still had, they sang joyful praises. However, what connected them all was the need for food. Whatever was in the kitchen had already been rationed. And seeing the improvised establishment of a second safe zone, the National Guard, who had partly used the large parking lot as one of several base camps, visited the church to address their needs.

Two armed, uniformed men entered the sanctuary and captured the attention of everyone in the room. Some perceived them as a beacon of hope, and others shifted uncomfortably in their seats.

Patrick and Sam, Bishop Dyer's appointed commanders, rushed to greet them.

"Officers," Patrick said.

"We wanted to stop in and give you all some updates."

"Okay."

"Initially, we were to take the people from here over to the stadium where they can be properly accounted for—maybe reunited with others."

"Questioned, if need be," the other officer chimed in.

"That's no problem," Sam spoke nervously.

"Right now, we're waiting on vehicles to transport them all. Some of the volunteers retired their services hours ago, so we're scrounging up what we can to get them all moved as quickly as possible."

"Anything you need us to do on this end, officer?" Patrick asked.

"Patience, maybe. Anything you need from us?"

"I can't think of it," Patrick said confidently.

His response caused the second officer's antennae to rise. "Really? Not even food?"

"Oh, yes, yes. Food. If you can."

"No problem. The Red Cross has a good grip on providing meals to people who are still stranded. I'll ask if someone can bring enough to sustain you all for at least the evening."

It was exactly what the men wanted to avoid—the officers' return. "Okay. Thank you," Patrick said, and led the men towards the exit. He closed the door tightly behind them.

The high-strung Sam moved close to Patrick's shoulder and spoke near his ear. "We can't wait anymore. It's only a matter of time before they come back here."

"You're right. Let's gather the others."

After she left her father's study, Monika embarked on a quest to find her niece and nephew. They were not in the sanctuary, and neither were any TAAR soldiers. She checked the children's ministry room. Not there. And she moved swiftly through the kitchen. They were not there either. She ventured down another hallway, and finally noticed them sitting Indian style outside an open conference room door.

Monika could hear the voices of people inside and wanted to avoid detection, so she waved and flailed around to get their attention, but to no avail. She moved closer to the door and, when they finally noticed, jumped from their positions on the floor.

"Sshh...," she said.

Sam stood guard right next to the door and saw her approach.

"Monika, come inside."

She nodded politely, and then looked to the children. "Don't move. Don't go anywhere with anyone. Stay here."

Monika stepped into the space furnished with a few roundtables and chairs, but no one sat. The 25 TAAR soldiers who remained, gloomily gathered around one table stacked with loaded pistols, and another lined with handmade petrol bombs. She moved close to Jabari. His eyes were glazed over, and he stood unresponsively.

"This is it. There isn't much to say that hasn't already been spoken," Patrick said. "While we're gathered here, the doors are being chained. I'm sure they'll soon grow suspicious, and they may want to attack. Grab a jar from the table; detonate it within five minutes of leaving this room. To ward off attack, or if you prefer a bullet to fire, or if you just can't stand to watch, take a pistol from the table."

When others moved robotically to collect a pistol, Monika followed suit and grabbed one for herself.

"We will live freely in paradise," Patrick concluded.

They offered silent goodbyes—took deep breaths, bounced a little and shook themselves, smiled even. Some smirked, others bowed their head slightly, but Jabari was unmoved. Monika hoped it had all gotten to him and that his defenses were lowered.

One after another, they grabbed a deadly cocktail from the table and rushed away. Jabari was amongst the last of them.

The National Guardsmen, who had recently paid a visit to the church, were perched next to an oxidized, pale green statue of a horse at the corner of the enormous lot when they received a distorted message over the radio.

"What was that?" the officer said as he placed the device close to his ear.

"The church. Get the people out," the voice said frantically over tinges of static.

"I don't understand. Come again."

"They're hostages. Get them out of the church now!" the voice ordered loud and clear.

"Aww man," one officer said to the other, "I knew something wasn't right. Let's go."

They were yards away but, on foot, it would take at least two minutes to get back to the front door if they ran full speed. Six others joined them, but it did not matter. When they pulled the door handles with all their strength, they would not budge. Each one had been chained. The officers could not get inside, nor could the innocent get out. They heard screams from within those walls and shuddered to think of the people's demise.

"No entry. No access," the officer spoke desperately over the airways.

"The tanks are nearby. They should be coming in now," the voice responded. "Hold your position until they break through."

The guardsmen looked across the lot and saw the immense vehicles encroach upon the building. They were tailed by a defensive line of police cars with lights and sirens ablaze. When they were near the entry, Valerie hopped from the passenger-side of one of the cars and unholstered her weapon.

"On my signal," a voice screeched over the handhelds. "Get ready guys. Once you've broken through the wall, back into the lot quickly so they can come through."

Someone aboard the gigantic vessel responded, "If there are several hundred inside, would the hole be large enough to get them all out safely?"

"It will have to be. We won't have time to plow another without jeopardizing their safety as they escape."

"Oh my God!" someone spoke. "There's smoke."

Valerie, antsy without access to Dyer's captives, ran hastily around the building and hoped to gain entry some other way. However, she underestimated the enormity of the facility, and was quickly winded. Her feet moved by her mind's cues and hard-wired affirmations, so she did not stop.

Inside, Jabari and Monika were the last to collect a petrol-filled container.

Monika grabbed his arm aggressively. "Don't do this," she said.

Screams roared from the sanctuary and startled the children from their seat on the floor. "Daddy!" they both called. "Come on!"

"We can leave here together—with the kids," Monika continued.

He said nothing but looked to his children who stood in the doorway. The clash of glass against the floor and walls commenced slight tremors in his body.

"Daddy, come on!" Shiloh gestured for him to come to her and, in the flutter of his gut, he thought to preserve their lives.

When he placed the cocktail back down on the table, Monika's observation of his softened heart had proven true. Jabari dashed out the door and took James into his usable arm as he sprinted to a nearby exit.

Monika pulled Shiloh along as smoke seeped into the hallway. Their plan for a secret escape may have gone undetected, but that area of the church was securely chained. Jabari pushed past the pain as he rammed against the door with his injured arm.

Every door in sight was attempted as smoke spread through the building. It became more difficult to breathe, and they started to cough. Monika lifted the neck of her shirt to her nose for a thin barrier that offered little resolve.

Trapped, Jabari had no cause to conjure hope, and was certain they would all die there. His willingness to survive was fully depleted. Monika saw the light go out within him when he placed his son's feet on the ground.

"No. No, wait," she said.

He looked at her with burning eyes, and rapidly overtook her with a firm kiss on the lips. She was open, and easily returned the sentiment. The kids looked on with stark expressions; and they all experienced the first kiss Jabari and Monika had ever shared.

Jabari released Monika from the passionate exchange and kneeled to his children. "I'm sorry," he said.

Monika, without a moment to fully bask or explore the meaning of their kiss, remembered a detail about the church's layout that had nearly escaped her.

"Wait. There could be another way out."

Jabari grabbed her arm. "No. Let's finish this. There's no other way."

"You serious?" She swatted his hand away. "Look at your children. They didn't ask for this. Neither did you, or me. We don't have to keep my father's secrets anymore."

Smoke in his eyes, he slid down the wall and sat on the floor. "There's no escape, Monika. There is no escape," he recited helplessly.

Monika got into a squat next to him. "You're not a machine. You have a choice. Amara's gone. That wasn't the plan. These kids will have no one." She coughed.

"That's why they're not going anywhere." Jabari grabbed both of his children and locked them in a firm grip.

"Don't!" Monika yelled.

Her words were powerless to Jabari's uncanny beliefs, and she realized he would not relinquish them—not even for his children. If she was all the children had, it was enough.

Monika drew her gun and aimed it at Jabari. "You may not want your life, but don't let them watch you die like this. Let them go."

He took in the visual of their frightened faces and released them both.

"I know you love them, Jabari. Come with me," she pleaded.

"If I don't stay, Amara would have died in vain."

"But you still have them—and me too."

"What kind of life would that be? It ends here for me." He stood to his feet, removed the string of jasper stones that wrapped his wrist, and solemnly handed it to his daughter. He patted her on the head.

"Loyalty trumped the love I've always had for you, but know that it was there," he said to his partner.

"Goodbye, Jabari."

"Go for the gold, Monika. Take good care of them." He slid down the wall again and sat dazed as if in a daydream.

With their consistent coughing, another moment could not be wasted. She grabbed the kids' hands and rushed away as Jabari became a shadow amid the smoke. Monika hurried towards the kitchen where there was a back door to the dumpsters, which was only known to those who worked in there.

Fortunately, her assumption was right. They pushed open the unchained door and urgently sucked in the clean air. When she regained her composure, Monika examined the youngsters.

"You okay? You good?"

"I'm fine." Shiloh panted.

James' cough was severe, but he was able to move about, and that was a good sign.

Monika checked her surroundings. Along the backside of the church, near the kitchen exit, was a single string of parking spaces surrounded by a wooded area that led to a busy intersection. It would be their only option since the front lot was lit with red and blue.

"Look, it's dark, and we may have a ways to walk, but stay close to me. We're going through these trees right here. Can you do that?"

They nodded their head.

"Come on."

Monika led the little ones towards the brush, but like a coyote with its eyes locked on its prey, Valerie noticed their movements as she rounded the corner.

"Freeze!" Valerie yelled. "Police!"

The children clung tightly to their aunt whose gun was raised in the officer's direction.

"You want to do this little dance again, Officer?"

"36," Valerie said.

"What was that?" Monika glanced over the gun.

"That was my name," Valerie said. "36. I know you, 18. I was there—in that muggy community center with chairs arranged in a circle, masked the entire time, and warned not to remove it no matter how hard it was to breathe. I was twelve years old," Valerie said.

The officer that held Monika at gunpoint was among those who went missing from their training class in her early years. They had been there one day, or many days, and completely vanished the next. Their sudden disappearance cautioned others to properly align with their trainers' demands. Monika remembered clearly.

"Then why are you doing this?"

"Because I'm not one of you," Valerie declared.

"You are. Please. Just let us go."

"I'm not. I despise what you are. My parents were forced to relocate when I failed to be their golden soldier. They were outcasted when they could not uphold their contribution to some raggedy ass revolution none of us understood. I trained for almost two years without knowing why, or who was in control. It was a phantom program."

"But you see now. Don't you?"

"Yes. But what do you see, Monika? Any clearer than all those years ago? A part of me thought it was only a dream—that it ever existed—but I couldn't deny it had already ripped my family apart."

"Don't think you're special. It destroyed mine too."

"I know. Monika, this is fate. I've kept my eyes peeled since I've been back, and sure enough—here is the key to my time capsule of unanswered questions."

Monika found it difficult to digest the idea that her fate was to spend her life in prison.

Valerie continued to speak, "I know if you could have it any other way, you wouldn't be here. But how could you sleep knowing all you've done?"

The kids tugged tearfully at Monika's shirt.

"I'm it for them, you know." She nodded towards them. "My sister's gone—so is my daddy. And I'm sure you'll find their father's charred remains by sunup. Please." Monika's voice was stripped of courage.

"You could have made a different choice. You didn't. Now put down the gun, Monika."

She kept her arm locked into position.

"Auntie, let's go," James begged.

Valerie did not relent. "Your options are for me to shoot you down, or for you to spare them the blood splatter and drop the gun."

It was indeed over. Monika was ready to make peace with it. Without another thought, she did as she was instructed and tossed the gun a couple of meters from her feet.

The boom of an explosion sounded through the night air and forced people to flee in all directions. Officers whipped their vehicles around the rear of the church and blasted their sirens. Valerie shuffled over to Monika before the lights of the cop car was close enough to illuminate their faces.

Monika turned, and placed her hands behind her head to await the cuffs as Valerie picked the gun up from the ground.

"Quick. Put your hands down," Valerie said, and Monika instantly complied.

The squad car swooped in and came to a complete stop near the women.

"Everything alright, officer?" the policeman asked from the open car door.

"Yes. They're all fine. None injured. These folks were lucky to find another way out," Valerie said.

"Alright. I'll see about the others." He hopped back into his seat and sped off.

Monika was moved beyond bewilderment. In her mind, she was already stretched over the thin, lumpy mattress in her prison cell.

"I know what it's like to lose everything you love to something you don't understand," Valerie said. "Get out of here. The farther the better. You won't have long."

Monika feared she was being tricked, so moved reluctantly to grab the children's hands; but when Valerie backed away, she ran quickly into the dark brush and disappeared.

Valerie reached the front of the building, and the hundreds of unsuspecting people liberated from Dyer's death trap watched as the gigantic church went up in flames. They could still see the burning interior from the gaping hole in the wall—their passageway to freedom. Firefighters available to respond were slow to arrive, and over 70% of the building was already consumed.

Valerie joined Sergeant near the rescue tank.

"To my understanding, we got them all out," he said. "At least those who wanted to live. A few evacuees saw several of them chain themselves to fixtures inside there."

"How could anyone see this coming?" she said.

"It's not the first time. Won't be the last. If we're so consumed with fanning away the smoke that we forget to put out the fire, we can expect the cycle to continue. But hey, why fight the flames if we can clear enough space to breathe."

"You know—nice analogy there, boss."

"I try," he blushed. "Seriously, good police work, Detective. A lot of lives were saved today."

Valerie humbly agreed, but it was not her assembly of facts or timely response that she found most gratifying. She finally understood the depth of sacrifice she avoided when she rebelled against TAAR—and ultimately, the parents who disowned her. The 14-year-old Valerie may not have fully understood what prompted her rebellion, but the adult Valerie discovered that her insistence to stand her ground was worth all she lost to become the woman that she was—a privilege not afforded to people like Monika Dyer.

With the chaos, firetrucks were unable to get close enough to the burning church to quench the fire. News helicopters flew overhead. Their cameras watched with zeal and offered viewers at home a bird's eye view of the disaster. The flames lit up the night sky like the 4th of July.

* * *

WHEN smoke cleared the region, when damaged buildings crumbled upon the concrete, when the last of the bodies were recovered from ditches, alleyways, dilapidated structures, and hospital hallways, 2,502 people were dead. Yet, no one could fully grasp why it had all occurred. The truth died with Michael Dyer, whose death, unlike his father's, was counted amongst the deceased; or it escaped on foot with Monika, who would have to make peace with her role in the calamity that snuffed out many lives.

While the outcome was measurable, blame was not fully placed. It was difficult to attribute the first swing to one side or the other, so civilians desired for justice to be dished out equally to the hate groups. To bystanders, there was no difference. If the mere color of someone's skin was enough to conjure deadly hatred, or if centuries of perpetual, uncured inequality triggered disgust, they were synonymous in the eyes of order-keepers.

Whichever way the pendulum would swing, a new level of respect, or fear, developed due to the existence of organized Blacks ready to die for a cause too imprecise to resonate with American lawmakers—coupled with the fact that the reach of its members and leaders was still unknown.

As buildings folded into themselves and streets were cleared of disfigured corpses, the people watched. All people watched. The scenes plastered over their television screens were as captivating as any box office flick. It spoke the universal language of suffering, and the desperation of a people fettered by legislature as they clashed with those who feared change. America failed to uphold its word as a land that extended total freedom and equality to Blacks or honor those who were brave enough to ratify change on their behalf.

To smooth over rocky public opinion beyond American borders, President Couper held a press release within days of the tragedy. In a staged press room within the White House, he stood behind his podium surrounded by people with limited, secondhand opinions, and read from his unsubstantiated list of facts.

"The incredible men and women at the FBI have worked diligently to unearth the truth behind terrorist organizations who struck one of our nation's most prominent capital cities. This group of radicals are now understood to have ties to jihadist terrorist organizations. These people are the greatest threat to the internal security of the country, and we are working around the clock to bring each of these perpetrators to justice. Remember, terrorism on any front will not be tolerated, and all involved parties will be prosecuted to the full extent of the law."

Nestled next to a brief report on the FBI Director's desk was the image of Bishop Michael Dyer, and his unexpected guest, Fatima Shamoon, taken the night of the ball. Bishop Dyer's body made the count, but his mission was completely undermined. Perhaps the truth of their existence was enough.

www.ingramcontent.com/pod-product-compliance
Lightning Source LLC
Chambersburg PA
CBHW022026240626
47154CB00007B/2279